"If this doesn't give you a chill, you'll never be in love or a hospital."

—Roy Blount, Jr.
author of CRACKERS

"WAVELENGTHS is a fast-paced, suspense-filled story . . . sure to hold the reader enthralled—and scared."

—Frank Slaughter
author of DOCTOR'S DAUGHTERS

". . . trapped by its surprise, and its final horror."

—Stephen Peters
author of THE PARK IS MINE

D1412803

WAVELENGTHS

DANIEL M. KLEIN

A JOVE BOOK

This Jove book contains the complete
text of the original hardcover edition.
It has been completely reset in a typeface
designed for easy reading, and was printed
from new film.

WAVELENGTHS

A Jove Book / published by arrangement with
Doubleday & Company, Inc.

PRINTING HISTORY
Doubleday edition published 1982
Jove edition / December 1984

ISBN: 0–515–08051–9

Acknowledgments

A number of people have been very generous to me with their time and knowledge, especially Charles and Susan Halpern, Peter Roemer, and Leslie Scallet. I also want to thank Ayub Ommaya, Fred Elias, David Lippman, Bridgit Potter, Susan Schwartz, and Mel Berger. As always, my wife Freke Vuijst, has aided me in every aspect of the writing of this book, and I am immensely grateful to her.

D.M.K.

FOR FREKE

Love is an ideal thing, marriage a real thing; a confusion of the real with the ideal never goes unpunished.

—Goethe

Prologue

" 'If this isn't love, the whole world is crazy.' " Harry Goodwin was singing in lusty off-key to the slapping rhythm of his windshield wipers. " 'If this isn't love, I'm as daft as a . . . as a . . .' "

" 'Daisy,' " Harry's wife, Florence, piped in on perfect pitch.

"Daisy, daisy, of course." Harry pounded the palm of his hand against the steering wheel and laughed. "Good God, Florey, I'm hopeless. I can't even get through a song without you. I'm doomed to duets."

He smiled happily to his wife, then craned his craggy, gray-fringed head forward, squinting through the streaked window at the highway, the lights from the oncoming traffic multiplying in miniature in the raindrops. Florence emitted a soft, humming sigh.

"Cozy night," she said.

Harry nodded, his eyes still fixed on the glistening macadam. For a few moments the husband and wife remained comfortably silent and then Harry's mouth broke into a wide, crooked smile.

"I've just had the most delicious thought," he said.

"Tell me." His wife's voice sounded almost girlish.

"I was thinking," Harry said, still grinning, "that what we ought to do tonight, Mrs. Goodwin, is spend the night in some little out-of-the-way motel somewhere."

"You must be kidding."

"Nope. In fact I've made up my mind. We are definitely staying in a motel tonight. Someplace with very bouncy beds."

"But what about Pam?"

"We'll call her. She's a big girl. Believe me, she'll be delighted to have us away for a night. Now how about a kiss?"

Florence kissed him on the neck, her tongue slipping between her lips to the little pocket of soft skin beneath his

Adam's apple. She lifted her head, smiling. "What if they don't believe we're married?"

Harry chuckled. "A couple of old farts like us?"

He put his arm around his wife's shoulders and pulled her toward him, now cupping her right breast in his hand and touching his lips to her ear, unaware that his car had drifted halfway across the yellow meridian of the highway into the path of the Appleton Dairy's first southbound milk truck of the morning.

The state policeman who pried open the left rear door of the Goodwin sedan found the driver, a man in his mid-fifties, impaled on the steering column as if stabbed in the chest by a giant ski pole. The other passenger, an attractive woman in her late forties, had only suffered cuts and abrasions of the knees and calves, yet she was spattered to the eyes with stripes of blood, some half dried to the color of clay, some fresh, a brilliant red. It was her husband's blood. The officer estimated that the last drops had spilled from the puncture in the dead man's throat only minutes before his arrival. He reached his arm over the back of the seat to the woman.

"Let me help you out of here," the policeman said.

Mrs. Goodwin looked back at him; her eyes were dry and serene.

"Thank you," she said softly. "But I'll stay with my husband."

The officer considered waiting for the medics to remove the woman when she abruptly grasped the dead man's head in both hands and fastened her lips to his, her tongue slipping into his mouth. As she pressed her body against her late husband's side, two more spurts of blood pumped from his neck onto her corpse. Instinctively, the policeman yanked her away from the corpse.

"Jesus, lady, stop that! The man is dead!"

The widow Goodwin slowly turned her head and smiled rapturously.

"Goodness, Officer, don't you understand?" she whispered. "Haven't you ever been in love?"

Sunday

9 A.M.

"Let us pray."

The senator from Arkansas was standing at the head of the long, linen-covered table, his arms extended in front of him, palms upturned. He smiled at the First Lady and then looked over the row of bowed congressional heads to Marshall Jeckman, the director of the National Institute of Mental Health. Jeckman was examining the cherry-topped grapefruit half on the plate in front of him; he quickly bowed his head and closed his eyes.

"Dear Lord," the senator intoned, "we are gathered here this morning in the spirit of Christian fellowship to seek your guidance that we may guide others.

"Lord, year after year we have sought some meaning in the pattern of evil drawing around us. We searched for some signpost to lead our people out of this labyrinth of iniquity. Yet, instead of signposts, everywhere we looked we saw our children drunk and stupefied. We saw our daughters fornicating guiltlessly and then demanding the right to murder their unborn babies. We saw our sons sadistically enslaved by homosexual teachers. We saw one sister locking her God-given husband from her door so that she could qualify for a government check while another sister lived in naked sin so that she could qualify for a tax benefit. We saw parenthood that was no longer natural, but planned by men with pills and test tubes. We saw children dragging their parents to court, whores demanding payment of palimony, adulterers demanding no-fault divorces. Yes, Lord, everywhere we looked we saw a Sodom where a man was no longer responsible for his wife and children, a Gomorrah where a woman did not need to honor and obey her husband. And we cried aloud in the words of Your Son, 'Why have you forsaken us?' "

The senator paused and, thinking that the prayer had concluded, Jeckman raised his head and opened his eyes. He saw the senator wet his lips with orange juice, then run his fingers through his silvery hair before bowing his head and going on.

5

Jeckman continued to gaze at him.

"And yet, Lord, in that moment of darkest doubt, when my faith in Your Divine Purpose had all but ebbed away, You did give me a sign.

"Lord, on a Sunday evening two years ago as I was working alone in my study, You came to me in a luminous, overwhelmingly beautiful vision, a vision of a Peaceable Kingdom on Earth. Families all over America were united, wives with husbands, children with parents, parents with grandparents. Drugs and drink had disappeared, replaced by a natural joy. Homosexuals had vanished, replaced by men who cherished their wives and supported their families. Child murderers were gone, replaced by wives swelling with the blessing of God-given children. Wedding vows were sacraments. Families were indivisible. Matrimony was holy again.

"Lord, I sank to my knees and cried like a child as I beheld this Heaven on Earth. I cried with joy because in that moment, Lord, I understood that there are not a million obstacles preventing us from founding Your Kingdom on Earth, but only one obstacle. And that is the barrier between a man and his wife. The barrier born of dying marital love. Yes, Lord, if every man and wife could truly love one another with all their hearts for all their lives, peace would reign on this Earth forever after."

As the senator again paused, Jeckman leaned forward, straining to get a better look at him. He believed he saw tears slipping from the corners of the senator's eyes.

"I asked for a sign, Lord," the senator continued. "And You gave it to me. The very next day a man came into my office who I would not normally have listened to, a man I had not before believed deserved our attention and certainly not our financial support. But, Lord, You gave me a sign and I understood then that this man, Marshall Jeckman, bless him, is doing your work on this Earth."

Jeckman suddenly realized that the senator's eyes were open and he was looking back at him, now one of his fluttering, as if batting back a tear. Or winking.

"In the name of Jesus Christ our Savior, we thank You, Lord. Amen."

4:10 P.M.

"Yesterday, love was such an easy game to play
Now I need a place to hide away
Oh I believe in yes—"

Laura Esposito shot her hand out to the car radio and snapped off Paul McCartney in midlament.

"Hey! What did you do that for?" Ted gave his wife his familiar hurt smile. "That's one of our favorite songs."

"It was." Laura slumped down in her seat. "Now it's just another golden oldie."

"Nothing wrong with that. Actually, it's got kind of a comforting ring to it. You know, like, 'Grow old along with me! The best is yet to be.' "

Laura looked across the seat at her husband. Somehow the way he rendered that line made her feel as if she already had one foot in the grave. Her married foot. Only last week at her cousin's wedding she had shuddered when the kids said, "Till death do us part." It had sounded to Laura more like a life sentence than a pledge of undying love.

"What do we do now, take Route One North?" Ted was squinting through the windshield. "Check it out, would you, hon?"

Laura picked a glossy folder embossed in gold with the monogram "I.M." off the dashboard and pulled out the map, a meticulously hand-drawn affair labeled "From Boston to the Institute of Marriage by car."

"Yes, One," she said. "Just like going to the seashore."

Ted took the turn and then sat back, glancing at his wife. He was grinning. "Hey, do you know what this route makes me think of?"

Laura said nothing. She could just guess, damn his handsome face.

"It reminds me of that time we cut out from school and drove up to Kennebunkport for the weekend." Ted pointed out the window. "We took this same highway, remember?"

7

"That was ten years ago, Ted."

"Yup." His dark eyes twinkled. "But it seems like only yesterday, Chérie."

Laura smiled in spite of herself. On that weekend a decade ago, Ted had registered them at a seaside guesthouse as Mr. and Mrs. Amedeo Modigliani and back at school they had called each other Amedeo and Chérie for weeks afterward, much to the annoyance of their friends. It was all terribly silly and wonderful and romantic, this tall, curly-haired Amedeo from the Bronx strolling around art school in his black leather jacket with his adoring, long-legged Chérie from Upper Montclair, New Jersey. Now Laura turned her head to the side window. No, damn it, she wasn't going to let Ted get to her with some sentimental reminiscence today. Not on their way to marriage camp for their last desperate attempt to avoid divorce. It was too easy. Amedeo and Chérie were long gone, like almost everything else that was mad and vital and fun in their marriage. For some time now Laura had stopped believing in yesterday.

"Hey, you aren't getting into one of your moods, are you, Laur? The back of your neck is turning an unfriendly color."

Another old family joke. Ted was really pulling them out of the hat today. She turned back to him.

"Ted, let's not try too hard today, know what I mean? If this thing is going to work, it's got to come naturally. Nothing forced, okay?"

Ted's eyes turned cold. "That was natural, damn it. Just a friendly observation. You can't even tell the difference anymore, can you?"

"Sorry."

"Forget it."

Silence.

Shit.

Laura closed her eyes. Another absurd argument about absolutely nothing. Not a lover's quarrel that left her furious or hurt, but a *former* lover's quarrel without fury or rancor or even blame. Just emptiness. The sad lack of any feeling at all.

On the Institute of Marriage's first questionnaire, they had asked, "What went wrong with your marriage?" and Laura had answered, "Nothing. And everything." She had written that the very same things which had once been so exciting in her relationship with Ted had gradually grown heavier and harder and suffocating, that what had been so joyously simple and spontaneous in those first golden years of their marriage had turned complicated and inhibited. From sex to talking in bed afterward, from choosing their Christmas card to choosing a place to live. It was, in fact, a simple after-dinner argument about whether to move to the suburbs that had brought their marriage to an end. Listening incredulously while Ted described his plans for a four-bedroom home in Beverly Farms, Laura had finally realized just how far apart their dreams had grown, that they were operating on totally different wavelengths. That very night she had suggested a trial separation and two months later, on a cool Saturday afternoon, Ted had rented a U-Haul trailer and moved his drawing board and chair, the guest bed, and two suitcases of clothing to his new apartment on Commonwealth Avenue.

That had been almost a year and a half ago.

"Say, do you mind if I turn this thing back on again?" Ted had switched on the car radio and was twirling the dial. He shot her a conciliatory grin. "This may be our last contact with outer civilization for a week."

It took Laura a moment to realize that he was referring to the no-radio rule at the Institute of Marriage. There were dozens of such rules listed in the I.M. folder they had received last week: no radios, no teevees, no cameras, no chocolates; there was even one forbidding microwave ovens, although Laura could not imagine what kind of compulsive hausfrau would lug a microwave oven to a marital therapy camp. All the rules came under the general rubic of leaving reminders of everyday life at home so a couple could freshly focus on each other. Probably not such a bad idea at that. And at least it wasn't as stringent as the weekend ashram retreat her friend Valerie had gone to where the swami had confiscated her books right out of her suitcase because, he had said, "Words confuse the spirit."

Ted found a station that was broadcasting *Rigoletto* and immediately began booming along with the bass. It was the first time she had heard him sing in Italian in years. He smiled at her.

"What do you say we stop for a drink when we get to Portsmouth?" Ted winked. "We can drink a toast to our new life."

Laura would have loved to wink back, to say, "Sure, let's

celebrate," and then to clink martini glasses with him in some sunny Portsmouth bistro toasting marital bliss everlasting, but it would have seemed so forced, so fraudulent, that Ted surely would have seen through it. Ever since depositing their six-year-old son, Jonah, at Valerie's, she had been feeling terribly shaky. Sitting in front of her brownstone waiting for Ted to pick her up, she had considered taking a cab to North Station and spending the week alone in some inn in Rockport, leaving her husband a note which said, "Let's not break our hearts again."

But she could not do that to him. Or to herself either. Not after all the preparations they had gone through, the Institute of Marriage questionnaires, the interviews, the medical check-up, the thousand-dollar deposit. And all the wonderful hopes they had built up. No, she did not have to feel celebratory. Just willing to give their marriage another try. One last try.

"What do you say, Laur? One for the road?"

That famous Italian smile of his again. His Amedeo smile. God, how she'd hate to think of losing that forever.

"Ted, this whole trip may be chancy, you know." Laura managed a weak smile back at her husband. "I mean, I don't think we should get our hopes up too high, do you?"

Ted's jaw went rigid. He steered the car past the Portsmouth exit without speaking. "I can't see any harm in having a positive attitude about this week, Laura."

"No. No, of course not. I just meant—"

"Hell, it was your idea in the first place, wasn't it?"

"Yes, Ted." She nodded. "My idea."

Well, not exactly. In the very first place, going to the Institute of Marriage had been Jerzy's idea. Her lover's—ex-lover's—idea. This was a detail Laura had never told Ted, but it really wasn't as bizarre as it would have sounded if she had confessed it. Because, in a way, that enchanting, dazzling affair with Jerzy was what had given her hope that she could work things out with Ted.

Laura had met Jerzy on her job at the Science Museum only months after Ted had moved out of their Bunker Hill brownstone. And she had immediately been captivated by the intense, bushy-browed professor. He was just what the doctor ordered for that point in her life: witty, warm, spontaneous.

Totally undemanding. He was a tender lover and a joyous companion. Laura felt alive, vibrantly alive as a woman, for the first time in years. And yet from the very start there had been a bittersweetness about their affair, an underlying sense that it would not last, that in the end it could never be combined with the rest of her life. Jerzy had never married, never even lived with a woman, and whenever Laura would tease him about that he would laugh, saying that the best time to get married was when you were old and impotent and had nothing left to argue about.

But there was something else too. Much to Laura's surprise, the more she saw of Jerzy, the more she found herself thinking about Ted—the old Ted who used to race home from work for lunch in bed. And, though Jerzy's no-strings attitude was liberating, she found herself missing the security of Ted's devotion, his commitment to being a family. Laura felt torn. And she felt ridiculous. Lying in bed with Jerzy after a bout of passionate lovemaking, she would catch her thoughts drifting off to Ted and she would be filled with regret over the failure of their marriage. At those moments, she would wish to God there were some way of infusing that marriage with the vital feelings she had rediscovered with her lover.

And, of course, there was Jonah.

Whenever the boy returned to her after a weekend at his father's apartment, he would have difficulty settling into a good sleep for one or two nights. He would awaken crying, calling first for Ted, then for Laura, confused, disoriented, angry. Sure, half the children in his school came from broken families and had two bedrooms at separate addresses neither of which felt quite like home. And, of course, the most recent theories said that there were so many of these divorce orphans that they no longer felt abnormal or cheated or unloved. But what did the theories have to say about waking in the middle of the night and not knowing whose house you lived in? Laura's heart ached for little Jonah. It was a rotten deal. And all because his mother had thought that her marriage was imperfect, because she had insisted on feeling some arcane emotion for her husband. Because she had contended that a man and a woman had to be on the same wavelength to live as husband and wife.

It was Jonah who had gotten them both to try again. One

Friday night when Ted had come by to take the boy back to his rooms on Commonwealth Avenue, Jonah had looked up at Laura and asked in pure innocence, "Hey, Mom, why don't you come with us this time?"

Why not, indeed?

Laura had cried for hours and late that night she and Ted had made a plan: they would continue to live separately, but they would seek professional help immediately.

Over the course of five months, they saw a total of two marriage counselors, a psychiatrist, and a pair of psychotherapists, one male and one female, who worked in tandem. They talked about the division of household tasks; they talked about Laura's relationship with her father and Ted's with his mother; they talked about new techniques for "pleasuring" each other in bed; and they talked *ad nauseam* about communication. Sitting on padded leather chairs with nodding professionals between them, they tried to negotiate their lives. But to Laura it all was so absurdly irrelevant because it all came down to one question: How in the name of God could she make herself fall in love with Ted again.

Finally, in the midst of their third session with the male-female psychotherapist duo, Laura interrupted a discussion about "listening to each other's needs" to say, "You know that song 'You've Lost That Loving Feeling?' That's what I'd really like to talk about today. I mean, what do you do when you've lost that loving feeling?"

The male therapist laughed softly, like a parent showing appreciation of a youngster's joke. Ted looked hurt. And the female therapist touched Laura gently on her sleeve and said, "It's funny how things like popular songs can get mixed up in our minds with our real lives and confuse us. Do you know what I mean, Laura?"

"I'm not talking about a song," Laura said sharply. "I'm talking about the magic that can happen between two people. The chemistry. The romance, for chrissake! Have any of you heard of romance?"

Again, the male therapist laughed, though less indulgently this time. "I think we all know what you are talking about, Laura. We've all experienced those dreamy moments at one time or another." He smiled patronizingly. "Especially when we were younger."

"But one cannot expect to sustain such feelings as those all the time," his cotherapist continued without missing a beat. "Any more than one can expect to laugh all the time or to feel orgastic pleasure every moment of the day." She smirked. "I think it would be difficult to lead a mature, fulfilling life if we did."

Both the male therapist and Ted smiled.

"Well, then, fuck the mature, fulfilling life!" Laura said.

They were all silent for a moment and then the male therapist looked seriously at Laura and said, quite calmly, "I think that was very good, Laura. I think we've had a breakthrough here today. I think we have something we can work with now."

Laura didn't. At that moment she felt like she was married to all three of them. And that she was about to die of suffocation.

That same week Laura ran into Jerzy at the museum. It was the first time she had seen him in almost six months, the first time she had spoken to him since that Friday night when she had called him at his office to tell him that she was getting back together with her husband. Jerzy embraced her and, taking her by the arm, suggested that they have a coffee together. Laura hesitated, wondering if she were breaching a trust with Ted, but a few minutes later they were sitting opposite one another at a corner table of the cafeteria. Over their first cup of coffee, they chatted rather breathlessly about their work: Laura told of her troubles getting a stuffed three-toed sloth to hang by its tail in the diorama she was constructing for the arboreals exhibit; Jerzy told her of his lectures at Harvard on penguin pecking orders. But when their second cup arrived, Jerzy looked directly with his dark eyes into Laura's and asked, "So, how goes it with Ted?"

Laura said, "Fine," shrugging noncommittally. And she was just about to launch into an anecdote about her latest field trip when she suddenly found herself recounting the "Fuck Maturity" episode. Jerzy and she had laughed so hard that people at the tables around them stopped talking and began to stare at them.

"I really shouldn't be talking about this with you of all people," Laura said, catching her breath.

"Why not? It's a marvelous story, truly marvelous. I must

find a way of working it into my lectures."

"In your course on penguins?"

"Don't worry, I'll change your names."

Again, they both laughed uproariously and then Jerzy abruptly leaned down from his chair and began rummaging in his bulging leather briefcase. Opened, it gave off the familiar, musky lab odor that Laura had so often smelled on his clothing.

"Here it is," Jerzy said, pulling out a crumpled envelope and flattening it on the table in front of him. "I knew I was saving this for something."

"What is it?"

Jerzy looked back at her somberly. He reached his hand out and lightly touched the top of hers. "Laura, are you still determined to work things out with Ted?"

Laura felt her face coloring. At that moment, she was feeling more excitement, magic, desire—all those feelings that the therapists had found so trivial—than she had felt with Ted in five months of psychological hard labor. She knew she could very easily lift Jerzy's hand to her lips and kiss it, then silently leave with him for his apartment where they would make glorious, rapturous love for the rest of the afternoon. She gently lifted her hand from under his and put it in her lap. "Yes," she said softly. "I'm committed to that. For a while, at least."

Jerzy sighed. And then he smiled warmly at Laura. "Well, if there's no chance left for us, maybe at least I can be of some help. It would give me pleasure to know that you are happy."

Laura gave a puzzled shrug.

"One of my colleagues showed this to me." He pushed the envelope across the table to her. "It's a week-long seminar given by Dr. Elizabeth Saxon. Remarkable woman. I've heard her speak several times. Very clear. Very insightful. Her reputation is well deserved."

Laura absently opened the envelope while he spoke.

"And she's a raving feminist as well. I thought you might like that." Jerzy smiled. "Anyway, she's involved in something new called radical love therapy. It might be worth a listen."

Laura looked down at the sheet in front of her, a notice of a lecture at the Sheraton Ballroom by a Dr. Elizabeth Saxon, director of the Institute of Marriage.

"Thanks, Jerzy," Laura mumbled. She was still thinking how nice it would have been if they had left for his apartment. Damn, they could have been in bed at that very moment.

Ted was singing again, pounding out the finale to the second act with gusto. One of his finest virtues was that he never lingered in a bad mood for long—a rare trait, judging by what most of her married friends told her. His face was full of life when he sang, younger, more the face she had instantly fallen in love with so long ago than the tight-jawed, anxious face of the driven careerist he had become after they moved to Boston.

What a puzzle it was. Underneath it all they were still the same people they had been at art school, that dark, muscular face was still the same face that had literally made her heart flutter when she first saw it next to her in Renaissance painting class.

Now Ted seemed to sense Laura looking at him and turned his head and smiled. She smiled back.

What a peculiar sensation it was to *want* to love someone.

More as an excuse for canceling a session with the double-teaming therapists than anything else, Laura had brought Ted at eight o'clock on that Thursday evening to the Boston Sheraton. But much to her surprise, Dr. Elizabeth Saxon turned out to be everything Jerzy had said she was. And more. Much more.

From the moment the tall, white-haired woman stepped behind the lectern, Laura knew that she was something special. Saxon's appearance alone was a welcome relief from the tennis-shoe chic of the therapists they had been seeing; Saxon wore a gray-and-blue tweed suit, an amber silk blouse, and a string of pearls. Her fine-boned face was at once patrician and grandmotherly, and her eyes, keen blue, were warm and intelligent. As far as Laura was concerned, the regal doctor could talk psychobabble for the next hour and she would listen attentively. But Dr. Saxon did not talk psychobabble. She talked about love and marriage and the human heart in a way that Laura had never heard before.

"Most of you are here tonight because you are caught in a contradiction," Saxon began. "You want to save a marriage that you are dying to be finished with. You want a fresh, exciting start with something that couldn't feel older or more boring. You want to experience and dream and strive together, but you couldn't feel more apart. You crave the comfort, the security and continuity of family life, yet your heart is set on romance, passion and mystery. In short, you will settle for nothing less than the impossible: to feel something for your spouse that at this moment you cannot possibly feel. The real thing—love."

Laura felt a tingle in her spine. Incredible. It was as if the doctor were speaking directly to her.

Dr. Saxon leaned forward on her lectern, looking more serious.

"If you had come into my office a few years ago with those kinds of demands, I would have told you what at least one psychiatrist has already told you long before your arrival here this evening. I would have told you that you can't have it both ways, not sexually or any other way. I would have told you that the fact is, domesticity inevitably deadens sexuality, that you cannot crawl into bed night after night with the same person and expect it to be an erotic adventure."

There was a scattering of nervous laughs in the room. Dr. Saxon waited for absolute silence before she went on.

"And what is more, I would have told you that you could go ahead and try a so-called open marriage or a secret love affair or even, God help you, a group marriage, but in the end instead of expanding your life and feelings, you would diminish them. Not for moral reasons, but because of the ineluctable laws of the human heart."

Sitting directly in front of Laura, a red-haired, rather smart looking woman turned to her husband and simpered.

"In short," Saxon went on, "I would have told you to make your choice. Either stay in your marriage, resign yourself to some lower expectations and make the best of it, or get out of your marriage before it is too late!"

Laura's shoulders shuddered. As she watched Dr. Saxon step out from behind the lectern, she was suddenly afraid that the lecture was over, but now Saxon was walking toward the front row of the audience, her face brightening, her forefinger raised.

"Yet today," Dr. Saxon said emphatically. "Right now I am able to tell you that with a great deal of hard work and perhaps a little bit of luck, you *can* have it both ways! You *can* create a marriage that combines the comforts of home with the excitement of an illicit affair, the warmth of family life with the cool romance of solo adventure. Yes, you have a very, very good chance of having it all!"

Laura had to restrain herself from rising to her feet and cheering. A number of people did begin to applaud, but Saxon immediately silenced them with a quick, shy wave.

"Before I go any further, I see I have a few friends here, a few of my prize graduates." The doctor looked down a second and then smiled mischievously. "Actually, they aren't exactly here by accident. I asked a few couples if they would come by tonight and say a few words to you. Aaron, Cassy, would you come up here, please?"

A sharp-featured man in his late forties with long, gray streaked hair ambled toward Dr. Saxon from the second row followed by a tall, elegant blond woman at least fifteen years his junior. In front of Laura, the red-haired woman rose a few inches in her seat, then turned to her husband and said in a stage whisper, "My God, it's Aaron Stein. I thought I'd read he was off on a shoot somewhere in Portugal."

Aaron Stein slipped his arm around his wife's slim waist as he faced the audience.

"Hello," he said. He smiled, showing a row of gleaming teeth. "I feel like I should sing a chorus of 'I Love My Wife,' or something."

Many people in the audience laughed brightly, as if they were in a television studio. Laura figured Aaron Stein was one of those show business celebrities she had never heard of because she never watched "The Tonight Show." Stein planted a kiss on his wife's cheek before continuing.

"It's no secret that Cassy and I went through a living hell together for years. It was the pits, as the kids say. We hurt each other in every ugly way you can. To tell the truth, it's still a wonder to me that we got ourselves up to the institute instead of going straight to divorce court. But, by God, I'm glad we chose the institute." He paused a second, looking out at the audience seriously. "A lot of people will tell you that marriage is a drag. Well, I'm here to tell you that there is nothing in the world that can make you higher."

A number of people applauded, but stopped as soon as Cassy Stein stepped forward.

"Aaron's always been a hard act to follow," she said, smiling. "I just want to say that these past four months have been

the happiest in my life.'' She looked over at Dr. Saxon. "And
now I want to do something that I've been dying to do ever
since I met her.''

Cassy walked over to Saxon and threw her arms around the
doctor, kissing her audibly on the cheek. Again, several people
clapped. Laura grimaced, mouthing the words "Show biz" to
Ted, but seconds later, when the next couple appeared, she
was sitting at the edge of her seat. It was Whit Bancroft, from
Harvard, one of the directors of the museum. And standing
beside him, her arm slipped through his, was Bancroft's wife,
Raquel Freely, the feminist writer.

Professor Bancroft took a step forward and shrugged dif-
fidently.

"As always, Shakespeare put it best,'' he said. " 'Let us not
to the marriage of true minds admit impediments.' I think Dr.
Saxon understands these words better than anyone I've met.
Thank you.''

Laura found that she had impulsively joined in the applause
this time.

"I believe the best thing I could do now would be to answer
whatever questions you have,'' Saxon said.

A man in a corduroy suit rose and asked how much the
treatment cost. Saxon said that there was a thousand-dollar
returnable application fee and that the week at the institute
cost three thousand dollars more. When a number of people
groaned, she said that she was very sorry about this high cost,
but she had a large staff to maintain and the upkeep on the
buildings and grounds alone was a small fortune. She added
that any couple who genuinely could not afford it should
speak with her privately.

Next, a plump, pretty-faced woman about Laura's age
stood and immediately blushed.

"I don't know exactly how to put this,'' she began, "but
have you ever worked with a couple who are really terrific
friends, you know, who get along together fabulously and
everything, but—'' She abruptly stopped and began fussing
with a strand of hair.

"But who don't sleep together?'' Saxon said matter-of-
factly.

The woman laughed. "Yup,'' she said.

"My friend,'' Saxon said, smiling. "If I didn't, I would

have long ago been out of business."

Laura thought she heard people sighing all around the room.

Dr. Saxon was striding back toward the lectern when the red-haired woman in front of Laura abruptly stood up.

"Since it looks like nobody else is going to do it, I guess I'll have to ask the obvious question," the woman said, throwing back her head, her earrings swinging. "How do you do it, Doctor? How do you patch up a marriage in one week that people haven't been able to put together in years? In other words, what's your gimmick?"

Several people turned their heads away in embarrassment. Laura did not much like her style either, but she had to admit that the woman was asking the very question she had been afraid to. Dr. Saxon did not seem at all offended.

"I was wondering who would be the one to ask that question tonight," she said. "Yet I'm afraid it's one that I cannot give you a totally satisfying answer to, at least not at this point. But I can tell you that I do not subscribe to the 'patching-up' school of marriage counseling. I'll leave that to the first-aiders. I'm not interested in marriages that are simply stuck together. I'm only interested in vital, passionate marriages."

Saxon leaned forward on the lectern.

"Now as far as the time period is concerned, I'm going to have to say something that will probably get me kicked out of the American Psychiatric Association if anyone tells on me." Saxon pushed back a strand of silver hair that had fallen across her eye. "Over the years I have found that the longer a course of therapy takes, the less likely it is to succeed. What happens, I think, is that the therapy begins to take on a life of its own. Instead of guiding your life or your marriage, it becomes the trip itself. That's good for our business, but bad for you."

Laura said a silent "Amen."

"Finally, I would like to say that I, for one, prefer not to think of my treatment as a 'gimmick' any more than I suppose Freud would have liked to have thought of psychoanalysis as a gimmick—although, of course, there were several doctors in Vienna who thought it was precisely that. The therapy I offer is a technique for refocusing your feelings, for taking a couple who have lost emotional contact with one another and putting them back on the same wavelength. And, as most of you know, this therapy has enjoyed an extraordinary success rate." She smiled. "I'm afraid that's all I can tell you at this point without giving away any trade secrets."

The red-haired woman sat down, a skeptical simper still playing on her lips. Nothing Saxon could say could satisfy her, Laura thought. But as far as Laura was concerned, she was ready to sign up immediately. She was positive that if anyone in the world were going to save her marriage, it would be Elizabeth Saxon.

Saxon answered a few more questions—two more about payment schedules, one about what clothing to bring—and then she stood silently a moment, looking from face to face in the room.

"I'm afraid I've had to save the bad news for the end," she said.

The room went dead quiet.

"Much as I'd like to, we are unable at this point to accommodate every couple who applies to the institute. We simply don't have the manpower or the facilities yet. The unhappy fact is that only one out of every seven of you who apply will be admitted to the institute this season. I am very sorry about this and I sincerely hope that in the near future I will have enough room for you all. Let me just say this, though: if you do fail to get in this time around, it will not be because of your financial abilities or your age, and it will in no way reflect on your potential for someday having a fulfilling marriage. Our selection is guided only by our evaluation of our own abilities to meet your needs right now." Dr. Saxon again looked silently around the room before saying, "I want to thank each of you very much for being with me this evening."

There was a burst of loud applause but, looking along her row, Laura saw that many people's faces expressed less optimism than they had just moments ago. Laura's heart had sunk too. She turned to Ted, who was applauding enthusiastically.

"What makes you so sure we'll get in?"

"I just feel it in my gut," Ted said. "We're just what she's looking for."

"I hope you're right."

On their way out, Laura noticed that the red-haired woman also stopped at the information table and quickly, almost furtively, slipped an application form into her handbag. Saxon had gotten to her too after all.

Getting into the Institute of Marriage turned out to be more complicated and difficult than Ted had expected. They spent countless evenings at the kitchen table filling out questionnaires, answering multiple-choice questions about everything from frequency of sexual intercourse to the average amount of time they spent watching television together. Laura's favorite had been, "How would you feel if you found that your spouse had used your toothbrush?—A) Furious; B) Somewhat angry; C) Flattered; D) Turned on; E) No reaction." Laura wondered what kind of a woman would check "Turned on." Maybe she was missing something. Next were three interviews, each with a different member of Saxon's staff, although they all covered more or less the same ground: When did your marriage go bad? What had you expected of it? What are your fondest hopes for it now? And finally there was the medical workup—more complete than the Army's, Ted said—at a private clinic just off Boston Common. By the day the institute mailed their acceptances Laura was in a frenzy of apprehension. She was so sure that she and Ted would not be admitted and so angry at Dr. Saxon for putting them through those months of probing their minds, souls, and bodies for absolutely nothing at all that she had already mentally composed a furious letter accusing the doctor of the worst kind of torture.

On April 18, both Ted and Laura received letters announcing that they had been selected for a seminar at the Institute of Marriage beginning the first week of June. They celebrated by getting drunk at Durgan Park and then, for the first time in many months, going back to Laura's and making cautious, comforting love.

"Bravo! Bravo fortissimo!"
The opera was over and Ted was cheering wildly.
"Bravo to you too," Laura said. "I haven't heard you sing like that in years. It was lovely."
"Grazie, grazie." Ted bowed his head, grinning, then drew in his breath, smacking his chest. "Umm, smell that, would you?"

Laura breathed in the salt air. It was good. She was feeling better, much lighter and happier than when they had left Boston. And Ted looked so much better to her too. By God, he looked an awful lot like sweet Amedeo.

"Hey, look at that!" Ted was pointing at a highway sign. Kennebunkport.

Suddenly, Laura leaned against her husband.

"Ted, let's turn off here," she blurted out excitedly. "Let's see if we can find that old guesthouse and we'll register as Mr. and Mrs. Modigliani and we'll stay the whole week."

"You're kidding."

"No, I'm not, Ted. I mean it. Let's just have fun. That's all we need. Just some good old fun together. We don't really need anyone to help us."

Ted smiled at her as if considering her proposal, then turned and stared through the windshield.

"Yes we do, Laura," he said very quietly. "I'm afraid we do need help."

Laura's hands clenched. She felt as if she could hit him.

"God damn it, Ted! Do you always have to bring me down? Don't you have any joy left in you?"

"Yes, I do," Ted said, still looking straight ahead. "But that's not what you're really talking about, Laur. What you're talking about is skipping out on the institute."

"Of course I am!" Laura shouted. "Of course—" But before she could finish she lurched back against the seat as Ted abruptly yanked the car off the turnpike onto the road's shoulder. He pulled the car to a halt and then turned to her, his face flushed.

"Not this time, Laura. You aren't going to pull out on me this time. Not—"

"Please!" Laura felt a sob welling in her throat. "You've got every right to be angry, Ted. But you have to understand, I'm only trying to save us from another letdown. From more pain."

"You and your goddamned pain!" Ted shouted. "That's all you ever think about. No wonder it's the only thing you can feel!"

"Ted, please try to—"

"You try, Laura. For once—for one damned week—you try!"

Laura's sob broke and with it came tears. Ted reached

across and held her by the shoulders, pressing his lips to her cheek.

"It's going to be good," he whispered. "We're going to make it, Laur. It'll be everything we hoped for. I just know it."

They sat this way for several minutes, cheek against cheek, both with their eyes closed, tears still slipping down Laura's face, gradually calming. Quiet.

And then, without warning, a sharp staccato rapping sound broke within inches of their faces. They sprang apart, opening their eyes. Laura saw it first, a gloved hand knocking against the windshield. She choked back a scream just as she heard the voice.

"Roll down your window," a man said.

Ted started to open his window, but Laura grabbed his arm. "Don't!"

And then she saw the large reflecting glasses and the slow grin of the state trooper as he leaned into Ted's window.

"Take the Biddeford exit," the policeman drawled with the unmistakable cadences of a Down Easter. "Then take your first right and follow the signs, the ones with the blue arrows. You're not more than five minutes from the institute."

"What makes you think we're—?"

The trooper showed all of his teeth.

"They most of them stop right along here to think about it one last time," he said. "Already had two others this afternoon."

He ambled back to his cruiser and Laura and Ted stared at each other dumbfounded. And then they laughed so hysterically that tears again gushed down Laura's face.

6:50 P.M.

The last of the blue arrows pointed down a gravel road bordered on one side by the bay and on the other by a ten-foot-high estate wall. The road ended at an elegant spike-topped gate which swung open automatically as their car approached and then slammed closed behind them.

"Hi."

A frizzy-haired man, college age, stepped out of a guard-house just inside the gate and held up a clipboard, signaling Ted to stop. Wearing jeans and a Grateful Dead T-shirt, the young man looked incongruously casual in this stately setting.

"Welcome to I.M.," he said, walking to the side of their Rabbit. He ran his finger down the clipboard, then leaned in Ted's window, just as the trooper had. Ted turned down the radio and said, "Hello, we're—"

"The Espositos," the young man said. "Ted and Laura, right?"

Laura squinted at him. "How did you know?"

"I'm psychic," the young man said, deadpan. Then he grinned and said, "But your license number was a little help."

Laura smiled. She noticed that under his clipboard he carried a worn copy of *Walden Two*. What a lovely summer job for a college student, just sitting alone in a little stone house reading. She envied him.

"What you do now," the young man was saying, "is keep going straight for about a quarter of a mile and you'll come to a parking lot on your left. Can't miss it, really." He reached across Ted and deposited a hand-drawn map on the dashboard. "Someone will get your baggage there and you can use my little artwork to find your way to your cabin." He dropped his hand to the car radio and flicked it off, grinning. "No more radio. From now on just think happy thoughts. Oh, and let me warn you about the food. It's calorie city up there. I've put on ten pounds in two weeks." He patted his stomach. "Have fun," he said, waving.

Laura waved back as the young man returned to the guard-

house. She craned her head. A video camera was swiveling on
the guardhouse roof.

"Jesus, they don't skimp on security, do they?" she said,
pointing.

Ted grinned. "Must be to keep all those rejected couples
out."

He slipped the car into gear and ground up the hill.
Glimpses of ocean shone through the majestic spruce which
lined the drive. On the sloping meadows between them,
patches of wild flowers—carefully avoided by the mowers
—dappled in the afternoon sun. It was all natural but without
the ragged edges, like an English country garden. Just what
Laura expected from Elizabeth Saxon.

"Well, here we are."

Ted had coasted down to a row of parked cars, among them
several Mercedeses and a Jaguar making it look like the parking lot of a posh restaurant. Apparently, the institute's admissions policy did not discriminate against the rich.

"Who says money can't buy happiness?" Laura said.

Ted laughed and pulled the car to a halt. They were no
sooner out of the car, stretching and breathing in the cool,
pine-scented air, than a pickup truck rattled down behind
them. A gray-haired man in a custodian's jacket got out and
came toward them with his hand outstretched.

"All your bags in the trunk?" he said.

"Yeh." Ted seemed puzzled for a moment before he realized that the man was waiting for his keys. He handed them to
him.

"Your cabin's just up the road a bit." The man started
toward the rear of their car, then turned and said, "We'll keep
your keys someplace safe. You better get started now."

"Right." Ted handed Laura the map. "You were a Girl
Scout. Lead away."

Laura stood still. She felt vaguely uncomfortable. Already
everything seemed so final—the slam of the gate, their keys in
safekeeping. They certainly made it difficult to have a last-
minute change of heart. That was the idea, she supposed. To
suck you right in and get on with it. For better or for worse.
Familiar words, those. She took a deep breath, looked down
at the map, and led the way back up to the main drive.

"Fabulous-looking place, isn't it?" Ted took her arm.
"Look at that. It's straight out of Versailles."

Laura could not help smiling as she gazed over at an ornate marble fountain capped with a winged Cupid which spewed water. To her it looked more like Disney than Louis Quatorze.

"Gorgeous," she said. But then she stopped short. Ahead of them a small garden had appeared between the firs containing wrought-iron benches arranged in a square. And on one of the benches a couple was tightly locked in a passionate embrace. Laura felt embarrassed, but she could not look away. The lovers were so intensely focused on each other that they did not move, as if they had even suspended their breathing.

"They look like an ad for the final product," Ted whispered.

Laura kept staring. "Don't they ever come up for air?"

Ted looked at her, then dropped his hand from her arm and sprinted over to the embracing couple. They still had not moved. Suddenly Ted let out a great hoot of a laugh which echoed in the hills behind them. He swung himself over the back of the bench and leaned his head against the woman's bosom.

"It's a gag!" Ted yelled. "They're statues. You know, super-realism. They're pure vinyl."

Laura was laughing now too, giggling as much from relief as at Saxon's peculiar sense of humor. Ted jogged up beside her.

"Plastic or not," he said, deadpan, "they do look terribly happy."

"You're ridiculous," Laura said. She almost added that he had looked awfully cute bounding over that bench like a schoolboy. Very cute. It seemed as if the place were working its magic already.

They walked on silently for a few moments, arm in arm, listening to the chatter of blue jays, and then turned off onto a footpath. A second later, Laura let out a cry of delight. Situated atop a pine-needle knoll was their cabin. Except "cabin" was hardly the word for it. Made of stone with a tile roof and a timber deck, it was the most exquisite country cottage Laura had ever seen. She ran to the deck steps.

"I'll take it! I'll take it! I'll work nights. Anything."

"Maybe I should carry you over the threshold."

"Let's save that for later."

Laura pushed open the cottage door and pulled Ted in after her. It was every bit as perfect inside as she had hoped, from

the wide oak floors and leaded glass windows to the white
wicker chairs gathered around a stone fireplace. They walked
through a stone archway past the kitchenette into the bedroom. With its beamed cathedral ceiling and graceful bay windows, this was clearly the principal room of the house.
Against one wall stood a huge oak bed covered with a lilac
quilt, to the side was a matching chest and opposite it was a
fireplace even larger than the one in the sitting room.

Gazing around her, Laura felt a pang in her heart. It was
almost too elegant. Too beautiful. Too romantic. Instead of
making her feel like lighting the fire, throwing her arms
around Ted, and falling into bed with him, it made her feel
sadly self-conscious. Instead of enchanting her, it only made
her long for genuine enchantment. She did not belong here
with Ted. Not yet, at any rate. This was a bedroom for lovers.

"Hey, how about this?" Ted was calling behind her. He
had opened the closet door and was staring inside.

Laura turned. Hung neatly on wooden hangers were their
blouses, shirts, slacks and jackets. And on the shelf above
were their bags, open and empty.

"You don't get service like this at the Plaza," Ted said.

"There's a reason for that." Laura plopped down in the
window seat. She wasn't too crazy about perfect strangers
poking around in her underwear. And besides, she could not
figure out how that old man had gotten in here ahead of them.
She didn't remember seeing the pickup truck pass them.

"Aha! Official greetings from the management." Ted
picked an envelope off the dresser and sat down beside her,
flourishing it in front of her. He certainly seemed to be in gay
spirits. Laura opened the envelope and pulled out a long white
sheet, perforated along the edges. A computer print-out.

"Welcome to I.M.," it said. "We hope you find your ac-
commodations satisfactory. If you need anything, please tell
Arnold or Wendy Stadler, your personal hosts. Drinks and a
light supper will be served on the Main Terrace of Hilltop
House at 7:30. Please be there promptly.

"We hope your stay with us will be fruitful. Do remember,
love cannot be forced. It can only take you by surprise. So we
would suggest that you do not try to make love tonight.

Cordially,
Dr. Elizabeth Saxon & Staff"

Laura laughed.

"Audacious little computer, isn't it?" she said.

"It certainly is."

Ted looked disappointed. Apparently, he had had plans for the big oak bed already. Laura leaned over and kissed his cheek. She was feeling remarkably grateful to the computer's message. It did take the pressure off.

"We've got exactly fifteen minutes to shower, get dressed, and get over there," she said, unbuttoning her blouse. "Never a dull moment at Camp Loads-a-Fun."

7:20 P.M.

Wade Hobson set his drink on the windowsill and considered the telephone on the table in front of him. Only ten minutes ago, while glancing at the *Post*, he had realized that today was his wedding anniversary. It was an occasion which had gone uncelebrated for all fifteen years of Wade's marriage to Rachel—she found rituals depressing—and toward the end they had made brittle, painful jokes about "celebrating their anniversary separately again this year." But tonight, more than two years after their marriage had ended, Wade had gotten the idea in his head that the time had finally come for them to celebrate it together.

He picked up the phone and dialed a local Washington exchange. At the very least, she would find his dinner offer amusing; Rachel had always appreciated Wade's humor, if nothing else. The phone rang once, then a second time.

But after the amusement, what? It was doubtful that she would accept—not right away. She would have to quiz him first, strip down his motives: What were his expectations? What did this mean about their relationship? In short, she would have to rob his impulse of every shred of its original spontaneity.

The phone was ringing for a fourth time.

Wade took a long sip of his vodka and tonic. Rachel's talent for ferreting out hidden agenda had actually once attracted him to her. At that time, the whole world of the unconscious had fascinated him; it had appeared as miraculous and mysterious to him as the notion of an immortal soul had centuries before to his Puritan ancestors. Only when he had begun his training psychoanalysis with a disciple of Freud had Wade's fascination faded: his own unconscious desires seemed so puny, so basically uninteresting. Somehow, he had expected to find that same grandeur that had thrilled him on his first reading of *Civilization and Its Discontents*. But by that time, of course, it was too late. He was married to Rachel and he had spent ten years of his adult life becoming a psychiatrist.

And, discontent with both, he had sought refuge with the government: he had taken a job at the National Institute of Mental Health.

Wade had lost count of the rings. He removed the phone from his ear and began to replace it on the cradle when he heard the ringing stop and a woman's voice say, "Hello." It was Rachel.

Wade hung up.

Dear Rachel could have spent hours analyzing that.

7:25 P.M.

When Laura and Ted emerged from the trail into the statuary garden and first saw the elegant mansion called Hilltop House rising above them, they both beamed with pleasure. Illuminated in the rose glow of the early-evening sun, the manor house radiated gentility. Laura looked down at the simple linen dress she had chosen for her introduction to I.M. society. It was just a frock, really.

"Maybe we ought to go in the servants' entrance," she said.

"You look terrific."

Ted led her by the hand up the open-air stairway to the main terrace, where a tall woman greeted them and pinned yellow buttons with their names on them over their hearts like corsages.

"I'm afraid these aren't terribly attractive," the woman said with a slight accent. "Rather more like a convention than a party. But it does save embarrassment on your first day."

"I think they're lovely." Laura squinted at Ted's button. "Don't you, *Fred*?"

Laura twirled around gaily, taking in the party. It was as stylish as everything else at I.M., complete with liveried servants and a tuxedoed combo playing Cole Porter tunes.

"We must thank Mr. Gatsby for inviting us," she laughed. Then she leaned against Ted and whispered in his ear, "I *am* glad we came. We haven't had fun like this in years."

Ted kissed her cheek.

"I'll drink to that," he said and guided her to the refreshment table.

A woman with a yellow button that said "Judy" was standing by the hors d'oeuvre, a watercress sandwich in each hand. Laura recognized her from Saxon's lecture as the wife who had said she had everything in her marriage except sex.

"Hi," Judy said. "Do you feel as out of place as I look?"

"It is a bit overwhelming, isn't it?" Laura said. "You'd think they'd have played up all this splendor in their brochure."

"Not at I.M. They'd rather surprise you," Judy said, grinning. "They're very big on surprises here." She leaned toward Laura. "As in 'Let love take you by surprise!' "

Laura laughed. "Oh, and I thought we were the only ones to get a personalized greeting."

"Ours told us not to make love tonight." Judy made a mock-disappointed face. "We were crestfallen."

John, Judy's husband, circled behind her with a goblet of sparkling punch in each hand. He had a cheerful, ruddy face, much like his wife's.

"I came to Casablanca for the waters," he said, handing one glass to Judy and offering the other to Laura.

Laura thanked him and they shook hands all around. It reminded Laura of the instant hotel friends Ted and she used to make on Caribbean holidays. At the end of their vacations they would always plan a reunion back in the States which somehow never happened. She wondered if it were the same with I.M. graduates.

"Who are your hosts?" John said.

"Arnold and Wendy Somethingorother," Ted said.

"Great," Judy said. "That means we all eat at the same table. The food is supposed to be yummy."

"There they are over there." John gestured with his head toward the far end of the terrace, where it gave off onto a magnificent vista of the Atlantic. "The tall ones. We met them before. Nice people."

Laura narrowed her eyes. All she could see was a group of eight or ten people with some sort of red-and-white bands around their arms above the elbow.

"What are those armbands about?" she asked.

"All the Soul Mates wear them," John said.

"That's what they call the grads who are on staff," Judy said. She rolled her eyes. "The bands have little red hearts on them, as in wearing your heart on your sleeve."

Laura groaned and both women laughed.

"They're somewhere between the Red Cross and the S.S.," John said. He lowered his head, grinning boyishly. "And I'll bet you it was one of those sweethearts who stole my radio."

"I told you you'd get caught," Judy said.

"I hid it in a hearing-aid box in the bottom of my trunk," John said, still smirking. "Same place I smuggled dirty pictures into Boy Scout camp." Suddenly he raised his head, putting a finger to his lips. "Cheese it," he whispered. "The cops."

Laura turned her head. A pair of the Soul Mates was passing behind them, their arms tightly laced around one another's waists. They both had placid, loving expressions on their faces and they took long, synchronized strides, like tango dancers. They smiled at Laura when they saw her looking at them and, automatically, Laura smiled back.

"How about something to eat?" Ted was saying. "I think I smell spareribs over in the corner there."

"Sounds good to me."

Laura followed Ted to the end of the table, gazing around her. All told, there seemed to be about twenty-five couples at the party, counting the staff. Most seemed to be about her own age, although there was one yellow-buttoned couple who were easily in their sixties and two others who were probably in their early twenties. None of them seemed particularly morose; one of the things Laura had dreaded about coming to the institute was being surrounded by desperately depressed couples who wore their marital misery on their faces. Tonight, on the contrary, everyone seemed excitedly happy. There was something about the sheer splendor of the place that promoted giddiness—that, and the promise of future happiness which hung in the air. Laura felt it too. She held out her plate as Ted ladled Swedish meatballs over her noodles. Behind her, a woman had burst into a throaty laugh.

"I'll tell you one thing," the woman said. "This place makes est look chintzy."

Laura turned her head. It was Ginger, the red-haired woman who had sat ahead of them at the lecture. Laura had met her once after that too, at the Boston clinic as Ginger was leaving. At that time, Ginger had announced to the room at large that it was probably easier to become an astronaut than to pass the physical for Saxon's funny farm. Laura had been the only one to laugh and so the two had chatted for a few minutes. Now Ginger winked at Laura before turning back to the bouncy little blonde beside her.

"Have you really been to est?" the blond woman asked, her blue eyes widening. She barely reached the bulging chest of the massive young man next to her. Her button said "Affy"; his,

"Guy." Guy had blank, perpetually blinking eyes.

"Yes, class of 'eighty," Ginger replied. "How about you—Daffy, is it?"

"Affy," the young woman said. "Affy or Daphne. A lot of people get it mixed up."

"I sometimes call her Daffy," Guy said, languidly.

Laura suppressed a smile.

"No, I've never been to est myself," Affy bubbled on. "But I've read quite a bit about it in magazines. Did you meet any celebrities?"

"I got to know several. *Intimately*." Ginger again broke into a sexy laugh. Beside her, a slender, refined-looking man laughed too, although with a bit of a sneer. Ted had turned from the serving table and smiled at this laughing, handsome pair. Ginger gave him a slow wink. She seemed to have winks for everyone.

"I think I'd better sit down before I spill this on somebody," Laura said.

"Right. I saw some tables near the band." Ted smiled again at Ginger and led the way to the tables. "A lot of nice people here," he said when they were seated.

"Yes." Laura was looking back at the serving table. Ginger and her husband were now chatting animatedly with another couple, a tall, square-shouldered man and his short, plumpish mate. A little behind them were Affy and Guy, looking abandoned. All the liveliness was gone from Affy's face and the two stood blank-faced with drinks in hand looking like wallflowers. They reminded Laura of couples she occasionally saw in Montclair when she visited her mother, old high school classmates who had married at eighteen and now walked zombielike around town, only coming to life when they ran into another couple in the street.

"The queen arrives." Judy was leaning down to their table. "I think we finally get to meet her."

Laura moved her head to one side. Standing in the center of the terrace in a simple pearl-gray gown, her hair pulled back in a bun, was Dr. Saxon. She did, indeed, look regal. Already, several couples were gathering around her like courtiers.

"Well, I guess we ought to pay our respects too," Laura said, starting to rise. She hadn't touched her food yet, but she was eager to meet the great Dr. Saxon.

"Do you mind if I tag along with you?" Judy said. "John

seems to have taken one of his powders. He heard there was dancing later and got a case of the willies." She held up her hands melodramatically. "God forbid the poor fellow should actually have to put his arms around me."

Laura slipped one arm through Judy's and the other through Ted's. "Her majesty is waiting," she said.

As they approached, Dr. Saxon looked up from the group surrounding her and smiled at Laura.

"Lovely to see you," Saxon said, extending her hand.

"It's lovely to be here."

Saxon's handshake was warm and direct, like everything else about her.

"I hope you got settled in all right."

"Yes, everything's wonderful," Ted said.

"I love your little home," Judy said, eyeing the mansion that adjoined the terrace.

Saxon's eyes twinkled.

"It's not much, but it's comfortable," she laughed. "Actually, we were incredibly fortunate to find Hilltop House. It had been empty for decades when they showed it to us. Some lovely old silver magnate had it built as a replica of his ancestral home in Wales. A present for his wife. We thought that was fitting, don't you?"

Everyone laughed and, bowing her head, Saxon excused herself and moved on to another group of people, among them two pairs of Soul Mates. Laura noticed that both of these couples continually fondled each other while they talked, fingertips caressing a neck, a tug at a waist, hands laced. They certainly were a good advertisement for the Saxon method, whatever it was. If you didn't wither from envy first.

"They certainly look happy enough," Judy said, sighing.

"Who wouldn't be happy with that one?" It was the tall man whom Laura had seen chatting with Ginger and her husband a moment ago. Up close, Laura saw that he had a thin-lipped, cruel mouth. He was staring brazenly at one of the Soul Mates, a quite beautiful woman with straight blond hair.

"It's not polite to stare, Gary," the woman next to him said, managing a smile. She looked at least five years older than her husband.

"God gave me eyes to look at beautiful women," Gary said, smiling pleasantly, though still eyeing the blonde. "Not even your great Dr. Saxon can change that." He grinned at Ginger who was standing beside him. "Am I wrong, Ginger?"

"Well, considering that God is a woman herself, you may have a point," Ginger said, smiling.

Gary laughed and returned to gazing at the blond woman. "Say, I wonder if there are any rules about dating the counselors," he said.

"I'm starved. Let's get something to eat, okay, Gare?" his wife said, slipping her arm through his. Laura saw that the poor woman's plump face was reddening.

"I've got a better idea," Gary said, simpering. "Why don't you go and eat for both of us, Sybil."

"Please, Gary."

"Please, Gary. Please, Gary," the man said in a mimicking voice. Then he looked coldly down at his wife and said, "Look, I'm here, aren't I? Isn't that enough? Now you do something for me. Let me have a little pleasure for once." He pulled his arm away and turned his back to her.

Laura reached for Ted's hand. She didn't feel like sticking around for the rest of this. But before she had moved, Sybil suddenly grabbed Gary's jacket and, with surprising strength, spun him around. Her face had puffed up and it was bright crimson.

"Don't talk to me like that!" she said, loudly.

"I'll talk to you any goddamned way I please!"

Instinctively, Laura, Ted, Judy, and the others backed away, yet they couldn't take their eyes off the squabbling couple. Around the terrace, everyone stopped talking. Even the band stopped playing.

"You're a stupid, heartless man," Sybil seethed. "I was a fool to bring you here."

"Bring me here?" Gary spat out the words in her face. "You dragged me here!" He exploded in a brutal laugh.

Sybil opened her mouth as if to scream, but before a sound came, two couples in armbands appeared on either side of them and, grasping them firmly by the arms, quickly escorted them off the terrace and through the oak door to Hilltop House.

Now it was so quiet that Laura could hear the surf slamming against the rocks hundreds of feet below them.

"I'm terribly sorry." It was Dr. Saxon. She wore a sad, apologetic expression as she looked from face to face. "Please. Don't let this ruin your first evening with us." She nodded to the musicians, who immediately resumed playing. "Now, if you'll excuse me, I must see if anything can be done for them."

Saxon bowed her head and quickly walked to Hilltop House and entered. The door locked loudly behind her.

For a moment, no one talked. Laura still cringed. It had been one of the ugliest fights she had ever witnessed.

"Oh, God," she murmured. "For a little while there, I'd actually forgotten what this place was all about."

"Not me," Judy said quietly. "I didn't forget for a minute."

Her husband was still nowhere to be seen.

8:35 P.M.

"Yaz is only one for six in this series. The big left-hander has been sliding them past him in the outside corner. . . . Okay . . . Guidry winds up and it's a fast breaking ball. High, for a ball. One and oh. . . ."

John lay sprawled on his back across the front seat of his car, his feet propped on the armrest.

"Yaz steps out of the box and looks over at the bench. The tying run is still on second. There may be a bunt in the works here. Yaz is back in the box now. . . ."

John reached over and turned up the volume just a tad. No harm. The old guy with the flashlight had been gone for ten minutes. Still, there was no sense in tempting fate. Not after he had practically broken his neck finding his way through the woods down to the parking lot. And then scrounging around in his wallet in the dark for his extra key to get into his own lousy car. What a pain in the ass. Although it was sort of fun too. Like reading comics under the blankets with a flashlight when he was a kid.

"It's a swing and a miss. One and one. Yaz missed that one by a good two inches. That slider has been the death of him."

He did feel guilty about Judy, though. She was having a ball at the party. Maybe one of the other guys would dance with her. And then, at the next party, he would dance with her until dawn, if that's what she wanted. She deserved all the happiness she could get. A wonderful person, his wife. The best. Even if they didn't have everything you were supposed to have in their marriage, it was still pretty damn good. Better than most, really. They understood each other. Like she knew how important this ball game was to him. She understood.

". . . a dropping ball . . . right across the plate . . . Yaz swings and—"

John suddenly sat up straight and smacked his hand against the radio. A high-pitched whining sound had completely eclipsed the announcer's voice and it was quickly building in

38

volume to a shrill whistle. John smacked the radio once more
and then snapped it off.

"Goddamn boondocks!" he said out loud. "What the hell
are we doing in the goddamned boondocks!"

Monday

8:15 A.M.

"Well, look what the mailman brought."

Laura removed an envelope from the basket which had arrived just inside their cottage door before they had awakened. The envelope was warm from nestling against a half dozen freshly baked croissants. The place really should be written up in *Gourmet* magazine.

"Another word from our sponsor?" Ted said, gliding through the door onto the deck with a tray held high in one hand.

Laura smiled at him as he set a glass of orange juice, a mug of coffee, and a butter and jam plate in front of her. He seemed more happy and attentive than he had been in years. Perhaps all they really had needed was a vacation after all.

"Sleep well?" Ted asked.

"Terrific."

Well, not entirely terrific. Laura had lain awake for better than an hour thinking about that miserable pair who had humiliated each other so horribly at the cocktail party. She could not get the image of that woman's face out of her mind. It was not only the hurt and anger which had gotten to Laura, it was something else in the woman's eyes: a desperate, bottomless loneliness. Laura had wondered what it was that tied that couple together at all, what combination of sex and money, fond memories and preposterous dreams had brought them to the institute to save their marriage. No matter what had gone wrong in her marriage with Ted, it had never been ugly.

"So what's the good word?" Ted was nodding toward the envelope.

Laura took a bite of her croissant before opening it.

" 'Good morning and welcome to your first full day at I.M.,' " Laura began reading out loud.

"Good morning. Good morning to you too," Ted chimed, grinning.

" 'Following is a list of today's activities,' " Laura con-

43

tinued, trying not to laugh. " 'At nine A.M. you are expected in the Game Room at Hilltop House to participate in the Personality Response Game. Your hosts, Wendy and Arnold, will explain the details of the game to you at that time. Please be there promptly.

" 'At noon, an informal lunch will be served in the garden.

" 'At three P.M., you are again expected in the Game Room for your Olfactory Index Test.

" 'Supper will be served at seven P.M. on the Main Terrace. Your hosts will lead a discussion on "Perfect Marriage" at your table.' "

"Jesus, does it mention when I'm scheduled to take a leak?" Ted said.

"Somewhere between two and two-fifteen," Laura said, laughing. "Hold on, I'm not finished yet." She looked down again at the print-out and read, " 'Do remember that love cannot be forced. You must let it surprise you. Again, we would advise against any lovemaking today.' "

"Thanks a whole lot," Ted said, sarcastically.

Laura smiled across the sunny table at her husband.

8:55 A.M.

"Here you go, Mr. Hobson."

"Thank you, Tulio."

Wade Hobson dropped two quarters on the counter, then reached in his attaché case and lifted out a silver flask. While he mixed vodka into his half-filled coffee container, Tulio busied himself with a mound of pizza dough, pretending not to notice. It was a daily ritual that warmed Wade's heart toward the young pizza maker. Ah pretense, it made the world a friendlier place.

Wade fitted the plastic cap onto the Styrofoam coffee cup, slipped it into a bag, and started for the door.

"Have a nice day, Mr. Hobson."

"You too, Tulio. May you sell a hundred mushroom specials today."

Wade heard the young man laugh as the door to the pizzeria swung closed. Like the coffee ritual, it was a joke they repeated every morning, funnier to Wade, no doubt, than to Tulio, who had once earnestly confided to him his impossible dream of merchandising a full hundred of the house specials in a single day. It was an ambition Wade envied. Specific. Concrete. One you'd know when you achieved. Wade's ambitions had always been of the nebulous, untestable variety. When he still had ambitions.

He made his way out of the shopping center onto Fishers Lane, which was already crowded with thousands of his cotoilers trudging toward a mammoth gray concrete-and-aluminum office building, that fitting tribute to the tombstone school of architecture which housed Rockville, Maryland's major industry, the National Institute of Mental Health.

"Morning, Hoby." A bearded man in his early thirties fell in alongside Wade as they mounted a ramp leading to one of the building's orifices. "Have an exciting weekend?"

"Restful. How about you, Greg?"

"So-so. Kept getting called out of the can on special sessions."

He gave Wade a knowing, amused look. As special assistant to the director, Gregory Horowitz was responsible for mental health emergencies of congressmen and their families. It was a little-heralded function of the director's office, one that consisted mainly of keeping dypsomaniacal legislators from becoming public embarrassments, but Horowitz reveled in it. Returning to the office from one of his "special sessions," he would wink at anyone who gave him a chance, intimating the scandalous stories he could tell if only his lips—and files—weren't sealed. Such stories would be wasted on Wade in any event. He felt only embarrassment on hearing other people's sad secrets, a serious liability for a trained psychiatrist. It was just one of the reasons why Wade Hobson had ended up as a functionary at NIMH.

As they jammed into the elevator, Wade felt two soft mounds pressing against his back, the breasts of an anonymous black clerk in data processing. It was one of the great pleasures the warm weather brought with it, these young, uncoated women pressing against him in elevators and buses. It was, in fact, the only remotely sexual pleasure Wade felt at all since Rachel was gone.

"Listen, Hoby, why don't you come straight up to HQ with me. The Wizard has a surprise for you."

Wade swallowed. It was far too early in the day to deal with Jeckman, the new director. Wade needed a few moments alone in his cubicle to prepare himself. He needed to read the *Post* first. And to have a drink.

"I'll come up in a few minutes, Greg."

"Come on! Save yourself an extra trip." Horowitz held on to Wade's arm and smiled as the elevator door opened and closed. He did not release him until they walked into Marshall Jeckman's office.

"Good morning, Greg. Wade. Glad you could spare me a minute."

Jeckman gestured to the chair on the other side of his desk and Wade sat down. He had once assumed that Jeckman's frizzy, electric red hair had earned him the monicker "The Wizard," but soon learned that it came, rather, from his crisp, direct way of making things happen. Among other things, the new director had garnered a fatter budget than any other department in the beleaguered agency since the new administration had come in. The Wizard.

"I'm sorry to spring this on you on such short notice, Wade, but we've got an 'on-site' over at the sanatorium in Baltimore this afternoon. Collins is tied up, so I wonder if you could fill in. We'll need someone from OPRR over there. It should be interesting. Okay with you?"

Wade managed a tight smile. He was more than relieved; he was pleased. No one had sent him on an on-site visit in half a year.

"Fine with me," he said. "I can clear up my afternoon easily enough."

"Good." Jeckman stood, handing Wade a thick file. "Here's the background. Cleary from Hopkins is the P.I. I don't think you'll find anything out of line."

Wade rose, taking the file from him.

"Thank you."

He started to turn toward the door.

"Oh, one more thing, Wade, while you're here. I need an OPRR signature on a late renewal. It's here somewhere."

Jeckman shuffled through a pile of papers on his desk before lifting a sheaf stapled in the corner and folded back to the last page.

"Here it is. One of the family communications projects." He set the papers in front of Wade. "Need a pen?"

"Thanks. I have one."

Wade looked down at the paper. It was a standard project renewal form, the kind he signed routinely several times a day. Clipped to the corner were receipts from the program's budget for the last year and the topmost, from Memlo Laboratories, was for the purchase of a liter of something called Tyrazepam. Eight thousand dollars' worth of it, whatever it was. Wade began to pick up the form.

"It's all in order, Wade. I've gone over it," Jeckman said and handed Wade his pen.

Wade looked at The Wizard for a second, then took the pen and signed his name in the space reserved for Program Analyst from the Office of Protection from Research Risks.

10:10 A.M.

She ran toward him, her arms outstretched, her face radiant, her glowing eyes for him only, oblivious to the other passengers in the station as they looked from him to her and back again, caught up in their ecstatic moment as the lovers floated into each other's arms.

And then the image of the lovers froze on the video console in front of Laura in her soundproof booth.

She sighed. It was pure schmaltz—stylishly French, but schmaltz nonetheless—and yet she still fell for it every time she saw that final scene of *A Man and a Woman*. It was the essence of every romantic dream she had ever had, lovers reunited, drawn to one another like magnets, an unbearable longing to touch, to caress, to kiss, to make love.

A message appeared superimposed over the image on the screen. It said: "Please rate your empathy with the characters in this scene on a scale of 1 to 5, with 5 as total identification. Press the appropriate button now."

The word "now" began pulsing.

Laura considered a moment. A "5" seemed a trifle extreme, she thought. It was, after all, still in the realm of fantasy. She pressed "4" and the screen immediately responded by flashing "Thank you."

Laura drew in her breath and sat back in her padded leather chair. She had been in the booth playing the Personality Response Game for almost an hour now and she was feeling more than a little claustrophobic. Not that she hadn't been enjoying herself. It was like being a contestant in one of those afternoon television games that pit husband against wife, revealing juicy bits of domestic gossip. Except, of course, this was on a much higher plane; she had already been through the suicide scene from Zeffirelli's *Romeo and Juliet*, the lovemaking scene in *Don't Look Now*, the beating scene in *Alice Doesn't Live Here Anymore*. Emotionally exhausting, actually.

Now, a new message appeared over the image of the embracing lovers on the screen.

"On a scale of 1 to 5, rate your *husband's* empathy with the characters in this scene. Press the appropriate button now."

A good question. Ten years ago, Laura would not have had to give it a second's thought. She could still remember staggering out of the theater at the student center with Ted after they first saw the film. They had clung to each other, sniffling, for half the evening. But what about now? Was Ted still a sucker for Gallic sentimentality?

The word "now" was pulsing.

Laura decided to hedge her bet. She pressed "3."

Immediately the screen responded: "Your husband selected number 5."

Wrong again. Either Ted was lying or she had been underestimating him for years. God knows, he certainly did not seem as sensitive or profound or full of humor as he was claiming to be.

The next message appeared on the screen. Ted had guessed that she had selected "4" as her response. Bingo! He had been right about her every time. The obvious conclusion was that Ted knew her better than she knew him. But Laura did not buy that theory for a minute. It was too simplistic. The whole test—or "game," as they insisted on calling it—did not get any closer to understanding genuine feelings than its teevee counterpart. And after Dr. Saxon's portentous introductory remarks—her whole rap about these games being designed to "discover areas of compatibility and incompatibility" and her admonition to respond as honestly as possible because "the more we can understand about you, the better chance we have of reactivating your innate capacity for love"—Laura felt short-changed. There had better be more to Saxon's technique than guessing games or a lot of people were going to return home as unhappily married as they had come. And four thousand dollars poorer.

Barbra Streisand appeared on the screen, parading back and forth with a "Ban the Bomb" picket; then, just across the street from her, Robert Redford exited from a cab. Oh Christ, it was the last scene from *The Way We Were*, and Laura could already feel the tears welling up behind her eyes. She had seen the film three times, once in a theater and twice on television, yet she still found herself hoping against hope that Streisand

and Redford would work things out this one last time. God knows, they still loved each other in some basic way. Laura had always identified with them—two well-meaning people who had made the world's oldest mistake: marrying their opposites. When Laura had fallen in love with Ted, she had secretly hoped that his streetwise Bronx background would help her break out of her middle-class Montclair mold; she never suspected that Wild Amedeo in his leather jacket yearned for a blue Oxford shirt, a son in prep school, and a house in Boston's chicest suburb. She could have just as well married the boy next door. Now Streisand and Redford were facing one another on the street corner, both trying to hide the pain in their eyes. Redford was asking about their daughter and Laura felt a lump swelling in her throat. Oh God, it wasn't fair; they both deserved to be happy. Redford said good-bye and the image froze with them turning away from one another.

Laura pressed "5" the moment the question appeared. And she guessed—hoped, really—that Ted had pressed "5" too. They were both right. The machine announced that the morning's game was over. Happy ending.

Laura pulled off her earphones, stood, and let herself out of the booth. For a moment, her legs felt wobbly and her eyes were dazzled by sunlight streaming in the windows. Across from her, the husbands were emerging from their row of booths, rubbing their eyes, yawning, looking like passengers arriving in a foreign airport in the middle of the night. Except for Ted. He wore a big grin as he looked over at Laura. The perfect husband for sure. No one could look quite as smug as Ted Esposito.

On both sides of Laura, the wives were beginning to chatter.

"Robert Redford, come back," Judy said, wiping a tear from her eyes and some of the others laughed.

"Oh, I've heard he's terrible in bed," Ginger chimed. "A good friend of mine—"

Laura turned. She was in no mood for Ginger's show biz gossip or Ted's overachiever grin just at the moment. She started for the Game Room door.

"Don't worry, Jane. We hardly expect our couples to match up perfectly on the first day. There would be little left for us to do, then, wouldn't there?"

In front of Laura Dr. Saxon was talking with Jane Pratt, an attractive if somewhat preppy-looking woman about Laura's age. Jane looked disturbed. Apparently, she had not fared very well in the Response Game either.

"No, Jane, I have no doubts at all that you and Donald are basically quite well suited to each other," Saxon went on. "We wouldn't have selected you otherwise. Believe me, you'll be enjoying a beautiful relationship with each other in every way once we get you reoriented a little bit. Once you reach the Final Session."

Dr. Saxon touched Jane on the shoulder and they both smiled. Next to Laura, Judy said, "I'm sure we'd all live happily ever after if we could only take that wonderful woman home with us."

Laura smiled as they continued together to the door.

"Can I help you?" It was Wendy, their hostess, who had escorted them into the Game Room from the entrance earlier that morning.

"Just thought we'd get a little air," Laura said.

"Fine. I'll show you the way."

"I think we can find it," Laura said, sharply.

"No trouble." Wendy smiled beautifully as she led them down the corridor.

Laura scowled. My God, they seemed to put more effort into security than into therapy around here. It really was obsessive. What did they think she would do if she were left alone for a minute inside Hilltop House—steal a portrait of the silver magnate's thin-lipped wife? She watched as Wendy pulled a key chain from her jeans pocket and unlocked both bolts of the rear door.

"I can't tell whether they're trying to keep us in or out," Judy said, once they were outside and the door closed and locked behind them.

They strolled together to the knoll overlooking the pond and sat down in the grass in silence, looking up now and then at the pair of swans gliding in perfect synchronization below them.

"If only it were that easy for people," Judy said, dreamily.

"They mate for life, you know," Laura said. "They pick each other out when they're just kids—cygnets—and then they stick together through thick and thin, through swamp and ice.

If one dies, the other doesn't even remarry. She stays celibate for the rest of her life.''

"I wonder what they know that we don't.''

"Probably nothing. They have the advantage of not knowing a thing. I guess love works best when you don't have a thought in your head, just like they say in the songs.''

The two women watched as the swans executed a flawless turn at the edge of the pond. It was no wonder that these birds had inspired so many ballets.

"I have a friend who just sat and watched swans every day for an entire year," Laura said quietly. "On the Vistula in Poland. He stared at them through binoculars, trying to catch that sign, that silent signal that passed between them which said, 'Okay, we're going to turn now . . . one, two, three—turn.' '' Laura smiled. "He never did see it.''

"What a lovely way to spend your time. John would be bored with it in two minutes. Your friend must be very patient. And gentle.''

"Yes.'' Laura lay down in the grass and looked up at the cloudless sky, thinking of Jerzy. "I suppose he is.''

Again, they were both silent a moment and then Judy said, "You know, it's not really the sex I miss with John. I can live without that. Hell, my mother lived without it most of her life.'' She sighed. "But the gentleness. A gentle hand on my belly. How I long for that some nights.'' Her face colored slightly. "Hey, I'm sorry. That test seems to have gone to my head.''

Laura looked up at Judy. Her eyes were damp.

"It never quite works out the way we thought it would when we were little girls, does it?'' Laura said.

"No. That's the worst part about growing up, isn't it? Finding out that nobody lives happily ever after.'' Judy shrugged, managing a smile. "I didn't mean to get maudlin. I'm much better off than most, I know. Like that hopeless couple last night. What a doomed pair they are. I heard he lives off of her money and she's hung up on his body. Some deal. They didn't show up this morning, did they? I suppose the doctor had to send them packing off to the divorce lawyers already.''

Laura nodded. She had wondered where Gary and Sybil were also.

A burst of feminine laughter came from the garden and both women turned their heads. A small van covered with

colorful supergraphics had stopped in the driveway near where
the other wives and their husbands were waiting for the lunch
buffet to be set up. A young man was leaning his handsome
head from the van and Ginger was standing in front of him,
hands on her slim hips, apparently joking with him. Flirting
with a stranger at a marriage camp. The woman was so out-
rageously shameless that Laura could only laugh herself. But
she stopped when she saw Saxon approaching the vehicle, the
doctor's mouth drawn tight, masklike.

The driver's face blanched. Abruptly he pulled his head in
and jerked the van to a start. It circled Hilltop House before
coming to a halt in front of an adjacent stone building, a small
Gothic structure which looked as if it had once been the
estate's chapel, but was now known by all as the Therapy
Pavilion.

"I don't think I'd like to get on that woman's bad side,"
Judy was saying.

Laura nodded absently. She was squinting at the Therapy
Pavilion. It was surrounded by a low stone wall, and sitting on
top of pillars in each corner were rotating video surveillance
cameras. As the van approached, two short-haired men peered
out from an iron gate before swinging it open. And before it
closed, Laura saw the young driver gingerly step down from
his van. He held a small brown parcel in each hand and carried
them like a man on a tightrope.

3:15 P.M.

"Tell me, Doctor, you got any children of your own?"

"Yes, Mr. Goldberg. Three. All grown up now."

"So, who doesn't? My grandchildren are grown."

Wade took a deep breath and let it out slowly. He glanced at his watch. In two hours, he had only interviewed three subjects. He should have had twelve done by now. Somehow, all these octogenarians ended up interviewing him. Was the doctor married? No, divorced. A doctor without a wife? He should marry again. He had. And divorced again.

"Mr. Goldberg, let's get back to the questions, shall we? I'm afraid I have a train to catch."

"So, ask." The old man blinked his eyes, his pathetic, abandoned look. It had already worked twice on Wade. "That's what I'm here for. So you young fellows can ask me questions."

"Good. Thank you."

Wade looked down at his clipboard. He had skimmed Roger Cleary's prospectus that morning in his office, carefully rationing his sips of vodka-laced coffee. Not that it mattered. He could have read the whole thing in a stupor and gotten its simplistic point. Cleary's two-hundred-thousand-dollar hypothesis was that geriatric depression could be relieved by slipping subliminal uplifting messages onto the teevee screens the old people watched in the sanatorium all day. Greeting card slogans like "Enjoy each day" and "The best is yet to come," flashing surreptitiously onto their unconscious minds as they huddled blinking in dark rooms. The best is yet to come, indeed. Cleary had gotten onto the geriatric mental health bandwagon just at the right moment: the new administration was funneling more money into it than into adolescent disorders research. And for good reason: most of the cabinet hovered near seventy.

But Wade's job was not to evaluate Cleary's experiment, only to ascertain if the research subjects were being treated

54

ethically, were not being subjected to risks. Most importantly, he had to determine if the subjects had known exactly what they were getting into when they volunteered and, the trickiest question of them all when it came to incarcerated patients, if they had volunteered of their own free will.

Wade unfastened a sheet of paper from his clipboard and handed it across the table to Mr. Goldberg. It was the subject's informed consent form.

"Is that your signature on the bottom there?"

"You tell me. You got better eyesight."

"I need you to confirm it."

"So, it's confirmed."

"Do you remember reading that sheet before you volunteered for Dr. Cleary's experiment?"

Goldberg grinned, showing his gold bicuspids. "Doctor, I can barely remember what I ate for breakfast."

Wade sighed. "Would you read it now then, please? Out loud, if you don't mind."

"Look, Doctor, I know all about Roger's little experiment. The flashing teevee. The feel-good messages. By now, I can spot them coming." Goldberg shoved the consent form back across the table. "And let me tell you, it doesn't do a bit of good. When you're old, nothing makes you feel good. That's a fact of life."

Wade could not resist smiling. Goldberg could have saved the taxpayers a lot of money. He glanced down at his questionnaire.

"Has anything happened during the course of the experiment that in any way surprised or alarmed you?"

Goldberg shrugged. "Nothing surprises me."

"Have you suffered any unusual headaches or sleeplessness since you began the experiment?"

"No," Goldberg said.

"Were you in any way threatened, bribed, or coerced to participate in the experiment?"

"What could they bribe me with? A beautiful woman?" Goldberg emitted a short, barking laugh that ended in a cough.

Wade replaced the consent form in his clipboard.

"Why did you volunteer then, Mr. Goldberg?" he asked.

Goldberg looked directly into Wade's eyes. Despite the

cataracts that were forming in the old man's eyes, there was an unmistakable alertness visible there, a sad, philosophical intelligence.

"Because they asked me, Doctor," he replied.

"Thank you very much, Mr. Goldberg."

"My pleasure, I'm sure."

"Please tell Mrs. Leinsdorf to come in on your way out."

7 P.M.

"Well, let's get started then," Arnold said as the waiter finished filling his goblet with white wine. He lifted the glass and smiled around the circular table, looking warmly from face to face. A touch too warmly for Laura's tastes. All of the staff, Dr. Saxon excepted, were a little too big in the sincerity department as far as she was concerned. They reminded her of those dewy-eyed evangelists who hung around airports with Bibles clutched to their breasts.

"I propose a toast to perfect marriage," Arnold said.

"I'll drink to that." Wendy clinked her husband's glass. With both of their arms raised, their heart-emblemed armbands were nicely displayed.

Everyone else clinked glasses around the table.

"I think you missed me," Ginger said, her eyes flashing at Ted.

"An oversight, I'm sure," Ted replied.

Ginger gave him one of her theatrically seductive smiles as Laura gazed at her. The woman seemed to persist in thinking she was on a singles holiday at Club Med.

"I believe now is a good time to begin our discussion of perfect marriage," Wendy said. She made it sound like an impromptu idea, although they had all been informed of the night's dinner-table conversation in their print-outs that morning.

"For each of us, the concept of perfect marriage carries a different meaning," Arnold said, not missing a beat. "For some, it's based on our earliest naîve perceptions of our parents. For others, the model comes from books or movies or even some couple met briefly at a party. But somehow this ideal couple gets implanted in our imaginations and flourishes there, getting more enviable each day."

Arnold paused while the waiter set a plate of linguine in pesto sauce in front of him. He smiled at the food and then at everyone around the table.

"For most of us," he went on, "our own marriages never
come close to this ideal pair who live in our minds. So let's
start this evening by each confessing who his or her perfect
couple is."

Laura waited one second longer and then dug her fork into
the pasta. She was mad for fresh pesto. And having it served
on a terrace overlooking the sea was her idea of heaven.
Arnold was looking expectantly around the table.

"Why don't you get things rolling for us, Laura?" he said.

God, these people certainly knew how to ruin a perfectly
delightful meal. Another disappointment in Elizabeth Saxon:
group therapy at supper hardly seemed her style, although
after a day here it was hard to know exactly what Saxon's style
was. Her simplistic truth games and hovering, "happy day"
staff hardly reflected the depth or originality Laura had expected from the Dr. Saxon who had lectured at the Sheraton.

"Laura?"

Laura touched her forehead like a grade schooler who'd
been caught daydreaming.

"I guess my very first perfect couple was Dagwood and
Blondie," she said. "They had nice kids, a terrific dog, and
they made each other laugh. When I was nine, they certainly
seemed a lot happier than my parents."

"Wonderful," Wendy said. "Who came next?"

Laura took a sip of her wine. She might as well tell all and
be done with this so she could get back to her food.

"Well, by the time I got to art school, it was Virginia Woolf
and her husband, Leonard. I mean, I thought they truly had a
wonderful life together. Stimulating friends. They helped each
other with their work. It seemed they did absolutely everything
together." Laura paused. "Of course, then I found out there
was one thing they didn't do together—make love! I haven't
believed in a perfect couple since."

Everyone laughed, John a little too loudly, Laura thought.

"How sad." It was Dr. Saxon. She had walked over from
one of the other tables. "It's like a final loss of innocence,
isn't it, Laura?"

Laura nodded, looking into Saxon's bright, penetrating
eyes. Perhaps she had misjudged her. The sheer intelligence in
the older woman's face went a long way toward renewing her
hope for this place.

"And how about you?" Saxon had shifted her gaze to Ted.

"Any perfect couples in your life?"

"Yes, as a matter of fact," Ted said earnestly. "When I was in art school there was a couple who seemed perfect to me too. They were very attracted to each other. And they had this way of naturally complementing each other's strengths and weaknesses. They really had it all."

"What was their tragic flaw?" Ginger asked.

"We got married," Laura blurted out.

"That'll ruin a good relationship every time," Ginger said.

While the others laughed, Laura looked over at Ted.

"Sorry," she mouthed.

Ted patted her knee. "It's okay," he whispered. "That's what we're here for."

Dr. Saxon wandered off to the next table and, as Arnold posed his question to a new couple, Laura wound a healthy mound of linguine onto her fork. Jane and Donald Pratt admitted that they shared the same ideal couple, Charles and Anne Lindbergh. Then Judy said that she thought Lillian Hellman and Dashiell Hammett had the most perfect relationship she had ever heard of, even though they had never married. And John, after much coaxing, conceded that he had always thought his parents had as good a marriage as anyone could hope for. While the waiter removed their pasta plates and replaced them with the entree of cold asparagus with lemon mayonnaise, Affy took her turn.

"Lately there's been this couple on teevee . . . I mean, they're just in an advertisement, but I'd sort of like to model our life after theirs." The young woman's usually vapid face had come to life; animated, she was really quite attractive. "You probably know the one; there's this woman who works all day at an office in a suit and then comes home, puts on an apron and whips up a great dinner. And then when her husband comes home, she's in this gorgeous gown and they go out dancing to a nightclub."

"What is it you envy about them?" Wendy asked.

"I don't know," Affy shrugged. "Because she gets to get out of the house a lot, I guess." Guy stretched his muscular arm and rested it across her shoulder. It might have been a tender gesture, but Laura noticed that Affy jerked her head to the side. A flinch. And her face immediately lost all its vitality again.

Ginger was laughing.

"How about you then, Ginger?" Arnold asked. "Has there ever been a couple you envied?"

"Not really," she said.

"Come now, dear. Everyone envies someone," her husband, Ralph, said. He arched his eyebrows sardonically.

"Well, come to think of it, maybe there is one couple, Ralph." Ginger narrowed her green eyes. "Some friends of ours. Eli and Alice Lukas."

Ralph laughed, but it did not hide the fact that his face was coloring.

"Is there something special about them?" Arnold asked.

"Oh, any number of things," Ginger said, blithely. "But mostly I think it's their nonpossessiveness I like. They're a very free couple." She turned to her husband, smiling. "Especially Eli. He's the most uninhibited man I know."

"That's enough," Ralph murmured, barely audibly.

Ginger burst into a brittle laugh.

"But, darling, you wanted me to be honest, didn't you?" she said loudly.

"Then why don't you tell our friends about your wave," Ralph said, sharply. "Your honest little wave at the orgy."

"Don't be absurd, Ralph."

Ginger's face was now red too. Everyone had set down their forks and were dead quiet. Laura knew that she should not be enjoying this, but she was in spite of herself.

"It's really a rather interesting story," Ralph was saying, looking around the table as if he were recounting the plot of some movie he had just seen. "We were out at the Lukases' beach house for the weekend and one evening after dinner we decided to switch partners for the night. Well, we never did make it to the bedrooms and in the midst of everything I saw Ginger waving across the living room to me from the sofa." Ralph mimicked a merry, finger-trilling wave. "It was the most truthful thing I'd ever seen her do. 'Not waving, but drowning,' as the poet said."

Ginger stared at him coldly.

"You could never understand," she said evenly. "I was merely thanking you for letting me have my own space."

"Bullshit, darling."

They were facing one another, their heads separated by only inches, their eyes locked in silent anger. Laura saw Wendy slip away to the next table, where she stooped down and whispered to Dr. Saxon, then both women looked up and seemed to critically study Ginger and Ralph. Laura felt a chill pass across her shoulders—Saxon was going to remove these two just the way she'd had that other couple carried away last night, sent home for misbehaving—but, no, Saxon was shaking her head and Wendy returned to the table.

"Well, how about some coffee?" Wendy said brightly.

For a moment, no one replied and then, plopping her napkin on the table, Judy said, "Actually, what I could use is a little walk."

"Me too," Laura said and both women stood and started to leave, followed by their husbands.

"Now I know how this place works," Judy said. "After you listen to enough of those poor wretches putting each other through the mincer, you start to believe you are happily married after all."

Laura smiled ruefully. Much to her surprise, she had found herself sympathizing with Ginger. The woman was so intent on being extraordinary, on living up to some hip ideal, that her ordinary heart was doomed to be forever broken.

"But then again, who knows?" Judy was saying. "Maybe that's how those two keep their sex life interesting."

"I wouldn't bet on it," Laura said.

They were walking past the pond to where the footpath joined the main drive, Ted and John a few yards behind them, cheerfully debating the Red Sox's chances for the pennant. To the casual observer, Laura mused, they would probably look like four old friends out for a stroll in the park, not two couples on the brink of divorce at a marriage camp. Laura came to a halt. She shaded her eyes with her hand.

"Judy, look! That couple!"

Laura was staring at a man and woman walking down the drive toward them, their arms laced around one another's waist. They seemed to glide, moving in effortless unison like dancers in an old romantic film skimming over the grass, levitated by loving joy. Except that Laura knew this couple. She had met them last night at the party. Just before they started ripping each other to pieces.

"My God! Gary and Sybil!"

Laura could not take her eyes off the couple. They had paused in the middle of the road to gaze into each other's faces and now they swept into each other's arms, pressing their mouths together in a deep, sensuous kiss. When they finally finished, Laura heard Gary murmur, "Oh, baby, baby. You are too much."

Judy and Laura had come to within a few steps of them. Sybil looked up and smiled.

"Hi," Sybil said. "What a glorious day it turned out to be, didn't it?"

She gazed up at the blue spruce trees which lined the drive, her eyes gem-bright, her cheeks glowing. It was, very clearly, the glow of a woman who was passionately in love.

"Yes, a lovely day," Ted replied. He and John had come up beside them.

"Well, have a nice evening, everyone," Gary said, nodding pleasantly, and the pair continued past them, immediately oblivious to everything but each other, as if they were being carried in a cloud.

Judy sighed deeply. "God, that's what it's all about, isn't it?" she said.

Laura did not reply. She had turned around and was staring after the loving couple, her jaw slack. She hesitated only a split second and then raced up to them.

"Excuse me."

"Oh, hi again." Sybil released her hand from her husband's waist and looked at Laura with an expression of concern. "Say, is anything wrong?"

"No. Not exactly." Laura felt embarrassed. These two were so obviously madly in love, what could she ask them without seeming as though she were trying to dampen their joy?

"We met last night, didn't we?" Gary was saying, his smile erasing the cruel creases on the sides of his mouth which had seemed indelibly imbedded there the night before. "Let me see, I'm usually pretty good at names. . . . Laura, right?"

"Right."

Laura searched Sybil's eyes and Sybil looked down shyly.

"I'm afraid we were pretty horrid last night, weren't we?" Sybil said softly.

"Trying to maul each other per usual," Gary said, smiling.

Laura could not resist smiling back. "Yes, well, that's one way of putting it, I suppose."

"A pretty mild way," Sybil said in a sincere tone. "We'd been trying to do each other in, one way or another, for years."

Laura's face softened with relief. So that was their story; they were one of those passionate, loving-it-up-one-minute, hating-each-other's-guts-the-next couples. It was, no doubt, an exhausting way to live on a day-to-day basis, but she had always secretly envied couples like that. Their highs and lows had to be better than the relentless monotone her marriage had fallen into. She hoped that whatever Dr. Saxon's therapy was, it did not deprive this pair of their dazzling romantic highs.

"Well, good luck," she said, starting to leave.

Sybil suddenly reached out a hand and touched Laura on the shoulder.

"Isn't it dumb?" Sybil said. "Two people who basically love each other treating each other the way we did?"

Laura cocked her head to one side. "I suppose so."

"But now it's like we're starting all over again," Gary said. He slid the tips of his fingers across the nape of his wife's neck.

"It's the truth," Sybil said. "It's exactly like we're starting all over again. But this time we aren't forcing anything, do you know what I mean? We're just letting it happen. I know that sounds terribly corny, but I'll tell you, there's nothing in the world quite like it."

"Nothing," Gary repeated. "I never would have believed that before the Final Session."

Laura looked from one rapturous face to the other.

"Final Session?"

"Yes, we had it last night," Sybil said. "After our brawl. Dr. Saxon said she was afraid if she waited any longer, there'd only be one of us left."

"And now, just like that, you two are happy together? No problems?"

"It's incredible, isn't it?" Subil said, smiling radiantly. "I wouldn't believe it myself if it weren't happening to me."

"What? What's happening?" Laura hadn't intended to raise her voice.

"Just this," Gary said. "Just simply being in love." He had leaned forward and was looking at Laura as if there might be something wrong with her powers of understanding.

"Yes, but how does it happen? How does Saxon do it?"

Gary and Sybil looked at each other for a second and then simultaneously broke into rippling laughter. When they stopped, Sybil looked at Laura patronizingly and said, "Dr. Saxon can't do it for you, Laura. You have to do it yourself."

Laura stared back at her, speechless. From the corner of her eye, she saw Judy and the men coming to join her. She had one more question and she did not want to ask it in front of them. "But what about the bad things? The infidelities. Your money. What's happened to them?"

For an instant, Sybil's face clouded, her brow trembling as if it were independently fumbling for an expression; the creases reappeared on Gary's cheeks. Then, abruptly, they were both smiling again, soft, affectionate smiles. Sybil leaned her head against Gary's shoulder.

"That's all in the past," she said quietly.

"The past," Gary said, echoing her.

Laura heard the others stop just behind her.

"It's funny," Sybil was saying. "It's like you get a little happy. And then you're so happy about being happy that you get even happier. And it just keeps on going."

"That's beautiful," Judy said with a sigh.

Laura said nothing.

"Hey, I guess we'd better be going now," Gary said. He lifted his wife's hand to his lips and kissed it, then smiled at Ted. "This takes a little getting used to, I can tell you."

"Take care now," Ted said.

Laura stood perfectly still as she watched the couple glide away, effortless, joyous. Enchanted. Everyone was silent a moment and then John murmured, "Well, I guess there's hope for us all."

Laura turned. Judy was looking up at her husband, tears in her eyes. She looked so very hopeful. Laura quickly stepped around her and started back up the drive. Ted followed behind her.

"Looks like we came to the right place," Ted said, resting a hand on her shoulder.

Reflexively, Laura pulled away from him. Gary and Sybil were everything she wanted to be, everything she longed for. The place worked, damn it. It worked. What in hell was she feeling so anxious about?

8 P.M.

It had taken Wade over six hours to complete the interviews he should have been able to do in three. He was hungry and, worse, he was very, very thirsty. He was stepping out of the elevator when Roger Cleary called to him. Cleary was a prematurely balding man in his early thirties, a tall, angular Irishman who looked as if he were better suited to an outdoor country life—on a farm perhaps—than to the gray-tiled corridors of experimental psychology.

"Everything look shipshape, Hoby?" Cleary asked, coming alongside him.

"I think so," Wade said. He was already looking forward to a gin fizz on the train.

"What do you think of my procedures?" Cleary asked, smiling.

Anyone from NIMH, even Wade, was worth a little professional flattery. They were, after all, close to the source which made it all possible. But Wade knew that secretly every principal investigator held the institute personnel in the lowest esteem. Just working there was like an admission of failure.

"Your procedures seem appropriate," Wade said.

"But not imaginative." Cleary forced a little laugh.

"I'm sure they are just fine," Wade said. He looked for the outside door.

"Look, I have no illusions about the outcome of the experiment," Cleary went on. "It won't come to much. I'm just treading water, really. There's only one solution to geriatric depression."

Wade smiled. "What's that—death?"

Cleary laughed longer than was necessary. Then he leaned toward Wade, a serious expression on his face, and said, "We've got to catch senility before it begins or we're lost. When they start to lose their memories, all their joy goes with it."

Wade looked back at the young psychologist. Perhaps he

had underestimated him. He looked genuinely concerned. "Good luck," he said.

"I'll need more than that," Cleary said, grasping him by the arm. "What I'd really like to get going here is a synthetic-acetylcholine project. You know, the memory drug. See how dosage correlates with depression. But the damn stuff is still phase one—strictly. The FDA has been holding it back for years now, trying to jog rats' memories. And meanwhile my people are dying here. Dying of unhappiness, really."

"I'm sorry to hear that, Roger."

Cleary still held on to him.

"You know Jeckman, don't you?" Cleary went on. "Couldn't you get him to give somebody a nudge over at Drug?"

"I'll mention it to him," Wade said. He took a step backward so that Cleary's hand slipped from his sleeve.

"Hell, he could get it for me just like that." Cleary snapped his fingers. "I heard he got the FDA to release Tyrazepam to him with just a phone call."

Wade stood still, furrowing his brow. The drug sounded familiar, but he couldn't place it.

"Of course, that's for his people working the other end of the street," Cleary was saying. "Anterograde amnesia. Single-episode suppressant. They let him have it just like that."

Wade started for the door. He had just remembered where he had seen the name of that drug before.

Midnight

Pamela heard her mother again. Heard the moans and whimpers, the sad sounds the poor bereaved woman held back until she was alone in her bedroom where no one, she thought, could hear her.

Pamela's heart ached when she heard these sounds, yet she was relieved that her mother had found some release at last. It had not been natural the way she had been bottling up all that grief, offering a serene smile to the world as if nothing had happened. As if her husband—the only man she had loved since Pam's father had divorced her—had not been killed in their car accident less than two weeks ago.

Pam sat up in her bed. She heard her mother pacing on the other side of the wall, opening and closing bureau drawers, slamming her closet door. Pam fitted her feet into her slippers and stood, silently listening. Her mother's bedroom door opened. Footsteps on the stairs, clicking. Heels. In the middle of the night, her mother was wearing high-heeled shoes.

Pam pulled open her bedroom door and looked out. She saw just a flash of her mother descending the stairs. A flash of blue satin. She was wearing her wedding dress. Pam was about to call after her when she heard the front door open and close.

Grabbing her robe, Pam dashed to the stairs and down. But by the time she reached the front door all she could see was the headlights of her mother's car as it disappeared at the end of the driveway. For a moment, Pam could not decide what to do. Calling the police was out of the question; it could only upset her mother more. She had the number of a doctor, the "grief specialist" her aunt Estelle had recommended after her mother's outburst at the funeral—that terrifying explosion of laughter in the middle of her husband's eulogy. But the doctor was in Boston. And it was midnight.

Pam raced through the door and got into her car. She backed to the road without turning on her lights. The moon was bright enough. There was no other traffic. Within minutes, she saw the taillights of her mother's car ahead of her. Her mother was driving slowly, her window open, a blue satin sleeve flapping outside it. Pam could even hear her mother's car radio in the still night, playing the theme from *Dr. Zhivago*. And then her mother's car came to a halt. Pam applied her brake gently, turned off the ignition, and quietly got out of her car. She realized that she had known where they were going all along.

The dew soaked through Pamela's slippers by the time she reached the gate to the cemetery. She did not have to go any farther. She could see her mother clearly in the moonlight standing in front of her husband's grave, now kneeling beside it. Pamela turned her head away. She did not belong here. It was cruel to be spying on her mother like this. She was entitled to be alone at her husband's grave. Unwatched. Communing with her memories, his spirit.

Pamela was halfway back to her car when she heard the first moan. She stood still. The sound was carrying to her from hundreds of feet away, yet it had an intimate quality, a breathiness. It was not the moan of a woman in mourning.

Pamela turned and saw her mother crouched beside the grave, her head thrown back, the skirts of her wedding dress pulled up around her waist.

She was moaning in ecstasy.

Tuesday

7:40 P.M.

The bronze stallion thundered under Laura, her hair flying in the flower-scented air, her thighs gripping the animal's muscular back as they skimmed across the field past Hilltop House and onto the slope to the sea. And here was Ted, waiting for her, reaching up to her, swinging her in a weightless arabesque that carried her to the ground, now stripping away her blouse, now covering her mouth with his.

Laura sat bolt upright in the oak bed, her hand covering her mouth. The sheet clung to her sweat-damp body and she was trembling. It had been an enchanting dream, wonderfully erotic, but laden with an ineffable foreboding.

"Good morning and welcome to your second full day at I.M."

Laura turned her head, startled. Ted stood in the archway to the kitchenette, bare-chested, a mug of coffee in one hand, the day's schedule in the other. He looked quite handsome there really, though tamer than he had been in the dream. Fortunately, Laura felt. Maybe she was mellowing with age after all.

"Sleep well?"

"So-so." Fitfully would be more like it. Laura had been awakened by disturbing dreams throughout the night, not all of them with the passionate gloss of the last. She could not remember the other dreams, though some sense of them lingered with her. All she could recall was that each time she had awakened, afraid that she was falling.

"How about you?" she asked.

"Like a top," Ted said. He smiled.

"And what's on the docket for today?" Laura touched her hand to her forehead. It was beaded with perspiration.

"More of the same," Ted replied. There was something off-hand in his tone that made her curious.

"Let me see."

Ted brought the print-out to her and sat down on the bed as she looked down at it. At nine-thirty there was an Honesty

73

Game in the Game Room. Lunch in the garden at noon. At three was the Style Game, whatever that could be. The evening's dinner-table topic was "Definitions of Love." And at night, in the privacy of their cabin, they would be provided with a tape recorder and a cassette for a programmed personal meditation on "Loving." Afterward, if the spirit moved them, "Sexual contact was permitted."

Oh, boy.

"Breakfast is served on the patio," Ted said, grinning broadly.

10:10 A.M.

"Dr. Jeckman will speak with you now."

"Oh, yes. Thank you."

Wade had been waiting for the director to return his call for better than an hour, but now he felt unprepared. He kicked the door to his cubicle closed and hunched over his desk. He wished he had saved some of Tulio's coffee.

"Hoby? Jeckman here. How did everything go yesterday?"

"Fine, sir. Everything seems kosher." Bad choice of words. Jeckman was reputedly sensitive about being taken for Jewish.

"Good," Jeckman said. "Listen, Hoby, just between a couple of old hands, what do you think of Cleary's work out there? I mean, apart from any risk factor."

Wade felt flattered in spite of himself. No one had asked his evaluation of a research project since the "friendly dog" episode. On that occasion, he had announced to a review board that in his opinion the only project left worth funding would be an experiment which compared psychotherapy with the companionship of a friendly dog in terms of patient effectiveness. No one on the board had been amused. Just as well. Wade had been more than half serious. He was sure the dog would win hands down.

"It seems like a fairly straightforward experiment," Wade said.

He heard The Wizard laugh into the phone.

"That bad, eh?"

Wade laughed too.

"Let me put it this way," Wade continued. "I don't think Cleary is going to come up with anything that we couldn't learn by questioning a McDonald's advertising executive."

Jeckman laughed again.

"Very good, Hoby," he said. "I'll remember that line when Cleary comes up for renewal. I'll be talking with you."

Wade tightened his grip on the phone.

"Sir, there's something else I wanted to, uh, to consult with you about."

"Yes?" Jeckman already sounded impatient.

"That family communications project I approved for OPRR in your office yesterday. I was just checking my files. There's no subject consent for the use of a phase one drug. Tyrazepam is still phase one, isn't it?"

There was no response on the other end.

"Dr. Jeckman?"

"Sorry, Hoby. Someone just stepped into my office." He cleared his throat. "Now about that family project, I'm glad you brought that oversight to my attention, but I don't think there's anything there to worry about. I know the P.I.'s reputation quite well. She runs a clean ship. I'm sure she would not administer any experimental drugs without advising her patients first."

"Yes." Wade knew he should let Jeckman go. "Do you want me to draw up a consent form just so she's covered in our records?"

"I'll take care of it," The Wizard said, and he hung up.

10:20 A.M.

"Do you ever wish you had married someone else?"

Laura read the question off the video console directly into the microphone in front of her, then looked through the glass partition at Ted. He scratched the back of his head in an exaggerated mime of puzzlement, the long red wires trailing from the metal clips on his fingers like puppet strings.

"No," he said, finally.

Next to Laura, the green light pulsed on, the "truth" light, and she smiled. It was nice to know. Sure, it was egotistical of her to care so much, considering her own ambivalence about their marriage, but it was very nice to know nonetheless.

"Do *you* ever wish you had married someone else?"

"Is that your question or theirs?"

"Just answer the question, lady," Ted said, winking through the glass.

"Okay, okay."

It was no surprise that the Honesty Game was infinitely more fun when she asked the questions than when she had to answer them. When asking, the metal finger clips which registered Ted's galvanic skin response—the lie detector—seemed like a perfectly sensible safeguard against the usual marital double-talk. But when she had to answer a question, the clips were clearly an invasion of her privacy. Of course, she did not have to answer any question she did not want to. Before Wendy and Arnold had wired them into the booth, Dr. Saxon had made a point of reminding them that if any game or part of a game offended them, they did not have to participate. But, of course, she had also repeated that the more information you supplied her with, the better able she would be to "package your data" for your Final Session. She made it sound like a merchandising campaign. She certainly had done one hell of a packaging job for Gary and Sybil.

"Do you want me to repeat the question?"

"Hold on. Hold on. I'm thinking about it."

Had she ever really wished she had married Jerzy? No. Not really. When she was with him and thoughts of marriage had crept into her mind, they were somehow always attached to Ted. But on the other hand, over the last few years she had often wished that she had never married at all. Sometimes it seemed like such an absurdly arbitrary idea, this business of selecting one mate for life, pledging undying love, sharing bed and bathroom, vacations and bank accounts, with another person—the *same* person—year in and out forever after. It was the kind of blind partnership which no businessman in his right mind would enter into, a deal with so many unpredictable contingencies that no contract, however loaded with clauses, could begin to guarantee. It was totally irrational and it wasn't even natural. Born into another culture she might have been part of a harem or, better yet, had one of her own. Monogamy simply was not programmed in the genes. Jerzy had once said that some minute locus of the swan's brain compelled it to mate loyally for life. And that that locus was obviously missing in the human species.

Yet that wasn't the question, was it?

Laura looked through the glass. Ted was clenching his jaw apprehensively. He really did care deeply, didn't he?

"No," Laura said. "I never really did wish I had married anyone else."

Automatically, she looked down at the light panel. The green light pulsed on and, strangely, she was relieved. She had hoped she was telling the truth. Across from her, Ted was grinning like a schoolboy and applauding manically. Suddenly, a buzzer went off. In his enthusiasm, Ted had clapped his lie-detector clips right off his fingers.

Both doors to their booth opened simultaneously, Arnold sticking his head into Laura's side and Wendy's face appearing in Ted's. Arnold immediately reached across Laura and flicked off a switch.

"Looks like somebody got carried away in here," Arnold said, smiling as usual.

"Yes," Laura replied. "A little polite applause would have been sufficient."

Arnold nodded, but his eyes were fixed intently on his wife as she refitted the clips onto Ted's fingers. Arnold frowned and leaned his head down to Laura's microphone.

"Wendy," he said, sharply. "Wrong fingers. First and third, first and third. Remember?"

"Oh, God, are you sure?" Wendy's face was agitated.

"Yes," Arnold barked. "Jesus, you'd think you'd remember by now."

Laura could barely suppress her grin. What a relief. So Soul Mates had their little tiffs too, just like regular married folks. They were human after all. She looked up from the corner of her eye at Arnold. And at that moment his angry expression instantly vanished and was replaced by a look of utter puzzlement, his eyes blinking, his cheeks trembling. Laura stared at him. That look of fumbling uncertainty on Arnold's face somehow seemed familiar.

Arnold and Wendy ducked out of the booth and, just outside her door, Laura saw them face one another smiling again, sweet tender smiles.

"Hey, I'm sorry," Arnold said, touching her face.

"My fault," Wendy said, "I never was good with my hands."

"Oh, yes you are," Arnold said. "But let me take care of it this time."

Laura watched Arnold enter Ted's side of the booth, attach the clips, and laughingly warn Ted to try to curb his enthusiasm. It was incredible how quickly he and Wendy had recovered from their little spat. Laura looked down. A new message had appeared on her video console.

"Free question," the screen said. "Ask that question which you have been afraid to know the answer to until now."

Well, well. Dr. Saxon strikes again. It was another one of those sneaky, presumptuous questions which the doctor was so adept at, loaded with assumptions it had no business having —and, of course, dead on target. Laura knew what her question would be immediately. It was the one she had avoided assiduously all those months with the marriage counselors and psychotherapists although, God knows, there had been more than one opportunity to bring it up. Just thinking about it made her feel ridiculous and giddy. And afraid. She had no right to ask it really. But it was the question.

"Did you"—Laura forced herself to look up and through the glass into Ted's eyes—"did you sleep with anybody while we were separated, Ted?"

Ted's face immediately colored and he looked down for a moment before gazing back at Laura, his brown eyes soft, worried.

"Yes," he said, quietly. "Several women. But none of them meant anything to me, Laura."

The green light pulsed on and stayed illuminated for a minute as if to assure Laura that her husband's entire answer were true. Laura sighed deeply. It was the best answer she could have hoped for, better than if he had said that he had slept with no one at all. For a moment, they smiled at one another warmly through the glass. Laura could not remember feeling this close to Ted in years.

It was already time for the next question—something about money—trivial when compared to what had come just before it, as were the half dozen remaining questions which took them to the end of the game. When Arnold dewired Laura and helped her out of her seat, she was still thinking about her "free question," the delicate yet direct way Ted had answered it, and her immense relief when he had.

"Hi," she said, feeling almost shy as she saw Ted duck his head out from his side of the booth.

"Hi."

"What do you say to a little swim during free-play period?"

"Sounds terrific to me."

"Great. I'll meet you in the garden in five minutes. I just have to powder my nose."

Laura turned and made her way to the Game Room door. On either side of her, the other couples stood awkwardly facing each other. An almost palpable atmosphere of embarrassment permeated the hushed room; honest talk was obviously easier to contend with with a sheet of glass between them. And Dr. Saxon knew that, too; she was certainly several steps ahead of them all. At the far wall, Jane Pratt and her husband, Donald, were huddled next to one another, both looking tense, talking to each other in anxious whispers. Laura heard Jane say something about Mysoline and that he should have told the truth before.

"It's none of their business," Donald said, his voice rising out of its whisper. "You know how people are."

Laura walked by them to the door.

"Aren't you going to stay? We were going to serve some

coffee before we broke." It was Wendy. She was standing just outside the door. Like a sentry, Laura thought.

"I think I'll pass it up," Laura said. "I've had enough stimulation for one morning already. I'm just looking for the john."

"I'll show you the way," Wendy said.

"Look, why don't you just give me directions, okay?" Laura said coldly. She was in no mood for being treated like a convict this morning. "I think I can find my way to the little girls' room all by myself."

Wendy smiled enchantingly. "It's no bother," she said. "I could use a little walk myself."

It wasn't worth an argument.

"The games can be a little draining, can't they?" Wendy said cheerfully as they started down the hallway.

Laura nodded.

"It all pays off though," Wendy went on. "Every bit of it."

They arrived at the end of the hallway, where it opened onto the airy vestibule of the manor house. Along the walls were tufted velvet love seats and massive chestnut tables and scattered here and there were palms and ferns in enameled urns. Laura stopped and looked around her.

"What a marvelous place this is," she said. "Do you live here all year round?"

"No, Arnold and I just help out in the summer," Wendy replied. She pointed to the rear of the vestibule. "The rest room is just over there."

She grasped Laura at the elbow, but Laura did not move. She was staring at the heavy oak door under the stairway which had just opened. The overalled man who had taken care of their luggage on Sunday was now pushing a large trash barrel through the door and behind him Laura glimpsed two figures dressed in white walking down a long tiled corridor. The man looked up. He immediately pulled the barrel back through the door and swung it closed behind him. It shut with a hollow thud, like the door of a vault. Wendy tugged at Laura's arm.

"I think I can find my way from here," Laura said, trying to sound matter-of-fact. But her eyes gave her away and she knew it. She was staring at the oak door.

"No bother," Wendy said blithely. "I'll come with you."

Minutes later, as Laura was walking toward Ted in the garden, she stopped and stared back at Hilltop House. At the east wall of the mansion. The corridor door had been flush up against that wall. And it was more than a corridor. It had to be some sort of underground passage connecting Hilltop House with the chapel. With the Therapy Pavilion.

"We just want to observe you for a few days, Mrs. Goodwin."

"I think it's awfully silly." The woman beamed at the admitting psychiatrist, giving him a dazzling smile. "But if it's going to make Pam, poor dear, feel any better, I'm not going to make any objections."

"Thank you, Mrs. Goodwin." Dr. Berman bent his head over his yellow pad. Under other circumstances, he would have found the middle-aged woman's smile quite normal—engaging, in fact—but given her history, in particular her daughter's account of the woman's inverted grief behavior, he felt confident in his preliminary diagnosis: trauma-induced manic state. She would have to be watched carefully. Monitored. Depression followed mania like night followed day. He made a note recommending a course of Haldol to begin immediately. They could wait until she leveled out to consider lithium. And, hopefully, ECT—shock—could be avoided if they caught her before she crashed. Berman looked up. "Do you have any food or drug allergies that we should be aware of?"

"I don't think so, Doctor." Again, that vivacious smile. "Although if it is not too much trouble, I am trying to watch my calories."

She smoothed her blouse against her torso and laughed softly.

"I'll see what we can do." Berman gave her his best professional smile. "Well, that's about all, then. I'll just need your signature authorizing a request for your records from Dr., uh—" Berman consulted his notes. "From Dr. Saxon, and then we can get you settled."

The widow hesitated before taking his pen and Berman saw that she blushed. Interesting. An unusual response in a manic state. He wondered if he had jumped to his diagnosis too quickly.

"She was only our marriage counselor, you know," Mrs.

Goodwin was saying. "I'm not sure Harry would want me to do this."

Berman looked directly back into the patient's eyes. If he were going to confirm his diagnosis, now was the time.

"I'm afraid there is no way we can tell what your husband would want now, is there, Mrs. Goodwin?"

"Oh, I think I can," the widow said, smiling blissfully. "Even now I feel we're still on the same wavelength."

4:15 P.M.

A receipt fluttered from the file folder and spun like a leaf to the floor.

Bracing himself against a file cabinet, Wade looked down and considered his alternatives for retrieving it. Leaning over at the waist was clearly out of the question. And a bended-knee stoop was risky at best—this had been a five-jigger afternoon already and the floor seemed to have a treacherous tilt to it. Wade decided to leave the slip of paper where it was until he had finished with his business. Except, of course, reading over the annual progress report of the "Intrafamilial Communications Project" was not his business at all. If Jeckman had not made that clear, Horowitz had. Coming back from lunch in the elevator, Horowitz had made a point of telling Wade that The Wizard had asked for a performance review of all personnel in OPRR.

"Just thought you ought to know," Horowitz had said, with a significant wag of his eyebrows. "Better keep your nose to the grindstone for a few weeks. And your coffee weak."

Horowitz had laughed as Wade bounded out of the elevator at the tenth floor and Wade thought he could still hear him laughing when he closed the door in his cubicle and emptied his flask of vodka down his throat. Psychiatrists were masters of intimidation. Born into a poorer family, Horowitz probably would have become a cop. Or a gangster. If Wade Hobson III had been born into a poor family, he was sure he would be a happier man today. And at the very least, he wouldn't be risking the only job left to him to go prowling around, half drunk, in the Records Room of the National Institute of Mental Health.

Wade sat down at the government-issue green metal table and opened the folder in front of him. "Intrafamilial Communications" was the latest psychoterm for marital problems. Today, failed communication was the culprit for everything from juvenile delinquency to dypsomania. If everyone could only learn how to express their feelings verbally they wouldn't have to act out so destructively. A neat theory, the product of middle-class men and women who had spent most of their lives in classrooms learning how to talk. In their ideal world everyone would be seated in a chair jabbering away, expressing in exquisite detail every emotion before it was completely felt. It was one more reason why Wade preferred solitude.

He flipped through the progress report, pausing every few minutes to lift his eyes toward the door. He was not up to performing for the Performance Review Committee if they found him there. He skimmed the report's summary. The principal investigator had employed "a multimethod analysis of social reinforcement exchange between maritally distressed and nondistressed spouse and stranger dyads" and had set up "contractual models for negotiation training in marital dyads." Wade smirked. He should send Rachel a copy of this with his next alimony check. She had taken a special interest in contracts toward the end of their marriage. The summary went on in this vein for over ten pages, the P.I. finally concluding that "Positive reinforcement of intrafamilial communication" could reactivate a flagging marriage. Marvelous. But not a word about Tyrazepam.

Wade turned to the grantee's *vita* and bibliography. Wellesley, B.A.; P&S, M.D.; UCLA, Ph.D.; MIT, Postdoctoral Fellow. A grant giver's dream. And the bibliography ran to six pages, beginning with papers on sexual dysfunction and ending, inevitably, with papers on "communication dyads." Stifling a yawn, Wade closed the folder and started shakily to rise. He was halfway out of his seat when he plopped down again, frowning. Something about the bibliography had just struck him. He reopened the folder and, turning to the end, traced his finger down the margin. "*Journal of Applied Psychology,* Fall, 1961; *Conference on Human Sexuality,* January, 1962 . . ." He turned the page, then another. Halfway down the third page he stopped. Between a paper entitled "Erotic Reinforcement of Secondary Impotency" and one called "Systematic Marital Distress Coding" there was a gap in publication dates of six years. Wade turned back to the *vita.* Between UCLA and MIT was the same gap. Six years unaccounted for in the life of Dr. Elizabeth Saxon. Peculiar. Damned peculiar.

Wade again closed the folder, stood, and ambled to the file cabinet. He was fitting the report back into the drawer when he saw the errant receipt lying on the floor below him. Cautiously he lowered himself to his knees and picked it up. At that moment, he heard the door to the Records Room open. Instinctively, Wade stuffed the receipt into his pocket and crawled behind the far end of the cabinet. For ten minutes he sat there, an old fool with vodka on his breath, waiting while drawers opened and closed above him, footsteps receded, and the door finally closed again. Then he painfully creaked to his feet and left as quickly as he could.

Sitting in his cubicle an hour later, Wade reached into his pocket for a cigarette that was not there and his fingers touched the receipt. He pulled it out and unfolded it on his desk. For a moment, he could not remember where it had come from. The P.I.'s name, a Professor Adonski at MIT, was unfamiliar. And the project clearly had been misplaced in the "Intrafamilial Communications" file.

The receipt was for the purchase of two dozen African Pan troglodytes. Chimpanzees.

9:45 P.M.

"Imagine a golden thread attached to the center of your foreheads stretching between you. . . . Concentrate on that thread. . . . Now center all your feelings and let them flow . . . flow across the thread . . . heart to heart . . . mind to mind . . . soul to soul . . . from deep inside you . . . flowing . . . flowing. . . ."

Laura sat cross-legged on the bedroom rug, her back warmed by the blaze in the fireplace, her eyes closed, her breathing slow and rhythmic as instructed by the hypnotic voice on the "Love Meditation" tape. But not much was flowing.

"Let that loneliness that dwells deep within you open. . . . Rise. . . . Reach out . . . touching your partner's loneliness . . . embracing it . . . flowing with it. . . ."

A face came into focus in Laura's mind's eye. Not Ted's, but Arnold's. It was formless at first, vague, wearing that expression of fumbling uncertainty she had glimpsed for a moment in the Game Room. And then it was suddenly smiling, a caricature of a smile, like one of those "Have a Happy Day" buttons. But now it was not Arnold's face at all, but Gary's, still smiling that loving smile. That interchangeable smile.

"Feel the love growing inside you . . . flowing out of you. . . . And feel your partner's love flowing toward you . . . mingling with yours . . . enveloping you in its warmth."

A shiver shook Laura's shoulders. It had been a bad day. All afternoon and evening she had been feeling shaky, jumpy, labile. On the way to the pool, she had told Ted about the tunnel. He had been intrigued, but only as an architect, going on for fifteen minutes about the underground corridors which connected old Roman palazzos with their treasure vaults. When Laura had said that the Hilltop House passageway gave her an uneasy feeling, he had just laughed, so she had dropped it. She had grown gradually quieter for the rest of the day, taking little interest in the Style Game—an odd exercise in restyling your partner's clothes and hair and facial expressions on a computer visualizer, the silliest "game" so far, she thought—and she had been bored to distraction by the dinner-table discussion on "Definitions of Love." For a group of well-heeled, intelligent people, the other couples' definitions owed more to Kahlil Gibran than, say, Dante. Even sophisti-cated Ginger described love as "two people leading separate lives together." It sounded like a California greeting card. And Judy, bright as she was, called love "a sensual contract." Ugh! When it had been Laura's turn, she had shrugged and then quoted the line from Proust which said, "Love is space and time measured by the heart." She had felt embarrassed immediately afterward, feeling like a show-off, and Ginger's laughing wink at Ted had not made her feel any better about it. Ted's definition had been "sexy friendship."

"Looooove," the taped voice intoned. "Breathe it in. . . . Looooove. . . . Breathe it out. . . . Looooove. . . ."

Laura opened her eyes. Sitting on the rug three feet in front of her, Ted inhaled and exhaled on cue, his eyes closed, a soft, happy smile playing on his lips. At that moment, Laura found nothing at all attractive about her husband. He seemed so or-dinary, complacent, obedient—a candidate for the Most Im-proved Camper award. She could not help imagining Jerzy viewing all these games and discussions; he would find them hilarious, despite Saxon's academic reputation. And, worse, he would have found it a waste of time. He had once joked that America was the only culture he knew where even mar-riage was something you were supposed to "work at."

"Slowly reenter the here and now," the tape said. "Mind . . . heart . . . body. . . . Slowly open your eyes and look at one another. . . . Feast on each other's beauty. . . ."

Ted's eyes blinked open. He looked back at Laura bliss-fully, as if still in the throes of some celestial dream.

"Now slowly reach out your hands. . . . Now touch finger-tip to fingertip . . . gently . . . tenderly . . . the love flowing between you."

Laura held out her hands. She did not want to be a bad sport. But she was not about to blame herself either if she did not feel love flowing.

"Looooove," the tape droned. "Loooooove. . . . Loooooove. . . . Loooooove."

The word gradually faded and then, with a click, the machine turned itself off. Laura dropped her hands. For a full minute, Ted continued to gaze into her eyes, that limpid, dreamy look still on his face. Laura wanted to look away—she was feeling more self-conscious by the second—but she made herself look back out of some sense of obligation.

"Hi," Ted said, finally. His voice sounded remarkably like the man's on the tape. "How do you feel, Laur?"

"Tired."

Ted smiled. "I guess I feel a little sleepy too." He reached out a hand to her face and traced its contours lightly with his fingertips. "Why don't we go to bed?"

Laura looked down.

"I thought I might read for a while," she said.

"Really?"

"Yes." Laura sighed, then looked up again at Ted, managing a slight smile. "Ted," she said softly, "I'm sorry. But I don't think the love meditation took very well with me."

"Hey, that's okay," Ted said.

"To tell you the truth, I'm not sure this whole place is really working for me. Know what I mean?"

"Don't try to force it, Laur," Ted said. "Just let it happen."

"Oh, Christ! You're starting to sound like the rest of them." Laura's own voice jolted her. She had not expected it to be so loud.

"Laur, I only meant—"

"Listen, I'm sorry, Ted. It's just that—" Laura shook her head. She had to say it. "It's just that I don't really think we belong here."

"That's funny. I was just thinking how glad I am that we found this place."

"Not really, Ted." Laura was straining to keep her tone calm, confidential. "This isn't for us. Think about it. We don't want to end up like one of those Soul Mates, do we?" She attempted a casual laugh.

"Why not? That's what we're here for, isn't it?"

"But it's not real. Not normal. People don't change overnight like that. You know that. It's too fast. Too easy."

"You mean too effective, don't you?" Ted was on his feet, wagging his finger like a schoolmaster, not a trace of tranquillity left in his voice. "You see couples smiling, kissing, really happy together, and you go livid. Why is that, Laura? Why is it that one minute ago I was sitting there happy, full of love for you, dying to take you in my arms, and you had to bring me down? Why, Laura? Is happiness too goddamned ordinary for you?"

"Ted, please. You don't understand." Laura's voice quavered. "It's got nothing to do with us. It's just this place. There's something off about it. You can see that. Those surveillance cameras everywhere you look. People following you to the bathroom. And all that secrecy about the big Final Session. It's not right. There's something peculiar about this place and you know it."

Ted took a step toward Laura, a vein in his forehead throbbing as he leaned his face down in front of hers.

"Oh, I understand all right, Laura. I see very clearly what's going on. You don't like this place anymore. Two days ago you were convinced that Dr. Saxon was the person we've always been looking for. But now . . . now you want to back out. Just the way you've backed out of everything else we've tried. You know, sometimes I'm a little slow catching on, but I think I'm finally getting it. You don't want to stick with anything that's really going to help us because you really don't want this marriage to work, do you?"

Laura put her hand to her head as if protecting herself.

"Of course I do, Ted—but—but—"

"Well, give it a chance then, damn it! We're running out of options, lady, and you owe me this one. You owe *us* this one."

Laura's whole body was trembling and tears had sprouted in the corners of her eyes. Ted knelt in front of her, rocking her head in his arms.

"I'm sorry," he was saying. "I know you haven't been feeling well all day. I'm—I'm sorry I had to tell you about those other women. I know how you must feel. I didn't want to hurt you."

Laura closed her eyes. He didn't understand a thing.

11:30 P.M.

Berman arched back his neck and let the warm water pour onto his head and dribble down his face. After fourteen consecutive hours on admissions—a special privilege of first-year residents—he was beginning to feel almost human again. Just in time to dress and leave the hospital for the all-night diner on Boylston, where he would gobble down double portions of the Tuesday special, walk to his apartment and crawl into bed for his allotted six and a half hours of sleep. An interesting life for a man whose job it was to judge other people's sanity.

Abruptly, the water turned cold and Berman danced out of the shower stall, grabbing for his towel. The hot water was running out earlier and earlier every night. Another of the hospital's innovative economies, no doubt, along with reduced coffee rations in the residents' lounge and a 20 percent cut back of the orderly staff. Even Berman's job had been affected. With the reduction of bed space, the parameters of normality had risen. Craziness varied with the gross national product. Six months ago, Russell, the admissions chief, would not have thought twice about accepting his preliminary diagnosis of the Goodwin woman, but today he challenged him. Russell had said it would be more effective to take her on as an outpatient. Cost-effective, he meant. Berman had bargained him up to two days of inpatient observation. A compromise. The next patient would pay for it.

Berman pulled his old Brandeis sweat shirt over his bare chest. After the peculiar conversation he had had with Mrs. Goodwin's marriage therapist, he was glad he had stuck to his guns with Russell. This psychiatrist, a Dr. Saxon, had seemed more than a little testy on the phone at the beginning, as if she took it as a professional insult that the patient's family had not called her first. She had said that as the Goodwins' family therapist, she should have been notified immediately when Mr. Goodwin died and that Mrs. Goodwin knew that. A rather overzealous reaction for a mere marriage counselor, but not that unusual these days. Professional competition was on the rise as families' discretionary incomes dwindled. When Berman had asked that the Goodwin records be sent to the hospital, Saxon had responded that it would make more sense to transfer the patient to her clinic. Enough. This was a ridiculous conversation for two psychiatrists to be having. Berman had been ready to drop the whole thing when Saxon had suddenly softened, saying that she felt a personal responsibility for Mrs. Goodwin's well-being, that she should have foreseen that her patient's defense structure was too fragile to withstand trauma and that she should have better prepared her for it. Spoken like a real *mensch*. Saxon had then promised to send Mrs. Goodwin's records immediately, but in the meantime she suggested a substantial dosage of Haldol to prevent her from crashing when her mania peaked. Berman had accepted the advice as if he had not thought of it himself several hours before. Now, he tied his tennis shoes, slipped on his windbreaker, and started for the locker room door. He was hungry and he was tired and he had his own well-being to think about.

"Dr. Berman, are you busy?" Luz Perez, the head night nurse on the third ward, was standing just outside the door as Berman exited. She was breathing hard.

"Very busy." Berman threw out his hands and backed away in mock fear from the young nurse.

Perez followed him. "I wouldn't bother you, Doctor, but Abernathy doesn't answer his beeper."

Berman picked up his pace, trying to concentrate on the Tuesday-night special at the Boylston Diner. The nurse clasped his arm.

"I need a seclusion order," she said. "Emergency."

"What's happening?"

"I don't know, Doctor. It's a new admission. She suddenly jumped out of bed and started screaming and banging her head against the wall."

Berman grabbed the woman's hand and started sprinting for the stairwell door.

"What are you doing for her?"

"Restraining her. I've got five orderlies just trying to hold her down."

They were no sooner inside the stairwell when Berman

heard a cacophony of voices cascading toward them, cries, screams, laughter. And rising above it all, a bleating sound, like an animal giving birth.

"My God, the whole ward is up."

They took the steps two at a time, and at the third-floor landing Berman pushed open the door and they sailed through. "Get me five hundred mills of Thorazine. I'll sign for it later."

Patients in gray smocks lined the corridor like ghosts, shuffling, weaving, barely moving for all the noise they were making. Berman pushed by them and dashed to the ward entrance.

He froze.

Lying stark naked on the ward floor with five black orderlies grasping her limbs was Mrs. Harry Goodwin, her pelvis undulating wildly, her mouth gaping, and issuing from it the terrifying animallike moan.

"Doctor!"

Perez was beside him, the syringe in her hand. Berman took it from her and started for the patient. But at that moment, her arching body suddenly shuddered; she screamed, and slammed back to the floor, limp.

Berman reached for her wrist. Pulse was erratic, but strong. He looked at her face. Her eyes were open, dark welts rising beneath them, tears flooding from their corners.

The widow was weeping.

Wednesday

7:15 A.M.

"Hello?"

Pam picked up the phone in the middle of the first ring, before she was completely awake. She had slept on the sofa in the living room, the extension on the table next to her head. Dr. Berman had promised to call if there were any change in her mother's condition.

"Mrs. Goodwin?" A man's voice, but it did not sound like Berman's. It was colder, sharper-edged.

"This is her daughter. Is my mother all right?"

There was a second of silence on the other end, just enough time for Pamela's heart to take an extra beat. Something was wrong. She knew something was wrong.

"This is Sergeant Ozmond at Braintree Headquarters. Let me speak with your mother, please."

"What are you talking about?" Pamela felt the panic rising in her throat. Choking her. "What's happened to my mother? Tell me!"

"Listen, young lady, take it easy, please. And then why don't you tell *me* where your mother is."

Pamela took a deep breath. What was he trying to do?

"My mother is in the hospital. Memorial. What do you want?"

"Can I speak with her there?"

"No. She's under sedation. I'll take any messages for her."

Again, silence.

"Listen, Officer, I'm twenty years old and I'm the only one left in this house. Now what's going on."

"It's about Mr. Goodwin . . . your father." The policeman's voice was suddenly soft, hesitant.

"My stepfather. He's dead "

"Yes. We know." He cleared his throat. "We're conducting an investigation and . . . and we didn't want any of you to hear about it first in the papers or anything."

"It was a car accident." Pam stood next to the sofa, a sheet draped over her shoulders.

"Oh, yes, we know that," the policeman said. "But something unpleasant has happened."

He paused. Pam gripped the phone tightly to her ear.

"Mr. Goodwin's grave was, uh, tampered with last night. . . . The coffin was opened."

Pam felt her head spinning.

"It's sick, Miss Goodwin. Only a sick person would do something like that."

"What?"

"The corpse. It was decapitated. The head is missing, Miss Goodwin."

The phone dropped from Pamela's hand to the floor.

"Miss Goodwin, I don't like to have to ask you this, but did your stepfather have any enemies that you know of?"

8 A.M.

"Good morning and welcome to your third full day at I.M. At 9 A.M. you are expected in the Game Room to participate in—"

Laura crumpled the print-out into a ball, tossed it off the bed, and fell back onto her pillow exhausted. She had not had a restful sleep for three nights now. Four, really. The night before they left for I.M. hadn't been much better. She pulled the sheet up to her neck and closed her eyes.

"Hey, sleepyhead, your croissants are getting cold."

Laura opened one eye. Ted was strolling toward the bathroom in his swim trunks. He was dripping wet.

"Ted, I'm going back to sleep."

"But we're due at—"

"I'm too tired for any games this morning. I'm too tired for anything. Tell them I had a nervous breakdown."

Ted walked to the foot of the bed. He reached down and touched her ankle under the sheet. He smelled of chlorine.

"Are you okay, baby?"

"Fine. Just let me get some sleep. Please?"

"Sure." Ted raised his eyebrows and attempted a smile. "But don't forget, I've reserved a tennis court for three this afternoon."

Laura did not reply. She was already spinning off to sleep.

10:10 A.M.

Berman replaced the phone on its cradle and assumed a benign expression on his face as if he had not just completed the most bizarre conversation of his young career with a certain Sergeant Ozmond of the Braintree Police Department. It had taken Berman ten minutes to convince the zealous detective that there was absolutely no way his patient could have left the hospital in the middle of the night, traveled to her late husband's grave, dug up his coffin, decapitated his corpse, and returned to her bed for breakfast at six. Ozmond had sounded disappointed. A lunatic wife was a perfect suspect.

Berman gave a neutral smile to the prospective patient sitting across the admissions table from him, a young health-food-store clerk with the habit of dropping his pants at the odd moment. Exhibitionism had always struck Berman as a questionable form of sociopathology even though it was clinically detailed in the *Diagnostic and Statistical Manual of Mental Disorders*. After all, what did the manual say about the bottomless bars and nude beaches which were quickly becoming commonplaces of the American scene? This man, the breadwinner for a vegetarian family of four, had been picked up for indecent exposure five times in the past year and now faced the choice of imprisonment or incarceration in a mental hospital. He had opted for the hospital, poor fellow, although here he could expose his hapless penis with impunity. It would hardly be noticed in these wards.

"Mr. Firband, do you understand that your stay here will be for an indefinite period? It's up to the board when you can be released again."

"I know," the man said, shrugging unhappily. "It just seems like the lesser of two evils."

A rational response if Berman had ever heard one. This fellow seemed no more unbalanced than Gypsy Rose Lee.

"But perhaps we can help you with your problem and have you back with your family in a fairly short time," Berman said.

"Good," the man replied, grinning. Then he looked in Berman's eyes sincerely and added, "Although I don't really think I have a problem."

"No?"

"Goodness no," the man said, still grinning. "I mean, I know I wave my cock at people now and then, but they seem to like it. It's just my way of saying hello, you know."

Berman looked down at the table. He was beginning to wonder if he were really cut out for this line of work. He had been jumping to wrong diagnoses for a few days now and it came from more than lack of sleep: it came from a growing distrust of APA labels. A bereaved widow shrieks in the night and she is called a hysteric. A friendly man unzips his fly and he is a pervert. In another time and place they might have been called saints and showmen. Berman rubbed his eyes, looked again at the form in front of him, and then signed it. Mr. Ronald Firband was now officially and certifiably an insane asylum inmate. Berman picked up the phone and dialed two digits.

"Admissions," he said into the receiver. "May I have someone to show Mr. Firband to his bed?"

"I'm sorry, Dr. Berman," the supervising nurse said. "But all personnel are tied up just now."

"My God, don't you have anyone? I've got a roomful of people to see."

"No one is available," the nurse said testily. "We've had a little emergency to contend with. A patient is missing."

Berman was silent for a moment. He did not really have to ask his next question.

"Can you give me that patient's name?" he said finally, avoiding Firband's friendly gaze.

"Goodwin," the nurse replied. "Florence. Ward three."

Berman slammed down the phone and stood.

"Mr. Firband, I've been called away for a moment. Would you mind staying here until I come back?"

"No problem," the man said.

Berman strode out of his office and into the hallway. He looked quickly to his left—no one—and then to his right. At the far end of the corridor he saw a group of nurses and orderlies running toward the stairwell. Berman sprinted after them, his white coat flapping at his sides. He reached them just as they entered the hospital's first basement.

"The kitchen," an orderly said, breathing hard. "One of the cooks found her in a storage closet."

Berman pushed his way to the front of the group as they passed through the swinging door into the kitchen. Three white-haired Irish women, their aprons splattered with tomato sauce, stood wide-eyed against the wall, two of them clutching butcher knives in their hands. And in front of them, sitting cross-legged against the open closet door, was the patient, Florence Goodwin, her hands and face covered with a shiny, viscous substance the color of bile.

"Cho—chocolate," one of the cooks stammered. "She's eaten up two pounds of it. Baker's chocolate. Right out of the package."

Berman walked slowly toward the patient, forcing a calm smile.

"Off your diet, Mrs. Goodwin?"

The widow looked up at him, her eyes puffed red with grief.

"It doesn't matter anymore," she said, softly.

"Wouldn't you like a sandwich or something?"

"No," she said. "This is what I need."

Berman nodded to the orderlies and they gently lifted her to her feet. Together, they silently led her to the elevator and then to bed. Berman administered an intravenous sedative and left orders for the patient to be washed and kept under strict surveillance.

When he returned to his office, Firband was sitting just where he had left him, bending over a worn copy of the *Journal of Applied Psychology*.

"Hi," the man said. "Everything okay?"

"Yes," Berman replied. "And thank you for waiting."

He took off his chocolate-spattered jacket and looked down at Firband's file, trying to remember where he was, but his mind was still on the Goodwin woman. Nothing about her made sense. Everyone connected to her—the jealous marriage counselor, some mad mutilator of her dead husband's corpse —was bizarre even by the standards of the admissions office of a hospital dedicated to understanding the vicissitudes of psychosis. And nothing about Florence Goodwin herself fit the conventional labels—the denials, the hysteria, the gluttony. The chocolates.

The chocolates. Berman reached back in his mind to his medical-school lectures in endocrinology. Pure chocolate contained a heavy concentration of an amphetamine-like chemical identical to one produced in the brain in a specific excited state. He picked up the phone and dialed.

"Laboratory. Pierson here."

"This is Dr. Berman. How long do you keep urine specimens of new admissions?"

"Twenty-four hours usually. Unless we're doing a steroid work-up."

"Do you have a spectrograph up there?"

"No, but they let us borrow theirs over in genetics if we ask nicely."

"Good," Berman said. "I admitted a patient named Florence Goodwin yesterday. I want her urine tested for phenylethylamine."

"Phenylethylamine?" Pierson chuckled into the phone. "What have you got, a case of lovesickness on your hands?"

"I don't know what I've got," Berman said. "But bring me your results personally as soon as you can."

As he set down the phone, a young Filipino nurse entered the office and looked from the jacketless Berman to Firband and back to Berman again. She was new and Berman realized that she was not sure which of the two men was the patient she was to pick up.

"This is Mr. Firband," Berman said, gesturing across from him.

Firband stood, smiling, and placed the magazine on Berman's table. His fly was open and his penis, no bigger than a thumb, sagged sadly out of it.

1 P.M.

Wade thanked the librarian and took the journal with him to a seat at the periodicals table. On either side of him somber-faced, bearded men in their thirties were scribbling copious notes on legal pads. Full Freudian beards were in again with the younger NIMH doctors, replacing the wispy, Jungian Vandykes of Wade's generation. Hirsute badges of orthodoxy. Wade could divine a man's psychological persuasion by the amount of hair on his face. These silent, concentrated note takers beside him were obviously believers in penis envy.

Wade opened his journal, *The Psychopharmacological Review*, and glanced down the table of contents. The first article was about a new Ritalin compound for hyperkinetic children; the second was a preliminary report on an ongoing ten-year experiment with megavitamins on schizophrenics; the third on the latest antidepressive breakthroughs from Ciba. Gradually, these chemists were putting the beards out of business, titrating psychic tranquillity out of vials in Swiss laboratories. It was somehow fitting that most of these psychopharmacologists were from Switzerland. Wade remembered the bright yellow signs that dotted the winding road down from Mont Blanc as it entered Geneva. "*Silence et Prudence*," they said. Be quiet and be careful.

The last article was entitled "Benzodiazepine Hypnotics and Anterograde Amnesia: The Chemistry of Episode Retention." It was the one he had been looking for. Wade pulled his spectacle case from his breast pocket and put on his horn-rimmed reading glasses, the same pair he had been wearing since medical school. He turned to the article's summary. The authors, Ph.D.s from Stanford, had assessed the effects of five milligrams of Tyrazepam in two memory tasks, short-term retention of digit strings and the free recall of highly charged events. In both cases, the drug produced significant isomorphic psychological deficits in memory. In fact, what it did was obliterate all traces of memory of specific events.

Remarkable. The authors suggested that the drug might prove
therapeutic if administered soon enough after a traumatic experience, such as a wound or a rape. It made no mention of its
possible usefulness in marriage counseling. Wade smiled. He
would have had to take the drug hourly to erase the traumas of
living with Rachel.

Wade jerked up his head. Immediately the bearded man
beside him hid behind his notes. He had been staring at Wade
ever since he sat down, craning his neck to see what Wade was
reading. The Wizard was rumored to have a goon squad of
young psychiatrists who submitted detailed reports to Performance Review. The S.S., Horowitz called them. The
Snooping Shrinks. Wade leaned toward the young man, nodding pleasantly.

"Terrific article in here," he said, tapping the journal.

The young doctor snapped up his head and frowned as if he
had been engrossed in his work.

"It's all about experimentally induced paranoia," Wade
went on, a trifle loudly. Then he leaned closer to the man and
whispered, "It's full of good tips."

The bearded young man scooped up his pad, stood, and
walked away, leaving Wade laughing softly to himself. Even if
he had not been one of The Wizard's spies, it was good to jab
these fellows off balance once in a while. Catch them by surprise. Otherwise, reading their journals and gazing at subjects
through one-way mirrors, they tended to believe that all of
human nature was predictable.

Wade looked up at the clock on the library wall. One fifteen. Weiss had promised to return his call at one-thirty. He
flipped to the end of the article. Under "authors' *vitae*" it was
noted that the two Stanford professors were the chief officers
of a company called Memlo. Typical. How quickly pure science was turning to gold these days. Biochemists were the new
class of millionaires. It was twentieth-century alchemy.

Wade dropped the journal on the librarian's desk and
headed for the hallway. Just as the elevator door separated in
front of him, he saw his bearded tablemate step out from the
shadows of the stairwell. Wade entered the elevator, turned,
and winked at the man as the doors closed between them. If
the fellow were from Performance Review, Wade would certainly get bad marks for today. He had not opened his mail for

two days now, let alone attend to his current OPRR files. He wasn't even sure why he was so preoccupied with this Dr. Saxon and her "marital dyads." Drugs of all kinds were routine in most experiments these days. And written consent could have been easily overlooked in an open setting. It would not be the first time. No, it was probably the subject of patching up marriages which had hooked him. At fifty-seven, he already had two marriages with miserable endings behind him. Mysterious endings as far as he was concerned.

The phone was ringing in Wade's cubicle when he entered. He pushed the door closed behind him before he picked it up.

"Dr. Hobson?"

"Yes."

"This is Avram Weiss. I'm sorry I couldn't get back to you sooner, but I got trapped in one of those interminable faculty confabs. No one can jabber like clinical psychologists. It's like a roomful of neglected children."

Wade laughed politely. He had spoken with Weiss just once before, five years ago, and the professor had made the same little joke then.

"So, what can I do for you, Doctor?" Weiss said.

Wade rolled his chair up to his desk and hunched over his notebook as if he were hiding it.

"I just need a little background information," Wade began, trying to keep his tone casual. He did not want to alarm Weiss, but he wanted all he could get over the phone. Unofficially. "Just a routine check we're doing."

"Of course. Any way I can be of help."

"Thank you." Wade cleared his throat. "Professor, you were at UCLA back in 'sixty-eight, weren't you?"

"I've been chairman of our department here for twenty-one years," Weiss said.

"Yes, of course. Then you'd probably remember a research fellow you had back then. An Elizabeth Saxon."

For a moment, no reply came, as if the phone had gone dead, then Weiss said, "I chaired the review board that dismissed Mrs. Saxon."

Wade smiled in spite of himself. Damn it, for an alcoholic old fool, his instincts were still sharp. His hunch was paying off.

"That was fifteen years ago, Dr. Hobson," Weiss continued, his tone edged with defensiveness. "We made a clean breast of it then, dismissed everyone concerned, and returned our grant stipend in full. I really think that's all old business now, don't you?"

"I do indeed," Wade said quickly. He would hate to lose Weiss's confidence now. "We all thought you performed admirably under the circumstances. Uh, that's exactly why I'm calling, in fact. A similar case has come up recently. At another major university. One of your rivals, as a matter of fact." Nice touch, that. Wade was lying with ease now, a skill learned from years of living in Washington. "Dr. Weiss, I trust we can keep all of this conversation just between the two of us."

"Of course, Doctor." Weiss sounded happier already.

"I just wondered if you could save me some time," Wade went on. "You know, just fill me in on some of the details of the Saxon case."

Wade heard Weiss take a deep breath and blow it out into the phone.

"It was an ugly business, really," Weiss began. "Sad for everyone concerned. I never held Mrs. Saxon completely responsible for the worst of it, actually."

Wade murmured, "Yes," the transcontinental equivalent of a nod.

"Violent behavior was a hot subject then," Weiss went on. "We had student riots on our hands, war protests, the Bobby Kennedy thing. Control of violent behavior was where the money was and Saxon just got on the bandwagon. She set up an aversion-therapy model. You know, the sort of thing they use these days to get people to stop smoking. Little shocks for negative behavior. No one had the slightest idea she was using drugs."

Wade shook his head. It was all there. Every bit of it.

"Do you remember what drugs she was using?" he asked, still maintaining an offhand tone.

"I could look it up," Weiss said. "Whatever it was, it's still phase one. Some kind of superimmobilizer. It makes monkeys walk around in circles all day. Actually, she got it through one of her grad students. Some fellow in animal behavior. He was the culprit behind it all as far as most of us were concerned."

"You wouldn't remember his name, would you?"

"Adonski," Weiss said. "A-d-o-n-s-k-i. Protégé of Lorenz, actually. We sent him right back to Europe." Weiss laughed softly.

"And Saxon? What action did you take on her?"

Wade heard Weiss sigh.

"We didn't have to do much," Weiss said. "Poor lady had to be institutionalized before it was time for us to pass judgment. It turned out she had an awfully messy home life to contend with. Her husband—he was on our arts faculty at the time—had been playing around with one of his students. Then left his wife in the middle of this crisis. A real bastard. He probably drove her to it in the first place. And then walked out just when she needed his support. I wouldn't be surprised if she were still in a sanatorium someplace. I never saw anybody fall apart like that before or since."

Wade said nothing for a moment. He could feel his old heart thumping inside his chest.

"Thank you, Professor Weiss," he said, finally. "You've been most helpful."

"One thing," Weiss said, his voice lighter again. "We've got a renewal on one of our dream studies that seems to be stalled. Atkins is the P.I. I wondered if you could check into what's holding it up."

Wade smiled. It was favor for favor, just like any other business, even if this was the human experimentation business.

"I'll look right into it," he said, then, "Good-bye." He heard Weiss hang up.

As Wade took the phone from his ear, he heard a second click, but thought nothing of it. He was already searching in the piles of papers on his desk for the receipt he had found yesterday. The one for the purchase of monkeys. He was sure he had seen the name Adonski before.

3:30 P.M.

"Jonah!"

Laura's eyes snapped open as she was awakened by the sound of her own voice. Jonah! In her dream he had been waving frantically to her from the roof of their brownstone, coming closer and closer to the edge as he tried to get her attention on the street below. Just a dream, thank God, yet a knot of guilt remained in her stomach. What day was it—Wednesday? She had promised to call him twice while she was away and the fact was she had barely thought about him at all since she had arrived at I.M. What the hell kind of mother was she, anyway?

She rolled off the bed and picked up her watch from the bed table. Jesus, half past three. She had not slept that late since her honeymoon. Her excuse then had been that they had made love all night. Hardly her excuse this time. She pulled her nightgown over her head and slipped into her bra and panties, jeans and T-shirt, without washing. Then, searching under the bed for her sandals, she saw the morning's print-out in a crumpled ball. It could tell her exactly where to be now and what emotions she could expect to take her by surprise. She left it there and walked out onto the deck.

A blackbird was pecking at what was left of Laura's croissants on the breakfast table. The bird looked back at her with a single beady eye on the side of his cocked head and promptly returned to his task. He had certainly found himself a cushy ecological niche—croissants and preserve for breakfast, shrimp salad in the garden for lunch. Laura wondered how many unhappy couples' breakfasts he had picked at over the years. The marriage camp was his source of sustenance; he literally fed on human misery.

Laura stepped off the deck onto the path. She could not really call herself miserable, could she? Disgruntled was more like it. Spoiled and disgruntled. The little upper-middle-class princess who wanted everything her own way, marriage and career, motherhood and adventure, all the greedy contradictions Saxon had promised in her lecture to satisfy. The princess wanted nothing less than to live happily ever after. Or did she? After a few days here, she was beginning to wonder what in the name of God she did want. Ted had accused her of thinking that happiness was too ordinary for her. No, that was not quite true. She remembered reading Gertrude Stein's comment after her visit to the then idyllic island of Majorca. "It's paradise if you can stand it," the poet had said. That was exactly how Laura felt about Gary and Sybil and Arnold and Wendy and all the other Soul Mates. That much bliss would be unbearable for her. She would miss the grit of married life, the unpredictability of it. The danger. Laura shook her head. Good God, she had gone back to Ted from Jerzy because she had missed the security of a family, and now she was yearning for the instability of marriage. No wonder Ted was disgusted. There was no way to win with her.

She reached the drive and automatically turned to her left. She was sure of only one thing today: she wanted to talk to her son. She wanted to tell him that his crazy old mother loved him very much and that she would be back with him soon. That thought made everything easier. She smiled. There was at least one relationship in her life about which she had no confusion.

Laura heard a car coming up behind her and she stepped down onto the shoulder to let it pass, but as it came up beside her it stopped. Laura turned her head. It was Jane Pratt and her husband. They both looked distraught. Jane was lowering her window. Laura could see that she had been crying.

"I just wanted to say good-bye," Jane said.

"Good-bye? What for?"

"We're leaving." Jane's voice trembled. "We've been asked to leave."

"Let's pick up our bags and get it over with," Donald said sharply, racing the motor.

"Wait a second." Laura leaned down so that her eyes were level with Jane's. "Who asked you to leave?"

"Dr. Saxon. She said"—Jane's eyes started to fill up with tears—"she said we were incompatible. Irreversibly incompatible."

"Who the hell does she think she is, saying that?" Laura

tried to hold her voice down. She could see that Donald was angry enough already.

"She was very nice about it, really," Jane said. "She said she was sorry and everything, but it had simply shown up on the tests."

"Bullshit!" Donald barked. "You know goddamned well what showed up on her fucking test. She's supposed to be a doctor and she's just as prejudiced as anyone else."

Donald glowered and slipped the car into gear.

"Wait, please." Laura put her hand on the window to hold them. "Prejudiced against what? What are you talking about?"

Jane looked at her husband, as if asking his permission to answer, and when he sighed she looked sadly at Laura and said, "Donald's epilepsy. It turns a lot of people off. Even educated people. It scares them, just like it did in the Middle Ages. It's gotten so he never mentions it on a job application anymore. Why, he hasn't had a seizure in ten years. His Mysoline gets him through his EEGs with flying colors, and if anyone bothers to pick up the medication in his blood, we've always been able to pass it off as a sleeping pill. I mean they wouldn't have found him out here if it hadn't been for that truth game—you know, that question about, What is the biggest secret in your life? That little red light kept flashing on until he told the truth."

"Who cares?" Donald snapped. "This place is ridiculous anyhow."

"Don't say that, dear," Jane said, attempting a hopeful smile at Laura. "I'm sure it's good for some people."

The car started to move and Laura pulled her hands away. She wanted to say something—"Good luck" or "Don't give up"—but the fact was just now she envied more than pitied them. She would be more than grateful if Saxon told her and Ted that they had to leave today; it was probably the only way she could pry Ted out of here. Laura raised her hand to wave when she saw the Pratts' car come to a jerking halt.

"Fuck it! What now?" Donald bellowed.

Laura dropped her hand. Sitting in the middle of the road blocking the Pratts' way was a white motorcycle, its sidecar loaded with luggage. The driver swung his foot over the motorcycle's saddle and removed his black-visored helmet. It was Arnold. He was smiling his pleasant Soul Mate smile and the red heart on his armband blazed prettily in the afternoon sun, but there was something in his eyes that was less than loving. Much less. Laura strode quickly toward the car.

"I told you we'd bring your bags to the gate," Arnold was saying.

"I'd rather do it myself," Donald said.

"Well, we've already done it for you," Arnold said, his smile widening. "Now, if you'd just back up, you can turn around over there. I'll follow you out." He looked up at Laura and said quietly, "I think it would be easier for them if you were on your way now."

Laura did not move. She felt her face redden as the anger rose up inside of her.

"What the hell would you know about easier and harder?" she said loudly, her voice breaking.

Arnold tilted his head to one side, like the little scavenger on her breakfast table.

"I know all about it, Laura," he said softly. "I made life hard for myself for years, too. Suspicious and angry about everything. Holding back love from the people who needed it the most. Unable to give any new feelings a chance." He reached out his hand and touched Laura's shoulder. "Oh, I know all about harder and easier, Laura."

Laura pulled back from him. His hand dropped.

"If you can start by loving one person," Arnold went on, "maybe you can find it in your heart to be charitable to other people too."

Laura felt like screaming. Love, the man said. But all she heard was his anger and manipulation.

Donald had turned his car around and it coasted by.

"Good luck," Laura called.

"Good luck to you," Jane's voice came back bravely. "You've still got a chance."

A chance. Laura marched contemptuously past Arnold without so much as looking at him. Of course, they wanted you to believe that when you'd failed at I.M., you'd failed altogether, that it was time to call the lawyers, split up the furniture, arrange for shared custody of the kids. Is that what Jane and Donald were going to do now? Did they believe that they were "irreversibly incompatible," as Saxon had told them, even though they suspected that they had been asked to leave because of Donald's epilepsy? Laura accelerated her pace, then broke into a half run when she saw Hilltop House looming ahead of her.

"Hi! We missed you this morning." It was Andrea, the striking blond Soul Mate who had caught Gary's eye that first night. She stood in front of the door.

"Yes, well—" Laura was breathing hard. She had taken the steps up to the main entrance two at a time. "I needed my beauty sleep."

"Your first few days can be tiring, can't they?" Andrea smiled, then shaded her eyes and pointed across the slope to her left. "Everyone's taking a little break now. I think Ted and some of your friends are waiting for you on the tennis courts."

"I'll catch up with them later," Laura said. She walked around Andrea and reached for the door, but Andrea quickly stepped backward, blocking her way.

"It's a mess in there," Andrea said. "We're just setting up for tomorrow morning's game."

Laura held tightly to the door handle.

"I'll stay out of their way," Laura said evenly. "I just have to make a phone call."

Andrea did not move.

"I don't believe there are any outgoing calls scheduled for this afternoon," she said. She spoke in that same tone they all seemed to use with her, as if addressing a recalcitrant child.

Laura took a deep breath and let it out slowly.

"Listen, I promised my son I'd call him. It won't take a minute."

"Oh, that's nice," Andrea said. "Maybe we can schedule it for tomorrow, okay?"

"No." Laura's voice trembled. "I want to call him today. Right now."

"I'm sorry—"

"God damn it, you've got a phone in there, don't you?" Laura tugged at the door.

"Andrea!"

Both women spun around. It was Dr. Saxon's voice issuing from a small circular grill just above the door. A speaker box.

"Please forgive us, Laura," Saxon's voice went on. "Some

rules are made to be broken. I'm sure your son is eager to hear from you. Show Mrs. Esposito to the ground-floor study, please, Andrea.''

"Of course.'' Andrea took a key ring from her pocket and unlocked the door without looking at Laura. "Follow me,'' she said.

Silently, the two women entered the spacious foyer and walked past the stairway to the hallway. Laura glanced at the oak door under the stairs as they passed by—it was closed— and then waited while Andrea unlocked a glass-paneled door next to the entrance to the Game Room.

"Just one phone call,'' Andrea said, stepping aside. "Dial nine first.''

Laura said nothing. She waited until Andrea had closed the door and then made her way to the small mahogany desk by the window. It was bare but for the telephone. She sat down and reached for the phone, then abruptly pulled her hand back. It was shaking. She closed her eyes. What in the name of God was she doing in a place that made her feel like this? She took several deep breaths in a row. Calm down, girl. You're overreacting again. You don't want to sound unhappy when you talk to Jonah, do you? She opened her eyes, dialed 9, then a 1, then a 617 for Boston and Valerie's number. Her friend picked up on the first ring.

"Hi. It's me, Laura.''

"Well, hello. How's everything on the love boat?''

How incredibly nice to hear a voice from the outside world.

"Fine, Val. Quite an adventure, really. I'll tell you all about it when I get back. How's Jonah behaving?''

"Oh, he's terrific. A good eater, that boy of yours. Listen, he's been waiting to hear from you. I'll go get him. He and David are outside playing something called Space Ball. Hang on.''

Laura clutched the phone to her ear, as if by holding it tightly she would stay connected with the world beyond I.M. The real world.

"Mom?''

"Hi, Jonah. How are you, sweetie?''

"Great, Mom. I'm winning. David can't catch so good.''

"Yes, well—'' Laura heard her voice throb. God, she wanted to be home. "Well, you've got to remember, David's younger than you are, hon.''

"I know. But still, I'm winning."

"Good for you."

"Hey," Jonah said. "How's camp, Mom? Do you like your counselors?"

The laughter rose in Laura so suddenly, so uncontrollably, that the receiver nearly dropped from her hand. What a ridiculous joke it all was, this deadly serious marriage camp, these humorless, rule-abiding converts to eternal love, and it took Jonah—little Jonah of the crooked smile—to put just how absurd it really was.

"Mom?"

"I'm still here, honey," Laura said, still laughing. "Oh God, I miss you."

"When are you coming back?"

"Saturday, hon. Just a few days more."

"Are you having a good time with Dad?"

"Uh—" Laura put her hand to her head. She had never once wondered what Jonah thought of their trip to the institute. She had only told him that it was a camp for grown-ups and she hoped that Valerie hadn't added anything to that. "Yes, Jonah, a terrific time."

"Hey, that's good. Can I talk to Dad?"

"He's not here just now, hon. He's playing tennis. But he'll call you another time, okay?"

"Sure." Jonah sounded hurt.

"And he told me to tell you that he loves you up to the sky," Laura said.

"Yeh, well, I better go out again. David's probably cheating or something."

"Okay." Laura wanted to hold on to him longer, but knew she might only upset him if she did. Upset them both. Already she could feel tears gathering in the corners of her eyes.

" 'Bye, kiddo. I love you."

" 'Bye."

Laura started to replace the phone but suddenly heard her name squeaking from the receiver. For a second, the sound frightened her, as if there were someone else in the room with her. Hidden. Slowly, she put the phone back to her ear.

"Laur, you still there?"

"Yes, Val. Look, I wanted to thank you for everything. I really appreciate it."

"Don't mention it." Valerie was silent a moment. Then,

quietly, she said, "Laur, are you okay?"

"Sure. Fine."

"Tell me if you can't talk now, okay?"

"What are you talking about?" Laura snapped out the words defensively. She immediately regretted it. "Hey, I'm sorry, Val. I just—"

"Don't worry about it," Valerie said. "Look, I've been through two broken marriages myself. I know just how you must feel."

Laura shook her head. Lately it seemed as if everybody knew just how she felt. Everybody except herself.

"I've got to go now," she said. "I'll see you Saturday."

"Sure. Hang in there. 'Bye."

"Good-bye."

Laura set the phone onto its cradle. She sat very still, only moving her eyes as she looked around the small room. There were pictures hanging on either side of the window in front of her, one, a reproduction of Picasso's "The Lovers," the other, an original, untitled oil still life of a pitcher of flowers and a gold pocket watch. The flowers had just begun to wilt. It was as if the watch were clocking their decline from full bloom. Laura stood and walked slowly to the door. She put her ear to the glass and listened. Nothing. She grasped the handle and turned it soundlessly, opening the door an inch. She put her eye to the crack. No one. Quickly, she shut the door and returned to the desk. She picked up the phone and dialed. It rang twice and then a woman's voice answered in staccato.

"The number you have reached, two four two, five six nine seven, has been changed. The new number is two four two—"

Laura automatically yanked open the top drawer of the desk and reached inside. She pulled out a folded newspaper and the nub of a pencil and jotted down the number in the paper's margin, then jiggled the button on the phone and dialed again.

"Hello."

"Jerzy? It's Laura."

"Well, hello there. Funny, I was just thinking about you."

"Must be telepathy. Are you busy?"

"Not for you, friend. How are you? Say, aren't you supposed to be up at that marriage seminar?"

"Yes. I'm here now."

"Well, well. How goes it? Terrible, I hope." Jerzy laughed.

Laura said nothing. At that moment, she could not remember why she had called Jerzy. All she could think was that she was sneaking a call to her former lover from a marriage camp and using a call to her son as her alibi. When it came to brazenness and disloyalty she was no better than Ginger. Worse, actually. She was sneakier.

"Laura, I was just making a joke, you know," Jerzy was saying. "I wish you and Ted all the best. Now what can I do for you?"

"I, uh, I—" Laura tried desperately to focus. "Actually, I wanted to ask you sort of a scientific question."

"Doing research?" Jerzy laughed again, softly.

"Sort of."

"Shoot."

"Well, I was wondering if . . . if there was any reason why somebody with epilepsy couldn't, you know, if it wouldn't be a good idea for them to undergo marital therapy?"

Jerzy did not answer immediately. "You aren't asking about yourself or about Ted, are you?"

"No." Laura told him briefly about her encounter with the Pratts. She even mentioned overhearing Dr. Saxon tell Jane two days ago that she thought they were perfectly well suited to one another.

When she finished, Jerzy was again quiet for a moment. Finally, he said, "It's hard to tell, really. I know some epileptics try to avoid stressful situations. They think it can trigger them off, although I don't think there's any evidence supporting that."

"But he hasn't had a seizure in years. He's on some sort of medication."

"Yes. Hmmm, it doesn't really make an awful lot of sense, does it? I think there was probably some other reason for asking them to leave. Something they weren't told about."

"I don't," Laura said. For some reason, she was sure of that.

"Laura?"

"Yes?"

"If you don't mind my saying so, it doesn't seem like you to get upset over a little incident like that. And you do sound very upset, Laura. Am I right?"

"Not really."

"I mean, is something else bothering you? Is everything okay up there, Laura?"

"I told you—" Laura did not finish her sentence. She couldn't. Her throat had tightened, holding back the sob that was lodged there. And now the tears came, running down her cheeks onto the desk top. She held the phone away from her, covering the mouthpiece. A few moments passed before she could talk again.

"I'm sorry, Jerzy. I guess . . . I guess I'm not myself today. I shouldn't have bothered you."

"Bother me? Please, Laura, I don't want to hear that. Not after all we've been through together. Now tell me, what's making you so unhappy?"

Laura paused a moment. And then for five straight minutes she told him everything she could think of, ending with the story of how Gary and Sybil had changed overnight from brawlers to lovers. Only when she had stopped talking did she realize that the fluttering sound she had been half hearing on the line was Jerzy's laughter.

"My God, is it that funny?" Laura was furious.

"No, no. I'm sorry, Laura," he said. "It's just that I was thinking about those born-again lovebirds. I'll bet you anything they don't last the week without another field-day battle."

Laura was about to retort that Soul Mates had a peculiar way of skirting all their fights, but she held her tongue. She had said enough already. She wished she had not told Jerzy a thing. She wished she had not called him.

"I have to go now," she said.

"Laura, hold on a second," Jerzy said, his voice serious again, concerned. "Look, friend, if you're upset, I am too. Listen, I can be up there in less than three hours. Why don't I get in my car and come up and get you?"

Laura felt her whole body trembling.

"Jerzy," she said, coldly. "I came here with my husband. And if I'm going to leave, I'll leave with him."

"Sure, of course," Jerzy said quickly. "I just want you to know I'm here if you need me."

"Yeh. 'Bye."

"Laura—"

Laura slammed down the phone. She was still shaking. God, what a fool she was. Jerzy had only given her what she had asked for. She grabbed the pencil from the desk top and furiously blackened out his number on the corner of the newspaper, then pulled open the drawer and stuffed it in. For a moment she sat there, trying to calm herself, her eyes staring blankly at the paper. It was the obituary section. Fitting, somehow. One of the obituaries had been circled in ink and a sentence had been underlined. A notice that a Mr. Harry Goodwin had been buried at the Braintree Memorial Cemetery, God bless him, whoever he was.

Laura pressed the drawer closed, stood, walked to the door, and opened it. To her left, the Game Room door was open and inside men and women were hefting sections of booths onto dollies. Tomorrow's games. She turned to her right. No one was in the corridor. Slowly she walked toward the foyer, staying close to the wall until she reached the stairway. There she ducked under the casing and crept to the oak door. She put her ear to it. There was no sound. She grasped the knob and turned it.

"Well, how was your little boy doing without you?"

Laura froze. It was Andrea. Slowly Laura turned to face her. Andrea's brows were arched in a look of concern.

"Are you all right, Laura?"

Laura stared at the blond woman. Without thinking, she started backing away, her palms held up between them.

"Stop following me," she said, her voice trembling. "Just stop following me around. Do you hear me?"

She spun around and raced through the foyer to the front door, slammed it open and sprinted down the steps, through the garden, and around the pond to the pine forest. She did not stop until she was sure—absolutely sure—that she was alone.

4:15 P.M.

"You won't believe what I've just been through."

Wade opened his eyes. He must have dozed off in the plush chair outside Jeckman's office. He raised his head. Hovering over him with a gnomelike grin on his flushed face was Gregory Horowitz.

"Hoby, can you keep your lips sealed if I tell you something in strict confidence?"

Wade nodded. He had not the slightest idea of what Horowitz was talking about. At that moment, he was not even sure what he was doing here, snoozing in the director's waiting room. A second ago he had been dreaming that he was on a bird walk at his father's estate in Concord.

"The sheer insanity of it all," Horowitz was saying, rolling his eyes. "It boggles the normal mind."

Wade yawned.

"Get this," Horowitz went on, leaning his large, bearded face down to Wade's, his tone confidential though loud enough to be heard across the hall. "I'm called out of an executive meeting for an emergency on the Hill. No prep, no files. Nothing. Just get your fat Jewish ass over here in a hurry."

Horowitz issued a soft, gurgling laugh. His specialty of self-depreciating humor was said to have endeared him to The Wizard. Wade nodded in an attempt to hide his boredom.

"So ten minutes later I'm escorted into this double-doored conference room somewhere in the attic of the Capitol. You wouldn't believe who was there." Horowitz squinted, shifting his eyes from side to side. "You understand I can't give you any actual names."

"I understand," Wade said.

"Well, this is it. This is what they've rushed me over there for. At the head of the table, sandwiched between two of the absolutely top men on the Hill, is this Georgetown shrink. You'd know who I was talking about if I told you. And this is what he's got to say. The son of one of these bigwigs has been seeing him secretly for the past year. For therapy, supposedly.

120

But actually what the boy has been doing is pestering this doctor to get him into the clinic at Hopkins. The gender-alteration clinic. The boy wants to be a girl. Terrific. Except that his father is the author of that famous white paper on the scourge of homosexuality! It always strikes those guys, doesn't it? The doers and shakers always have a little hophead or fag in the closet, don't they?''

Wade tried to pull himself out of his chair, but there was no getting around Horowitz's hulk.

''And what do they want me for?'' Horowitz said, raising his arms in a pose of surrender. ''They want to know what kind of alternatives we have cooking over here at Mental Health. Anything will do. Drugs, shock. Whatever we've got, they want it. They just want this young fellow to stop wanting to own a pair of tits. And, mind you, these are the same guys who won't vote us a plugged nickel to fund a juvenile rehab project. No, juvenile problems should be solved in the home. Or church. I should have told them to take their boy to church. Maybe he could become a nun.''

Horowitz covered his mouth to hold down his laughter. Behind him, Wade saw Jeckman's secretary coming toward them. Wade waved at her with both hands, afraid she would miss him behind Horowitz.

''Yes, Dr. Hobson. I was just coming to find you. I'm afraid Dr. Jeckman is still tied up and he has to leave directly for another appointment. Can I take a message for him?''

''No,'' Wade said, leaning to one side. ''It's really something I'd need to talk to him about in person. How's tomorrow morning?''

''Not good,'' the secretary replied. ''Why don't I schedule you for early next week?''

Wade rocked to his feet, almost colliding with Horowitz.

''I just need a few moments,'' he said. ''It's rather important. Very important, actually.''

''I'll see what I can do. But today is out.''

''Thank you.''

Wade gave the secretary an earnest smile as she returned to her desk in front of Jeckman's office, then he turned and started for the corridor door.

''It boggles the normal mind, doesn't it?''

''Yes, Greg. Boggles.'' Wade continued to the door.

''You know, if you've really got an emergency, I might be

able to help you," Horowitz said deliberately, almost cooing his words.

Wade stopped and turned to look at Horowitz's florid face. The man represented everything that appalled him about the new rank of NIMH doctors: the gossipiness, the superciliousness, the contempt for human weakness unconvincingly masked by a glossy rhetoric of social do-goodism. They had spent their lives in institutions—college, medical school, analytic institutes, and now the grandest institution of them all. Not for a single day had they been forced to improvise their lives and as a result they knew nothing about the terror of waking up and not knowing what to do next, of not knowing why it was worth it to get out of bed this or any other morning, of reflexively reaching for a bottle instead of a briefcase. These were the caretakers for the desperate of the nation.

And yet, of course, Horowitz wielded the power which Wade needed at this moment. As special assistant to the director, he held the scepter which opened classified files, granted emergency funds, and enjoined funds. And which scheduled emergency on-site visits.

"Yes, maybe you can be of help at that," Wade said. "Do you think we could talk in your office?"

"Of course, Hoby." Horowitz gestured toward his door at the other end of the waiting room.

When they were inside and both seated behind the closed door, Wade presented his case. He began by telling about the absence of informed consent for the phase one memory drug at the Intrafamilial Communications Project, but seeing that he was losing Horowitz's attention, he quickly switched to the P.I.'s fiasco with the aversion-therapy experiment at UCLA in 1968. And then, hating himself for it, he added the juicy details of her philandering husband and subsequent breakdown. He concluded by recommending that they schedule an on-site investigation of her current project immediately.

Throughout, Horowitz said nothing, tapping the fingertips of each hand against one another, nodding rhythmically. All these young men seemed to nod in the same way, as if they had taken a special tutorial in nodding at their analytic institute. It was meant to communicate attentiveness; to Wade, it communicated nothing at all. When Wade had finished, Horowitz sat silently for a moment, stroking his beard, his brow puckered as if in deep thought, and then he planted his palms in the corners of his desk and leaned across it.

"You know, Hoby," he said quietly. "I've been doing my level best for you these past few days, but there's only so much I can hold back from The Wizard."

Wade stared incredulously at Horowitz. The man had not heard a word he had said.

Horowitz pulled himself back against his chair, paused a second, and then pulled open the top drawer of his desk. He lifted out a manila folder.

"I'll give it to you straight, Hoby. You're in trouble. Serious trouble, to tell you the truth." He held up the folder and waved it like a semaphore. "If Performance Review ever gets their hands on this, you'd have an hour to clean out your desk. And forget your GS rating. I don't even think you'd get away with your pension."

Wade felt nothing but an immense fatigue descending on him. The thought occurred to him that if he were to close his eyes he could continue with his bird walk in Concord. That was realer, much realer, than what was happening here.

Horowitz had opened the folder and was squinting down at it. He began reading rapidly out loud.

"Failure to respond to interoffice memoranda. . . . Insufficient data for your Cleary report. . . . Unauthorized perusal of confidential files. . . . Drinking of intoxicating beverages on institute premises and accompanying unprofessional behavior."

Horowitz raised his small eyes.

"But this is the one they'll nail you on, Hoby," he said, shaking his head. "Unauthorized communication with a Principal Investigator on classified material. Jesus Christ, Hoby, that's a cardinal breach of ethics and you know it. We can't allow our people to call up independent researchers willy-nilly and risk intimidating them. That's nothing less than government interference. Good God, that's the only thing that separates us from being a government that controls scientific thought. You know what I'm talking about. I'm surprised Weiss even talked with you."

Wade suddenly broke into a roaring laugh. It was too absurd, too ridiculously absurd, to even pretend to do anything else. They monitored your phone calls and then accused you of breach of ethics. They funded a scientist with a record of dangerous human experimentation and then lectured you about government interference. It was a joke, an insane joke in the name of mental health. Wade abruptly stood up, still gasping with laughter.

"Hoby, get ahold of yourself before you leave this room. Listen to me, you're lucky I caught you before you got to Jeckman with your cockamamie suspicions about somebody's research. Do you think he'd listen to you after the performance you've been turning in?"

Wade walked to the door.

"God damn it, Hobson, the family projects are the main reason this agency is still in business. They come straight from the top, Hoby. The top!"

Wade let himself out of the door, through the waiting room to the elevator in the corridor. He was no longer laughing when, in the privacy of his cubicle in the Office of Protection from Research Risks, he emptied his silver flask down his throat.

6:45 P.M.

From the garden Laura saw them filing two by two up the long, open-air stairway to the terrace, talking and laughing animatedly, eager vacationers at the end of the afternoon ready for drinks and supper, another festive evening at the Institute of Marriage. They did look happy, most of them, Soul Mates and novitiates alike. Exhilarated. Hopeful. There was a camaraderie between them, a communal optimism, a shared happiness in their good luck to be there, like freshmen at an exclusive college. Laura sighed. She felt none of it. Standing there, half hidden behind a lilac bush, she did not feel connected to any of them.

Laura stepped onto the path, turning back to the road which led to her cabin. She had not yet eaten a thing today but she was not up to dinner on the terrace. The oranges and cheese in her kitchenette refrigerator would have to do. She started slowly along the path.

She stopped short.

Racing up the hill ahead of her, laughing like teenagers in their white tennis shorts and sweaters, a final couple appeared. They looked like high school sweethearts, so gay they seemed, so free.

It was Ted and Ginger.

Instinctively, Laura braced herself against a tree trunk. The pit of her stomach cramped like a fist. She shook her head as if that could dispel the image of the two of them dancing up the stairway swinging their tennis rackets in unison. It was obvious what had happened. Laura had given Ted nothing since they had arrived here, not even hope.

"Laur? Is that you?"

Laura froze. Ted stood near the top of the stairs, shading his eyes with his hand. If she did not move, perhaps he would think she were someone else.

"Laur? What's wrong?"

Laura opened her mouth, but no words came. She wanted to turn and run, but she could not do that either. It was something worse than jealousy she felt. She felt totally alone. She saw her husband sprinting toward her as if in a dream.

"Laura, what are you doing here? What's the matter? Where have you been all day?"

Ted put a hand on each of her shoulders. She did not move. "Laura?"

"Nothing's wrong," Laura said in a monotone. She shook her shoulders and Ted's hands dropped away. "I'm fine."

"Terrific," Ted said, reaching for her hand. "Let's get something to eat then. I'm starved. God, I haven't played that hard in years. Ginger murdered me."

Laura let him lead her toward the stairs; she did not have the strength to resist. She barely listened as he chattered on about how he had waited for her at the tennis courts, how he had taken Ralph's place after his wife had beaten him in straight sets, what a fine day it was. Laura was too numb to even wonder if he were telling the truth. But she was not too numb to care.

"Well, look who the truant officer caught." Ginger had been waiting for them at the top of the stairs with Ted's racket. Her skin was silky with sweat and her shorts clung to her slim bottom like a wet napkin. "We all missed you terribly."

Laura said nothing. She had just glimpsed her reflection in one of the mansion's windows. Her T-shirt was rumpled and stuck with pine needles from lying on the forest floor and her face was puffed and blotchy. She looked like one of the middle-aged women she had often seen at the museum wandering around in twos and threes, killing time until it was safe to have the first cocktail of the day. Lonely women, she had always thought. Divorced women.

At their table, the waiter was filling their glasses with sangria from a glass pitcher. Laura immediately reached for her glass, then remembered that she was supposed to wait for the toast from Wendy and Arnold. Looking up, she saw that Gary and Sybil were sitting at Donald and Jane's places. Even now, their heads were leaning toward one another, touching at the temples. Happy. Happier than they had any right to be.

"Well, as the poet said, *In vino veritas*." Arnold raised his glass and hooked arms with Wendy. Around the table, several of the couples imitated them.

"Here's to truth and honesty in marriage," Wendy said,

smiling. "The first step to getting on the same wavelength."

"Hear, hear," Ted said.

Laura gulped down the fruity drink in two quick swallows. She could feel it tingle as it hit her empty stomach; it seemed to enter her bloodstream immediately.

"That's our topic for tonight," Arnold was saying. "Honesty in marriage. Sharing the truth. Who'd like to get the ball rolling? Affy, why don't you get us started tonight?"

"Gee, I don't know." Affy's pert face sprang to life. "I mean, I always think that honesty is the best policy of course. But sometimes, you know, you can catch more flies with honey than with vinegar."

Wendy smiled encouragingly at Affy. "Perhaps, but what happens when we hold back the truth from one another? The truth about anything—how we feel, what we've done. What happens to those secrets we keep inside of us? Do they just go away? Or do they fester and come out later in anger or sabotage?"

Affy shrugged.

"I don't know," she said. "I mean, I guess you're right about most things, the important things. But sometimes a little white lie just makes life easier, doesn't it? You know, like you say you'd rather go to the ball game than a movie even though you'd really kind of like to go to the movies. I mean, it doesn't really—"

Next to her, Guy leaned forward in his chair and Affy stopped blushing. For a moment, everyone was silent as the waiter deposited bowls of gazpacho in front of them. Laura signaled him to refill her wine glass.

"Those white lies only make life easier for the moment," Arnold said. "But in the long run they have a way of building up frustrations and resentments."

Laura wondered what kind of man Arnold had been before his conversion to goody-goodiness. A real bastard, she guessed. They always made the most fanatic converts. She took a spoonful of the chilled soup, but then returned to her sangria. She had never really given alcohol its due before. It did have a way of clarifying things.

"That's very true, Arny," a man said. "But isn't the real point that if you lie you can't build up a real spirit of trust with each other? That's the bottom line, isn't it?"

Laura raised her eyes from her glass. It was Gary who had

been speaking, a soft, smug, sincere look on his long face. Before she could set down her glass, she burst into a silly giggle and some of her wine spilled onto the tablecloth. Everyone turned to look at her.

"Sorry," she said grinning. "You can send me the laundry bill." She took another sip of her drink and looked Gary straight in the eye. "But you are the king of bullshit, aren't you?"

"Beg your pardon?"

"Oh, come now, Gary, I'm only speaking the truth. Cementing our spirit of trust, don't you know?" Laura's words came automatically. Uncensored. *In vino veritas* indeed. She felt exhilarated for the first time since she had arrived in this dismal place. "I mean, the fact is, you wouldn't be married to the little woman in the first place if it weren't for a few well-placed lies, would you?" Again, she lifted her glass. "So here's to bullshit, Gary. It can be very profitable, can't it?"

"I think you're out of line," Arnold said sternly.

"You're another one," Laura said, giving her host a wave of dismissal. "Full of love and beauty and truth. And the heart of a fascist. I saw you barking orders from your little motorcycle."

Ted touched her arm lightly, but she pulled it away without looking at him. Everyone was quiet, their eyes down, busy with their soup.

"Hey, come on," Laura said, cheerily. "This is an open forum, right? I thought what we ought to discuss tonight is honesty in the marriage of Gary and Sybil. You all know Gary and Sybil, don't you? The couple who specialized in humiliating each other right up until Dr. Saxon waved her magic wand."

"I feel sorry for you, Laura." Sybil's voice piped across the table. She was shaking her head slowly, like a parent reluctantly disciplining her child. "I mean that. You must be terribly unhappy or our happiness wouldn't upset you so much. You wouldn't be trying so pathetically to bring us down."

Gary lifted his wife's hand to his lips and kissed it.

"You're so right, darling," he said. "Jealousy makes people do the most pathetic things."

"You two are a riot," Laura laughed. "What do you do, hold it all in until you get back to your cabin? I bet it looks like hell in there."

Someone at the table laughed and Laura turned her head. It was Ginger and she smiled at Laura. Peculiar, who your allies turn out to be. Laura noticed that Arnold was out of his chair, walking toward another table. He leaned down and spoke to Dr. Saxon. They were both staring at her.

Laura had raised her glass to toast them when she saw Saxon rise and start toward her. She felt a sudden stab of panic. Oh, God, they were coming to get her. To take her away. She felt the blood draining from her face. She had to get out of here. She pushed her chair away from the table and tried to stand. But Saxon's hand grasped her shoulder, pushing her down. A chill ran down her spine.

"Is anything wrong, Laura?"

Laura craned back her head. The doctor wore a kindly, concerned expression on her face, but the grip on Laura's shoulder was quite different. It was the real message. Laura felt dizzy. She wished to God she were not drunk now. Someone had to help her. She looked around the table. At Ginger, Judy. Ted. She needed them. They had to believe her.

"We were just talking about the evils of secrecy," Laura said, her voice suddenly calm, sober. "And some of us were wondering why there were so many secrets around here. You know what I mean, Doctor, don't you? All those surveillance cameras and sentries and bolted doors."

She felt Saxon's hand tighten on her shoulder and again the panic shot to her stomach. She forced herself to go on.

"And, of course, the biggest secret of them all. The Final Session. The presto chango that can make happy lovers out of even our friends Gary and Sybil."

Abruptly Saxon's hand left her shoulder and Laura snapped her head around, terrified. But above her, both hands clasped to her face, Dr. Saxon was laughing, her blue eyes bright with humor.

"Oh, I love that," she said, catching her breath. "Presto chango. Would that it were as simple as that. Wouldn't that be nice? What a happy place this world would be if it were as easy as that."

Around the table, several people laughed; not just the Soul Mates, but Guy and Affy and John and Ralph too.

"But I think I know just what you are talking about, Laura," the doctor went on, her hand now back on Laura's shoulder. "We do have our secrets here, for a little while at least, and they must be maddening. But we've just found some things work so much better when they can take you by surprise. And genuine love is certainly one of those things. As you must know, you can't just go out and make love happen. Yes, I admit we have some surprises at I.M., but I can assure you we have no lies. Does that sound fair enough, Laura?''

For a long moment, Laura said nothing. The hand on her shoulder was relaxed now, gentle. The danger had passed. She did not have to say anything more. She could go back to her gazpacho and the delicious entree that was sure to follow. She could talk earnestly about honesty and love and happily ever after. And then what? Wait. Patiently wait for the Big Surprise.

Laura reached out her hand and calmly sipped wine from her glass. And then she looked up at Saxon and said, "But you do lie, Doctor. You lied to Jane and Donald. You told them they had to leave the institute because they were incompatible, but the real reason was because of Donald's epilepsy, wasn't it?''

Saxon's hand closed so tightly on her shoulder that her skin smarted from the pain. Everyone at the table—on the entire terrace—was silent, their eyes flicking from Dr. Saxon to Laura and back again. And despite her fear, Laura felt a thrill of triumph welling up inside of her. Her dare was paying off. They were all with her.

"You put me in a peculiar position," Dr. Saxon said. She paused and Laura smiled up at her. For the first time, Saxon appeared at a loss of words. She stared intently at Arnold and Arnold nodded to her and again Laura felt a surge of panic, the terror that she would be yanked from her chair like a prisoner.

"A very peculiar position," Saxon went on. "We have our professional ethics to consider here. Our confidences. The trust with which you must all expect us to treat the personal information you convey to us, consciously and even unconsciously."

She was stalling. Laura was sure she was stalling.

"But I'm afraid you force me to make an exception this evening," Saxon said, her voice louder now so that it carried across the entire terrace. "No, Laura, we did not lie to Jane and Donald. They are indeed incompatible. Irreversibly so, I'm afraid. And it has nothing at all to do with his epilepsy.

That presents no problem in marital therapy, I can assure you. No, Laura, Donald Pratt's problem is much more difficult than that. . . . He is homosexual."

Several people gasped audibly and with that sound the tension seemed to be cut immediately. A slight smile played on Dr. Saxon's lips.

"Good as we are at the Institute of Marriage," she said, "that is one problem I'm afraid we cannot deal with."

For a second, no one reacted. Then Arnold uttered a soft laugh, followed by Wendy and Gary and Sybil, and soon laughter filled the entire dining room, rolling laughter, growing in waves. Next to Laura, even Ted was laughing. Everyone was, but Laura. Finally, as the room quieted, Saxon spoke again.

"You present quite a different problem, Laura," the doctor said, her voice softer again, confident. "You're so suspicious of everything and everyone. It must be terribly isolating for you. It must make it very difficult for you to love."

Laura felt eyes all over the room staring at her.

"But perhaps we can help you," Saxon went on. "You see, we've often found that suspiciousness of others comes from having something to be suspect of yourself. When you have your own secrets, you are sure other people are keeping secrets from you. I think you know what I mean, don't you, Laura?"

Laura sucked in her breath.

"I don't have the vaguest idea what you are talking about," she said, but her heart was beating wildly in her chest.

"I'm afraid you force me to make another exception this evening," Dr. Saxon said. "But I only do it because I think it might help you. Because it might allow you to start building a spirit of trust between you and your husband. Because the secret you are keeping from him can only fester and prevent you from truly reaching out to him."

Saxon released her hand from Laura's shoulder and walked slowly around the table until she was facing Laura and Ted. The only sound that could be heard was the waves breaking against the rocks far below them.

"Laura," Saxon said quietly, "when you telephoned your lover this afternoon, you were breaking a solemn trust with your husband and with us."

The terrace seemed to spin in front of Laura. She grasped

the edge of the table and pulled herself shakily to her feet. Around the terrace, everyone stared at her as if she were completely mad.

"How the hell would you know that if you weren't spying on me?" Laura cried.

"Your friend Jerzy tried to call you back," Saxon said quietly. "He was worried about you, Laura. I spoke with him for a moment. We're all worried—"

But Laura did not hear Saxon finish. She backed away, knocking over her chair, and raced to the stairs. Terrified. Terrified and humiliated.

8:40 P.M.

"Laur?"

Laura continued walking, her eyes half closed, stumbling over roots and rocks as she blindly made her way deeper into the pine forest. The sun had just dropped below the mountain in front of her, casting refracted ocher light that filtered through the pines and gave the woodland world a surreal glow. For a long while now she had heard Ted following her, never coming any closer than fifteen feet, calling her name softly every minute or so like a shepherd cautiously trailing a frightened lamb. She could not face him. She could not tell him to go away. In some selfish, shameful way, it comforted her to have him there behind her. In some selfish, shameful way, she loved him for it.

"Laur? I—I'd like to be with you . . . if you'd let me."

She walked on, not turning.

"We—we don't have to talk," her husband said.

Laura slowed her pace ever so slightly, a half signal, a half wish, and she heard Ted gradually come nearer, the good shepherd. She smelled his musky odor; she saw his Roman profile illuminated in her peripheral vision, strong, kind, noble. They continued walking together slowly without turning their heads to one another, without speaking, now crossing a trickling brook, their hands brushing, now clasped, gently clasped. With each step, Laura felt calmer, almost as if some grace of innocence had descended upon them. If they could only continue walking this way forever, fresh, natural, unconnected to the rest of the world . . .

A cardinal swooped in front of them, a flash of crimson, and all at once Laura was crying, softly, tears slipping down her cheeks, a sweet sorrowfulness spilling out of her, shaking her, and she turned and fell into her husband's arms, pressing her face against his warm chest. They stood this way, barely moving, for several minutes.

"I'm sorry, Ted," she whispered, finally. "The last thing I

wanted to do was hurt you. Honest to God, the very last thing.''

''I know . . . I know.'' He stroked her hair.

''I only called him because I was frightened,'' Laura said. ''About Jane and Donald. I couldn't think of anyone else, you know, anyone who would know about epilepsy.''

The moment she said those words they sounded false to her. There were other people she could have called, any number of them. She pulled her head back and looked up into Ted's eyes.

''Ted, there's something I never told you,'' she said. ''Jerzy—'' She hesitated a second. ''I ran into him at the museum once after you and I were together again. He'd gotten a notice in the mail about Saxon's lecture at the Sheraton. That's where I heard about it.''

Ted smiled at her shyly.

''Well,'' he said. ''I guess I have something to thank him for then, after all.''

Laura smiled back and squeezed his hand. She felt lighter, so very much lighter than she had felt in days, no, longer than that, weeks, months. My God, maybe they were right, secrets do fester. She had carried that one around so long it had grown inside her like an ulcer, blocking her feelings, making her suspicious. Without saying a word, they turned around in unison and started back through the forest. They were thinking the same thing, she was sure. She wanted to be in bed with him.

''I guess I ought to make my little confession too,'' Ted said, quietly.

Laura felt her heart skip a beat. She had almost forgotten: she did have one suspicion left.

''I told everyone you didn't know how to play tennis,'' Ted said, smiling, ''so that I could get Ginger for my partner in the doubles tournament.''

Laura kept walking, not daring to look at him. Waiting. Ted said nothing.

''That's it?'' she said, finally, her voice rising like a child's.

''What do you mean?''

''That's your whole confession?''

''I'm afraid it's the best I can do on such short notice.''

Ted laughed and in a second Laura joined him and soon they were both laughing so hard that they had to stop walking until the last rolling giggle had left them.

When they reached the driveway, Ted guided her to the right, toward Hilltop House. Laura held back.

"Why don't we just go back to the cabin," she said. "I haven't really been alone with you all day."

"Time for that," Ted said, tugging at her waist. "But right now I think a drink is in order. A toast, huh?"

"I think I've probably had enough for one night," Laura said.

Ted took both of her hands in his.

"Hon, you're going to have to face all those people sooner or later," he said. "It's probably best to do it now. You know, get right back on the horse that threw you."

Laura still did not move.

"Actually, they might give you a standing ovation," Ted said, his grin widening. "I mean it. Most of the stuff you said up there has been on everybody's minds since they got here. But you were the only one with the guts to say it."

Laura tilted her head to one side.

"Well," Ted said, "guts and a little sangria."

This time when he tugged at her, Laura did not resist.

As they climbed the stairs to the terrace hearing the music and laughter above them, Laura had a *déjà vu* of their first night at I.M. How long ago had that been—three, four nights? It seemed longer than that; she could barely remember not being here. Not so strange, really. On ships and in foreign cities, she had felt that same isolation in time. Most likely that was part of Dr. Saxon's design, to disconnect them for a little while from all the bad memories and habits which had brought them there. And why not? In Paris, the year before Jonah was born, they had felt like they had fallen in love all over again, although that feeling had gradually faded after they returned to their old routines. That was the rub, of course. Certainly, the best Saxon could do was goose up a marriage for a month or two until the old ways of hurting and disappointing and numbing each other crept ineluctably back into their lives.

"Hi. Welcome to Fiesta del Torres." It was John. He and Judy were coming toward them. "I hope you two don't rumba either. We need somebody to sit out Spanish Night with."

"That's us," Ted said.

Laura looked up shyly. Judy was smiling at her, but there was something guarded about her look; she was still embarrassed for her, no doubt. This was not going to be an easy social evening.

The four of them took their seats at a long table on the open side of the terrace, and as the combo came to an end of a set of rumbas, the table began to fill with couples. Ginger and Ralph made directly for the seats across from Laura and Ted.

"You missed the paella, poor dears," Ginger said. Her face glistened prettily with perspiration; the woman seemed to be in a perpetual sweat. "It was loaded with all kinds of goodies."

She gazed at Ted, but tonight, happily, he merely looked away. Ralph reached for the pitcher of margaritas and began filling everyone's glasses. Laura quickly covered hers.

"No, thanks," she said. "I'm driving."

Everyone laughed, a little more loudly than the joke deserved, she thought, but at least they were trying to make her comfortable. She picked a taco chip out of the bowl.

"There's something I've been dying to ask you," Ginger said, smiling at her. "The good doctor said your friend's name was Jerzy. Is that with a z, or is it an s, as in New?"

A nervous quiet settled over the group. Laura felt her face reddening.

"A z," Ted snapped, "not that it's any of your business."

"Thanks," Laura whispered.

"Sorry I asked," Ginger went on coyly. "It's just that I know a Jerzy too, a gorgeous Slav with a lovely Old World way about him. I was only wondering if we had a little something in common."

"I doubt it," Laura said through her teeth. She hoped to God she was right. Jerzy had better taste than that.

Everyone began talking again, as if to blot out the awkward moment. Next to Ralph, Affy emptied her glass and reached it out for a refill.

"You've had enough," Guy said, in a thick-tongued voice. It was the first complete sentence Laura had heard the large, sullen man utter.

"Oh, don't be a pooper," Ginger said, poking Guy in the ribs. She pulled back her hand and pretended to nurse her fingers at her lips. "My goodness, what do you have under there, a bulletproof vest? You're hard as a rock."

"I try to keep in shape." Guy grinned boyishly.

"He was all-state in high school," Affy chirped, still

holding her glass in front of Ralph. He filled it quickly. Clever girl, Laura thought.

The band struck up a tango and several couples left the table. Ralph had risen too, but Ginger remained in her seat and stretched voluptuously.

"It's too hot to dance anymore, darling." She threw back her head and shook her long red hair. "But I've just had the loveliest idea. Why don't we all go swimming? We can skinny-dip with the swans."

"Don't be ridiculous." Ralph sank back into his chair.

"Oh, please," Ginger said, smiling around the table. "It will be terribly therapeutic. Help us loosen up our hang-ups. Who's coming with me?" She stood.

For a moment nobody moved, but then Guy popped up from his chair.

"Wonderful!" Ginger took Guy's big hand. "My very own lifeguard."

She pulled him across the floor and in a second they had disappeared down the stairs. Instinctively, Laura looked to the far end of the table where the Soul Mates sat in a cluster to see if any of them had observed Ginger and Guy's exit—surely impromptu swims were against the rules—but the Soul Mates were obviously too preoccupied with each other to have noticed.

"How does one become 'all-state'?" Ralph said, arching his brows as he refilled Affy's glass.

"By tackling people," Affy replied, smirking drunkenly. She really had had enough to drink. Laura felt like an expert on that subject.

"To . . . tackling people," Ralph said, clinking her glass.

"That's how we got married," Affy slurred. "He tackled me. After the big homecoming dance. He was the captain and I was the queen and he tackled me in my daddy's rumpus room and knocked me up."

Laura dropped her eyes. It seemed to be everybody's night to say regrettable things.

"What a romantic story," Ralph said. "Now Ginger and I never had that problem. Ginger cannot, as you say, get knocked up."

"Oh, that's a real shame." Affy leaned her pert little face into both of her hands like a cherub. "Children are such a blessing. They're what makes a family, you know."

Laura put her hand on Ted's arm. "Let's go," she said quietly.

Ted nodded and they both started to rise. They were halfway out of their seats when they heard the scream.

The band stopped. Everyone on the terrace stopped moving. For a split second they darted their heads around, unable to tell from where the terrified cry had come. Laura was the first to see Ginger as she appeared at the top of the stairs, naked except for a pair of bikini panties, her small, upturned breasts bobbling as she ran across the dance floor, tears streaming from her eyes.

"Ape!" she cried. "That ape!"

Ralph was immediately on his feet, racing toward her. He took Ginger into his slender arms and enveloped her.

"Baby," he crooned. "Poor baby."

"He grabbed me," Ginger whimpered. "He tried to—"

"It's all right now," Ralph said, petting her hair. "It's all over now, baby."

Gazing at them, it struck Laura that these two had played this scene countless times before, poor Ginger, naked and scared, rocking in her husband's paternal arms. If Laura had ever wondered what kept this pair together at all, she was sure now.

Suddenly everyone turned their heads back toward the stairs. Loping onto the terrace in his nylon briefs with his massive chest and overdeveloped arms, Guy did indeed look apelike. He wore a dumb half smile on his face.

"You stupid bastard!" Affy rose shakily from her seat, her eyes blazing. "You don't really think she wanted you, do you? She called you an ape! An—"

Guy's open hand caught her on the jaw and her head spun like a marionette's. Instantly Ted sprang toward the big man and seized one arm. On his other side, John grasped him around the waist. But no sooner had they restrained him when Arnold and two other Soul Mates shoved them aside and expertly pulled Guy's arms behind him in a full nelson. At the same moment, Wendy and Andrea latched their arms under Affy's and led her, stumbling, to the side door of Hilltop House. The door opened and Guy and Affy were rushed inside. It all happened in less than a minute.

Laura stared after them, her mouth half open, her pulse beating in her ears. And just before the door closed, she saw Dr. Saxon standing inside. For a split second, the two women's eyes met. Saxon's gaze burned.

Laura grabbed Ted's hand. They walked quickly to the stairs and down to the garden without speaking. As they neared the pond she saw Guy's and Ginger's clothes piled neatly side by side on the embankment.

"Laura? Ted? Over here."

Laura stopped. Lurking next to the same lilac bush she had huddled behind earlier was Judy. She was alone.

"Judy? What are you doing there?"

"Can I talk to you a second? Just a second."

Laura hesitated.

"I'll be right back," she whispered to Ted. She strode quickly over to Judy.

"What is it?"

"I, uh, I'm sorry I didn't stick up for you at dinner tonight," Judy said. Her voice sounded shaky. "I just couldn't get myself to do it."

"That's okay. But it's nice of you to say so anyhow." Laura smiled. "I'll see you tomorrow."

Judy touched Laura's arm.

"I wanted to show you this," she said.

Laura looked down. A small silver object glinted between Judy's fingertips in the moonlight. It looked like the tip of a basketball pump.

"It dropped out of a trash bin," Judy went on. "You know that old guy, the janitor. He was dumping stuff into a truck and it dropped out. I waited until he was gone before I picked it up."

"What is it?"

"A needle," Judy whispered. "For a syringe."

8:40 P.M.

"You sure pick 'em, Doctor. Last time we had a count like this it was for a sixteen-year-old girl who'd just lost her virginity." Pierson dropped the lab report on Berman's table and pointed at a figure in a column on the right-hand side. "That's four times the concentration of phenylethylamine for a normal white female her age."

Berman placed his thumbs in the corners of his eyes and rubbed. It had been a bad day and a worse evening. Despite professional protestations to the contrary, there had never been a doubt in his mind that a full moon pulled in the most bedeviled cases of the month. Tonight had been no exception. Since sundown he'd already admitted four schizophrenics with occult paranoid delusions. One had screamed when Berman touched her. She had called him—rather poetically, he thought—"Lucifer."

Pierson was pointing at a second figure.

"That's today's count," he said. "Yesterday's sample ran so high that I took the liberty of ordering a second urine specimen this afternoon and running it through the spectograph. Phenomenal, isn't it?"

Berman tried to focus. He had meant to read up on phenylethylamine on his lunch break, but as things went, he had not even had time for a sandwich.

"Your Mrs. Goodwin has dropped a couple of points below normal in less than twenty-four hours," Pierson went on. "And that's even with that two pounds of chocolate in her. Somebody must have broken the old gal's heart right in two."

"She's recently widowed," Berman murmured.

"How recently?"

"A week. Ten days. She's had a delayed response to it."

Pierson sat down on the corner of Berman's desk.

"Look, Doctor," he said. "I'm a mere lowly chemist, but I can tell you this is no normal bereavement you're dealing with. This isn't the chemistry of someone who's in mourning. It's somebody who's just been jilted."

Berman yanked up his head.

"We'll determine that," he snapped.

Pierson pulled a cigarette from his breast pocket and simpered down at Berman.

"Actually, it doesn't look like anybody at Memorial will be determining anything." Pierson put a gold lighter to his cigarette, lit it, and drew in slowly. The lanky lab supervisor was clearly enjoying himself. "When I dropped the dupe of this in Mrs. Goodwin's file, I saw that she's being transferred out of here Friday. To a private clinic up in Maine."

Berman narrowed his eyes.

"Who authorized that?"

Pierson shrugged.

"Search me. But nobody's denied a transfer request out of here since the new budget came through. Bed space is pure gold these days."

Berman picked up the lab report, folded it lengthwise, and stuffed it in his pocket.

"Thank you for your trouble, Pierson."

Pierson eased his haunch off of the desk and started for the door.

"Sorry it turned out to be a waste of time," he said and left.

Berman crossed his arms on his desk and leaned down his head. The hell with it. He was too tired to care about a brokenhearted widow on a full moon night.

9:15 P.M.

"So, what's the verdict, Mr. Hobson?"

Wade sucked a stray onion scrap from the back of his hand and smiled contentedly.

"You're a genius, Tulio," he said. "I can honestly say that I have never eaten a better pizza in my life. I hope you've patented the mushroom special."

The corpulent Italian laughed, then pulled out the vinyl-covered chair across from Wade and seated himself.

"Let me tell you a secret, Mr. Hobson," he said, his dark eyes sparkling. "If I served one of these at home—in Napoli— they'd throw me in the street. It's not a pizza, they'd say. It's an apple pie. This is not real Italian food, Mr. Hobson. It's a bad American imitation."

"I thought it was superb."

Again, Tulio laughed.

"Thank you, my American friend," he said. He stood, bowed formally from the waist, and returned to his position behind the counter.

Wade looked at his watch. He had been postponing his mission for two hours now. Two hours and two pizzas. It was time to either go home or get on with it. He pulled himself slowly out of his chair. Surely, he was everything that Rachel had said he was in her final litany: morose, lazy, bitter, alcoholic. Yet by the grace of God and his patrician upbringing there was one vice that had not touched him. Wade Hobson III was not a coward.

"Tonight it's on the house," Tulio said, as Wade approached the counter fumbling for his wallet.

"Please, Tulio, you're in business."

"I'm here sixteen hours a day," the Italian said, brushing his hands on his apron. "It's my home. And tonight you are my guest."

"You're a prince, Tulio."

"Tomorrow I will charge you double, Mr. Hobson."

Wade could still hear the young pizza maker laughing when

he was out of the shop in the parking lot. He lumbered slowly to the sidewalk, his stomach bubbling noisily inside him. He turned right. In the light of the full moon, the NIMH building looked even more ghastly than in daylight. The gray monolith did not so much reflect light as absorb it. Like most of the people who populated it by day, it lacked definition.

Wade waved his identification card at the entrance guard, an Indian whose policelike security uniform was topped with an elaborately wound turban, then he signed the after-hours register choosing the name Larry Friedlander from his Harvard class of thirty-five years ago. The guard would surely not know the difference. He took the elevator to the sixth floor and made directly for the file room.

It was locked.

Wade stared at the door, his hand resting on the knob. A mushroom-and-onion belch struggled to escape from his esophagus, a fitting climax to his bungled cloak-and-dagger escapade. He started to turn, then paused and on an impulse pulled his wallet from his jacket, removed his expired American Express card, and fitted it between the door and the jamb. He slid it down to the lock. In a moment, the door swung open —testimony to the instructiveness of late-night television movies. He closed the door behind him and turned on the light.

The subjects file was also locked but required less ingenuity to open: the key dangled from the lock of the neighboring cabinet. Wade pulled the drawer toward him and immediately located Saxon's "Intrafamilial Communications Project." He lifted the folder out and carried it to the metal table in the center of the room. He opened it. All the names were there, typed in alphabetical order, husbands' names first, complete with home addresses and phone numbers, Dr. Elizabeth Saxon's experimentees, going back for two full summers. Graduates in the skill of "marital dyad communication" and God knows what else. The list ran to twelve pages.

Wade walked across the room and switched on the copying machine, then leaned his back against the wall while the machine warmed up. It pleased him how calm he felt, how efficiently he was performing his little secret operation. It was as if at fifty-seven he were discovering an untapped skill, a well of unused energy. Perhaps when the institute let him go he should apply for employment with the CIA. Wade laughed softly to himself, then crossed to the oak card catalog near the door. There was one other item he wanted to check out. He ran his eye down the first column of drawers, then yanked open the fourth and walked his fingers through the cards until he came to Professor Adonski's.

Wade craned his head down. Baccalaureate, University of Warsaw; Ph.D., Université de Genève; postdoctoral studies, UCLA; associate professor, MIT; visiting professor, Harvard.

Wade froze. On the other side of the wall, he heard footsteps. Instinctively he lifted his feet out of his loafers and slipped quickly across the floor in his stockinged feet, snapped off the light, and slowly closed the lock on the door. A moment later the doorknob turned, the door rattled, and finally the footsteps receded. Throughout, Wade's heart had not so much as accelerated a beat. Again, he smiled to himself. Yes, the old fool was made for this kind of work.

He flipped on the light and returned to the card catalog. Adonski had received his first NIMH grant in June of 1980, his renewal in May of '81, both for violence-control experiments using animal subjects. Better than using humans, to be sure. Wade slid the door closed, paused a moment with his hand on the handle, and then abruptly pulled it open again. Those dates—June '80 and May '81—corresponded exactly with the Saxon experiment's grants. Of course, so did hundreds of others in those drawers, but the two researchers had worked together at UCLA. And there was that receipt in Saxon's file for Adonski's chimps. What did the experimental psychologists say—two corresponding events are random, but three makes a pattern?

It took only a few minutes to reproduce the list of names and return Saxon's file to the cabinet. He locked the drawer, walked to the door, unlocked it, turned off the light, and stepped out into the corridor, closing the door quietly behind him.

"Hello. I thought I heard someone in there."

Wade snapped his head around. The turbaned security guard stood smiling behind him in the darkness.

"Uh, yes." Wade smiled stiffly back at the man. "Report due in the morning." He waved the sheaf of papers in his hand at him.

"Did you lock up?" The guard reached for the file room door.

"Oh, sorry. I'm afraid not." Wade smacked at his pockets, as if searching for his keys.

"No matter," the Indian said, pulling a large ring of keys from his pocket. "I'll take care of it."

Wade nodded and strode quickly toward the elevator stuffing the papers in his pocket. He had played it well. He pressed the button to the elevator and waited. The guard was walking toward him. The elevator door opened and he stepped in and turned, facing the guard.

"Good night," Wade said, as the door closed.

"Good night, Dr. Hobson," the man replied.

10:35 P.M.

Wade fed the cats and poured himself a drink before he sat down by the telephone. It was late, but tomorrow was too far away. Tomorrow they would all know about his nocturnal activities. Performance Review, Horowitz, Jeckman. His desk would be cleared by the time he got there. If he went in at all. He dialed a local number.

"Hello?"

"Hello. Mr. Josephson?"

"Yes."

"I'm sorry to be calling so late." Wade set his drink down on the floor. "My name is Larry Friedlander and Dr. Saxon, Elizabeth Saxon, gave me your name. You see, my wife and I have been having, you know, some difficulties and we were thinking of applying for her program. But I guess I'm overly cautious or something; I kind of wanted to talk to someone who'd gone through it before I committed myself."

"I can understand that," Mr. Josephson said warmly.

"I wondered if we could get together," Wade said. "Say, tomorrow sometime?"

"Tomorrow's a bit of a tight day for us," Josephson said. "But how about breakfast; would that be all right? You can join us at our place."

"You're very kind," Wade said.

"It's our pleasure," Mr. Josephson said. "We're always happy to help other people who are in the same situation we were."

"Thank you."

"And I can tell you this right now," Mr. Josephson went on. "Dr. Saxon's program is the most wonderful thing that ever happened to us."

Thursday

6:10 A.M.

The bluebird took three quick hops in a row, cocked its delicate head, and then, as if it were making a critical selection, darted its beak to the ground, picking up a single pine needle from the thousands scattered there, and swiftly disappeared. Although she had been watching this process from her bedroom window for almost an hour, Laura always failed to catch that instant when the little bird leaped into flight. Now the bird returned, its secret—the whereabouts of its nest—still intact, and seemed to look up at Laura triumphantly. Laura nodded back, smiling, and as the process again began, she found herself thinking of a favorite poem from school:

> He who binds to himself a joy
> Does the winged life destroy
> But he who kisses the joy as it flies
> Lives in eternity's sun rise.

So be it. Let the bluebird disappear and perhaps it will return. Let love pick its own moment and perhaps it will reappear from time to time. Wanting anything else would be greedy. Anything else would be unnatural.

Laura sat back in the window seat. It was unnatural, whatever Saxon was doing. She was positive of that now. She had really been sure of it since Monday, but strangely what had finally confirmed it for her was not anything she had seen or heard at the institute, but those few moments of grace she had spent with Ted in the forest. That is all she wanted from her marriage, moments now and then, unexpected moments of knowing with perfect clarity that they belonged to one another. She did not crave eternal bliss. She had learned her lesson. She did not want to become a Soul Mate, however Dr. Saxon effected that enraptured state.

In the bed, Ted turned, his muscular calf jutting from under the sheet, his large, well-shaped head facing her, his eyes still closed.

We have to leave here, Ted, she said silently. Believe me. Make the decision. Make it yourself. But please take me away from here. Now.

Ted stirred, smiling in his sleep.

9:15 A.M.

"It's a shame about your wife, Larry," Tillie Josephson said, refilling Wade's mug with coffee. "Are you sure you won't let me ring her up? I still might be able to convince her to come over. You know, woman to woman."

"Thank you, but don't bother. Once Rachel has made up her mind, there's no budging her. It's part of our problem, really."

Wade smiled. "Rachel" had been a natural choice for "Larry Friedlander's" wife. In fact, for one mad moment earlier this morning, he had considered calling Rachel and asking her to pose as his wife for his investigations. He hadn't, of course. She would have only suspected him of something devious, another desperate attempt at getting her back, perhaps; and actually, there might have been a touch of truth in that. What if this Dr. Saxon were onto something with her "marital dyads"? Wade shook his head. Foolish thoughts.

Sam Josephson was laughing softly. A large man about Wade's age, he had a boyish face and bright, merry eyes much like his wife's. Happy people, both of them, sitting comfortably side by side in the sunny breakfast room of their Georgetown flat.

"Don't talk to me about stubbornness," Sam said grinning. "Tillie was the all-time champ at that. If I said black, she'd say white and that was it. End of argument."

Tillie Josephson gave her husband a mock jab with her elbow.

"What he neglected to tell you was that I was always right," she said.

"Still is," Sam said. "What a maddening woman to live with." He leaned his head to his side and planted a wet kiss on her cheek.

Wade automatically lowered his eyes. Open affection had always made him feel uncomfortable. Another of Rachel's complaints, in fact. She had often said that for all his so-called rebelliousness, Wade was still his father's patrician son. Stiff,

151

formal, cold. True enough. Wade had never once seen his parents so much as hold hands when he was a child. Yet he envied these two. He wished he had forced himself with Rachel. After a while, public kisses and caresses might have come naturally to him. It would have been worth it. Wade took a sip of his coffee, glancing at his watch. Nine-twenty. He wondered if anyone had missed him at the office yet. Or if someone were waiting at the door with the contents of his desk in a brown paper bag. He looked up at the Josephsons.

"There's still one question I have, although I feel a little silly asking it." Wade shrugged shyly. It was not completely an act. He did feel embarrassed pressing these two happy people, perfect strangers who had graciously invited him into their home.

"Shoot," Sam said. "I don't think we have any secrets, do we, hon?"

"None to speak of," Tillie said and laughed. What a charming woman she was. Wade felt his envy swelling.

"It's about Dr. Saxon's technique," Wade said. "I don't exactly know how to put this, but I heard a rumor—well Rachel heard it actually—that the doctor's therapy involves drugs."

Both Josephsons immediately burst into laughter and for a moment Wade could not help himself from joining them. What a perfect idiot he was. He had risked his job—lost it, most likely—and now he was laughing gaily at the absurdity of his own suspicions.

"So that's how Elizabeth does it," Tillie said, finally. "Drugs. I should have guessed it."

"I'll bet she laces those delicious raspberry tarts with aphrodisiacs," Sam said, smiling at Wade. "She serves such marvelous food up there. You couldn't keep me away from it if I knew it were filled with arsenic."

"There's no truth in it, then," Wade said.

"None whatsoever," Sam replied, seriously.

Wade again sipped at his coffee. There was one unanswerable question, of course. If they had been administered Tyrazepam, they could not possibly have any recollection of it. The drug erased all memory of having taken it. Or of anything else that had happened to them while they were under it. But what could that be—another drug? There was none in the current literature, not even a phase one drug,

which could effect such a specific, long-range reorientation of
subjects. And be their own testimony, the Josephsons had
gone to Dr. Saxon's "clinic" fighting tooth and nail and
returned to Georgetown a joyful and very much in love
couple. Amazing. But a drug could not do that, not unless it
were readministered daily. Not even shock was capable of
that. Only the recent radical therapies made such claims, the
ests and Scientologies of the psyche marketplace, the "brain-
washers," as the orthodoxy at NIMH dubbed them as if to
distinguish these sudden-personality-change techniques from
their five- and ten-year courses of classical analysis.

"How exactly does she do it then?" Wade asked, setting
down his cup. "I mean, how could she possibly get Rachel and
me to the point where we actually felt good about each other
again—and in just one week?"

Sam and Tillie looked at one another, slow, almost mis-
chievous grins growing in duplicate on their faces.

"Wouldn't you rather have it come as a surprise?" Tillie
said.

"Not me," Wade said. "I come from a long line of skeptical Yankees. We hate surprises."

Sam looked back at him, frowning, and Wade felt his face
coloring. He wasn't very good at this at all. Surely "Larry
Friedlander" did not come from old New England stock.

"All I can tell you is this, Larry," Sam said, leaning his
large head forward. "Dr. Saxon does not do anything that you
would not do yourself if you were able to without her help."

A good answer, Wade thought. Philosophical, really. And
totally unenlightening.

"What she does is get you to take a leap of faith," Tillie
said. "That leap of faith that's necessary to love anybody."

"You make it sound positively theological." Wade smiled.

"Well, I suppose it is in a way," Tillie said seriously. "I
mean, whether you're dealing with God or love, you've got to
leave rational explanations behind you, don't you?"

Wade nodded. He was fascinated. These two were discuss-
ing Dr. Saxon's crash marital counseling as if it were a course
in transcendentalism. Well, why not? He had come across
wilder synergisms in the field of mental health these past ten
years, those odd mixtures of Hinduism and Pavlov which were
garnering cult followings on college campuses. Perhaps in the
midst of her postmarital depression Elizabeth Saxon had had

an epiphany: she had seen the ultimate abyss which separates
Man from Woman and discovered a spiritual technique for
taking that existential leap across it. And then, like any good
psychologist, she had universalized her personal experience.
Patented it, in effect. Wade smiled inwardly. A lovely
thought, that. If he could believe it. He picked the napkin off
of his lap, folded it neatly, and inserted it into the napkin ring
beside his plate.

"You've both been very kind," he said. "I can't thank you
enough."

"Our pleasure," Sam said as they all stood.

The Josephsons leaned toward one another as they accom-
panied Wade to the door.

"Good luck," Sam said, shaking Wade's hand firmly.

"And do bring Rachel around once you've straightened
things out," Tillie said. She took Wade's hand and then, very
naturally it seemed, leaned her face to his.

Before Wade realized what was happening, Tillie Josephson
was kissing him, her soft, womanly lips pressed sensuously
against his. For a moment he felt himself surrendering to the
kiss, unable to pull himself away, but just as suddenly Tillie's
head jerked back. Her husband had yanked her away by the
shoulders. The Josephsons stared at one another, their faces
quivering, a puzzled look in their eyes, their hands fumbling.
But in a split second, like a fog suddenly dispersed by a warm
breeze, they were smiling again, their heads tilted toward one
another, their arms snugly fitted around each other's waists.

"Do keep in touch," Sam said, opening the door.

Out on the street, Wade strode briskly for three blocks
before he allowed himself a single thought. It had easily been
the most bizarre experience he had ever had, including his own
inappropriate response to Mrs. Josephson's kiss. He could not
make sense out of any of it. Except that fumbling business.
That, and the confused look in their eyes. There was something hauntingly familiar about it.

Five blocks later it struck him. He had seen that exact type
of disoriented behavior once before, thirty years ago during
his residency at Bellevue Hospital. One second later the patient had succumbed to an epileptic seizure.

11 A.M.

The buzzer rang signaling the end of the final round of the Visual Contact Game and Laura immediately shut her eyes, exhausted. On her right, she heard Wendy make some notations on her clipboard. With any luck she had failed this test. The instructions had been to lock gazes with your husband across the table and then, without looking away for so much as a second, to communicate your deepest feelings using your eyes only. A childish game really, of the see-who-laughs-first variety. For a while Laura had played it the same way she had as a child; occupying her mind with banalities—laundry lists and anagrams—while she stared blankly at the pair of eyes in front of her. But then she realized that she could make use of the game; she could try to communicate to Ted the depth of her feelings about this place. Perhaps if she pleaded to him with her eyes he would understand, he would nod back saying with *his* eyes, Of course, we'll leave immediately. It could not work any worse than words had. As of yesterday, her words lacked any semblance of credibility. She had not even bothered to tell Ted about the hypodermic needle.

She had tried to focus all her anxieties into her gaze, widening her eyes, arching her brows, but somehow it had all come out like bad acting. Ted had merely grinned back. To him, her expression must have looked like a Buster Keaton take and in the end she had returned to her laundry lists and blank stares, deliberately looking away from time to time, hoping that Wendy would take note and recommend that she and Ted be dismissed as irreversibly incompatible.

"God, that was terrific."

Laura opened her eyes. Ted was smiling across the table at her.

"Don't you think so, Laur?" he went on. "I mean, I really felt a lot of good stuff going back and forth between us, didn't you?"

Laura cringed. It was too sadly absurd to even laugh. She wondered how many significant looks and knowing smiles passed between lovers around the world without either party having the foggiest idea of what was really going on in the other's mind. Maybe that was the swan's secret of eternal love: they misunderstood each other completely.

"Well, I think you two should be very pleased," Wendy was saying. "The Final Session will be a snap for you."

"Great," Ted said. "How about that swim before lunch, hon?"

Laura rose slowly from her chair, looking again around the Game Room to see if Judy had arrived yet. She could not find her and John was still standing by the door looking impatient and embarrassed. She nodded to him as she filed with Ted and the rest of the group through the door to the hallway.

"I wonder when they've got us scheduled," Ted said. They were on the path, heading for the pool house.

"Scheduled for what?" Laura said absently.

"You know, Laur," Ted said, using the slightly patronizing tone he seemed to have acquired at the camp. "The Final Session. I wonder when we're scheduled for the Final Session."

Laura said nothing. She wondered too. Because she was determined to convince Ted to leave before then. It was Thursday already, two days to their week's end. She was running out of time.

"Here, catch." Ted had pulled her swimsuit from his canvas bag and tossed it to her. "Last one in is a rotten egg."

Laura walked around to the women's entrance of the stucco-and-wood pool house, a cute miniature facsimile of Hilltop House, entered, and sat down on a wooden bench. She kicked off her sandals. She had spent half the night trying to figure what her options were. Leaving without Ted was out of the question, of course. It would end every chance left between them. He would never trust her again and their trust was the final connection between them. But what did that leave? She could not argue with him again, not after yesterday and the fool her suspicions had made of her at dinner. Laura pulled her T-shirt over her head, dropped it on the bench beside her, then reached behind her and unfastened her brassiere. There was one idea which had occurred to her early in the morning while she was watching the fragile bluebird gather its nesting. What if she were to get sick? Ted would be forced to take her away then. But how in hell could she fake that? She unbuttoned her jeans and slid them over her hips. She shook her head. A moment ago she had been privately pledging her trust to Ted and now she was working on an elaborate scheme to deceive him.

Laura rolled down her panties, kicking them off at the ankle and catching them just the way Jonah did. She looked at herself in the full-length mirror next to the sink. Not bad. Not bad at all really, for a thirty-year-old mother with an insomnia problem. Her skin was still taut except for the tiny rivulets of stretch marks that radiated like a sunrise from her pubes, her emblem of motherhood. She turned to her side, flexing the muscles in her buttocks. Just a hint of a sag there and another hint at the side of her breasts. Still, they were fuller, more womanly than those neat, upturned buttons on Ginger. Laura blew out her breath. Silly woman. She could be on her deathbed and she'd be comparing her body with that of the woman next to her. She returned to the bench and began pulling on her swimsuit. She had just pulled it over her thighs when she stopped, suddenly sure that someone was looking at her. She covered her breasts with her arms, pivoting her eyes back and forth. There was no one at the door or at the window either. She sat down, feeling her heart thumping under her hands. Perhaps Saxon was right: she was overly suspicious, paranoid. She eased her swimsuit over her hips and had put one arm through the strap when her mouth dropped open.

A pair of eyes was looking at her from the mirror.

"Laura?"

Laura spun her head around just as Judy walked through the door. Her round face looked puffy, her eyes frightened.

"Jesus! You scared the hell out of me."

"Sorry. I had to be sure you were alone."

"Why? What's wrong?"

"Come with me. Quickly."

Laura slipped her other arm into the bathing suit and followed Judy out the door in her bare feet.

Ted was in the pool, taking little dolphinlike surface dives. Laura hesitated until his head was underwater, then sprinted up the hill behind Judy.

"They're over there," Judy said, her eyes straight ahead. "Just beyond that grove."

Laura followed a step behind as Judy walked stealthily to

the edge of the grove and pointed: romping like playful ponies in the tall grass and wild flowers on the slope in front of them were Affy and Guy.

"Look at them," Judy said, grimly. "One night with Saxon and instant love. I almost got myself to believe it with Gary and Sybil, but not these two. Look at them, Laura. It's sick."

Laura stared. Even from this distance, she thought she could see the gleam in their eyes, the sparkle. The dazzled look of love. But then she heard Guy's growl.

"Wait a second," Laura whispered.

Guy was racing toward Affy, his arms spread wide, growling like a wild animal as Affy, her hands in front of her, yelped in protest. But it was too late. Guy scooped her off the ground and tossed her effortlessly into the air, caught her and swung her around and around, her yelps turning to piercing shrieks, louder and shriller as he spun her helplessly like a doll. Laura let out a huge sigh of relief.

"You're wrong," she said, half aloud. "They haven't changed one bit."

Laura saw Judy's jaw set rigidly. Judy desperately did not want to be wrong—that was obvious—and in that moment Laura saw how Saxon and Ted, even Arnold, could be right about herself. Maybe all these suspicions were just resistance. Maybe she and Judy were inventing phantoms to keep from making a deep and lasting commitment.

Judy pointed again.

Guy was now running down the hill with Affy clutched to his chest, her arms and legs thrashing wildly. In a second, Laura and Judy were racing down the slope after them. They reached the drive and looked both ways. Judy nodded to the right.

"Their cabin," she said.

They walked quickly down the road, then turned left onto a footpath, Laura cringing as the dirt dug into the scratches on the balls of her feet. They slowed to a halt. The cabin was just ten yards ahead of them, its door half open, animallike sounds issuing from it. Grunts. Whimpers. Laura shivered. My God, that poor woman.

One slow step at a time, Judy and Laura approached the stairs to the cabin's deck, crouched like Russian dancers, and waddled up the steps, then crawled on all fours around the perimeter of the deck until they reached a window. Laura slowly raised herself on her haunches and peered inside.

On the chair directly in front of her was Affy's blouse, or rather what was left of it. Its tatters fluttered in the warm breeze like a battlefield flag. Just below were her shorts, ripped too, split symmetrically at the crotch. Laura hesitated before she raised herself any higher. It was horrifying to realize that what she desperately hoped to see was Guy beating his wife. She stared into the cabin.

The two naked young bodies lay side by side on the rug, Affy's legs locked around Guy's waist, her hands tenderly pulling his head to her own, lips to lips in a rapturous kiss. Laura put her hand to her mouth, gripping her fingers tightly between her teeth. No, this was not an assault, not a rape. Not at all. This was that rare kind of lovemaking, that total sensual contact, unhurried, uninhibited, complete, that married couples experience perhaps once a year on a marvelous night which makes all those other routine, mechanical nights such a letdown. It was exactly what Laura had been afraid she would see and yet her first reaction was envy. Why should these two—this brutal, stupid man and his cowering wife, people who barely looked at one another from one day to the next— why should they be enjoying this extraordinary ecstasy together? But immediately the answer chided Laura: Guy and Affy were not the same people they had been last night, last week, or ever before. They had indeed changed completely. They were totally in love.

Judy tapped Laura on the shoulder and gestured for them to leave, but Laura raised a finger, signaling that she wanted to look one moment more and again both women stared through the window. A minute passed, another. The couple's bodies undulated in unison, their skin glistened, their mutual gaze was full of wonder. Laura could not take her eyes away from them. She had never seen people make love before, never been to an X-rated movie, certainly never even considered installing a mirror over her bed. But this was a genuine wonder to behold. It was not sordid or ugly; it was the most beautiful thing she had ever seen and, by God, it had somehow been given to these two by Dr. Saxon. Was it just Laura's resistance, her defensiveness, that was keeping her from enjoying this ecstasy too?

There was a sudden blast behind them; both women spun around. At the point where the path met the road a white motorcycle abruptly came to a halt. The rider tilted up the visor on his helmet; it was Arnold. The women sprang to their feet, ran to the railing and vaulted it. And as Laura's bare feet struck the ground, she heard two voices rising in a single deep-throated cry. For an instant, she was sure they had been seen, but then, as she raced after Judy into the woods, she realized that the cry had had nothing to do with her. It had only been Guy and Affy reaching orgasm.

2:20 P.M.

Wade raised his glass, extending two fingers from the side, the universal sign for a double refill. A moment later, the bartender, a tall, collegiately dressed black man, delivered the scotch to him at his booth in the rear of the Georgetown saloon, the booth next to the phone. The bartender looked down at the lists of names and addresses and the scattered coins spread out in front of Wade.

"Not easy getting a date like this late in the week, is it?" he said.

Wade laughed. "Nobody loves you when you're down and out," he replied.

The bartender snatched up Wade's empty glass. "Nobody loves anybody," he said smiling. "Not if they can help it."

Wade looked after the man as he returned to the bar. The world seemed to be populated with cryptic philosophers today. All he had to do was mention the word *love*, and out came worldly wisdom from perfect strangers. He couldn't say his luck with graduates of the Saxon project was quite so good. The Josephsons had been an anomaly in more than one way. Of the twenty people he had called in the past two hours, only one had even suggested that she would be willing to talk with the Larry Friedlanders about her experience at "I.M.," as she called it, and she had said she would have to consult her husband first. Most of the others had been quite short with him and more than one seemed as if they had almost been expecting his call, although that hardly seemed possible. Wade took a gulp of his drink and looked down at the papers in front of him. He had exhausted all of metropolitan Washington, as well as the Philadelphia and New York areas, at least of those who answered. He traced his pen along the margin. Madison . . . Fort Worth . . . Tallahassee . . . Sacramento . . . Braintree . . . Braintree, Massachusetts. That was right out of Boston. He lifted the paper, a dime and his glass, and walked to the wallphone. He dialed, charged the call to his home number, then waited while a phone rang in Braintree. On the tenth ring a woman answered.

"Hello. Mrs. Goodwin?"

"No. This is her daughter."

"May I speak with your mother, please?"

"She's not here." The girl sounded testy, like so many of the others, and Wade had not even identified himself yet. Could it be something in his voice? He sipped his drink, managing to spill a drop of the brown liquid on his tie. He looked at his list.

"Can you tell me when I might reach Florence, please?" He was trying to sound like an old friend.

"You can't. She's still in the hospital."

"Really? I hope it's nothing serious."

No answer. Wade could practically hear the phone being returned to its cradle.

"Which hospital?" he said loudly.

Again no reply, just a long audible sigh.

"I think I can help her," Wade said quickly, not really knowing what had put those words in his mouth.

"Memorial."

The phone clicked and, a second later, went dead.

2:35 P.M.

Berman chewed mechanically on his doughy sandwich, the Irish kitchen staff's facsimile of an Italian grinder. He let the phone ring. Someone else could pick it up; someone else could handle it whatever it was. As of six-fifteen this morning when he had pulled himself out of bed for his tenth fourteen-hour-day on admissions in a row, he was living by a new set of resolutions: Don't do unnecessary work. Don't make waves. Just get through the next three weeks until the new, hopefully easier, rotation. The phone stopped ringing.

With the tip of his tongue, Berman scraped at the gobs of oil-soaked bread which adhered to the roof of his mouth. He opened the file in front of him.

"Peabody, Monroe Adams. Age, 36. Occupation, banker. Married, two children. Address, Beacon Hill. . . . Presenting complaint, hallucinations. . . . "

Berman inserted his forefinger into his mouth and loosened a chunk of salami from a molar. Peabody, another Boston Brahmin with a sudden crack in his consciousness. The third this week, a sign of the times. Economic historians could graph the stock market with the admissions rate from Beacon Hill. Berman reached for the button which would signal the receptionist to usher in Mr. Peabody when the phone rang again. He picked it up.

"Dr. Berman?"

"Yes, speaking."

"My name is Hobson. Dr. Wade Hobson, from the National Institute of Mental Health. May I speak with you a moment?"

"It depends on what you want, Doctor." Resolution number one.

"I understand you admitted a patient by the name of Florence Goodwin earlier this week and I—"

"I believe you want to speak with Dr. Clark Russell," Berman said, cutting him off. "He's admissions chief here."

"I already did," Dr. Hobson said. "That's why I'm calling

you. My conversation with Dr. Russell was—how should I put it?—short. Very short."

Berman smiled in spite of himself. His own conversation with Russell about Mrs. Goodwin's imminent transfer had also been short. About three words.

"This is an unofficial call," Hobson was saying. "I'm doing some follow-up work on my own time. May I speak confidentially?"

Berman found himself nodding. There was no way he could make himself terminate this conversation now.

"Yes," he said.

"Good, thank you." Berman heard Dr. Hobson take a deep breath. "About two years ago, Mrs. Goodwin and her husband were subjects of a NIMH-funded experiment on marital relations."

"Her late husband," Berman interjected. He felt a thrill of excitement. And apprehension. All resolutions were off.

"I see," Hobson said. "Dr. Berman, I know you cannot give me too much detail over the phone, but in your opinion do you find anything out of the ordinary about Mrs. Goodwin's behavior—I mean, in the context of her presenting complaint, of course."

Berman paused a moment.

"Yes, Doctor," he said finally. "I find everything about Mrs. Goodwin out of the ordinary."

7:20 P.M.

"How about you, Laura? What are your goals in intrafamilial communication?"

Laura looked from Wendy to Arnold to the plate of baklava in front of her. Arnold had been giving her sidelong stares throughout the meal, but if he had seen her and Judy this morning peeping at the lovers, he apparently was going to wait before he said anything about it.

"Well, let me see." Laura tried to focus on Wendy's question. Tonight, of all nights, she had to give the impression of being a serious, cooperative I.M. novitiate. "I guess my biggest goal is learning how to communicate what is really important to me. You know, there's so much who'll-take-out-the-garbage talk when you're married, sometimes it's hard to get across what really counts."

Laura managed a sincere-looking smile. The fact was, she really did believe what she had said.

"I know exactly what you mean," Wendy responded enthusiastically. The woman agreed with everyone, the ideal marriage counselor. She smiled at Ted. "What do you think, Ted? You've been very quiet tonight."

Ted rubbed his jaw. He had indeed been taciturn all evening. Sullen, actually. When Laura had finally caught up with him after her escapade with Judy, he had been furious with her for having left him waiting in the pool. "What's the goddamned story with you, Laura?" he had snapped. "Can't you stand to spend five minutes alone with me?" Laura had started to explain about Affy and Guy, but then stopped herself; she knew it would only sound like one more excuse, just more resistance to I.M. and, ultimately, to him. She had vowed to herself that the next time she explained anything to Ted, she would have something to say which could leave no doubt in his mind that there was something seriously wrong with this place. Either that or it was time for Laura Esposito to drop her defenses once and for all and see what Dr. Saxon could do to save her marriage.

165

"For me, the bottom line is what a man and wife say to each other in bed," Ted was saying. "That is, if they ever go to bed together anymore."

He turned and looked directly at Laura.

"I know just what you mean," Wendy responded.

While the band set up—tonight including a *bouzoukis*-playing mandolinist to complete the evening's Greek motif—Laura saw Judy slip away from the table on schedule. Laura sat out the first verse of "Never on Sunday" in silence and then asked Ted to excuse her while she went to the bathroom. Ted shrugged, not saying a word; he looked as if he did not expect her to come back and he was right. Judy was waiting at the bottom of the terrace stairway.

"Hi. How do you feel?"

"Scared. How about you?"

"The same. But I know we're doing the right thing, Laur." Judy's eyes shifted in the dark. "I saw them taking off another couple just a few minutes ago," she whispered. "That older couple from the table behind ours. They whisked them away while everyone was watching the band come in. This is as good a chance as we'll get to find out what they do in there."

Laura looked at her friend.

"We'd better get going," she whispered and the two made their way silently along the east wing wall of Hilltop House.

Judy mounted the steps to the service door ahead of Laura. Last night, she had seen the band come and go freely through this door during their breaks and now, as she turned the brass knob, it opened easily. She leaned forward, swiveling her eyes from right to left before signaling Laura to join her. They were in the corridor behind the Game Room and there was no one else there. Pressing their backs against the wall, they moved crablike toward the foyer.

Moonlight shone bright as a streetlamp through the leaded windows, reflecting on the gilt-framed portraits of Hilltop House's first occupant, the silver magnate's wife. And Laura could hear the accelerating beat of the Theodorakis melody the band was playing on the terrace, a freedom song, one the Colonels had forbidden during their reign in Greece, now background music for two unhappy American wives out prowling at their luxury marriage camp. It was not even ironic, Laura thought. It was pathetic.

When they reached the foyer, Laura stopped and held up her hand. Sounds were coming from the top of the stairs, voices, magnified, mechanical. She signaled Judy to remain behind her, then dropped to her knees and crawled across the parquet floor to the foot of the stairs. She tilted her head, straining to hear, and then she broke into a smile: one of the voices clearly belonged to Gregory Peck. Someone up there had the good sense to be watching an old movie this evening. Laura crawled around and under the stairway to the edge of yellow light which framed the door to the tunnel. She stood and reached for the knob when she heard voices on the other side of the door. These voices were live and they could not be more than ten feet away.

Laura's heart accelerated. For a moment she stood paralyzed, her fingers still on the knob.

"Judy!" Laura whispered as loud as she dared.

Immediately, Judy ran across the foyer and together they flattened themselves against the wall, holding their breath. The oak door snapped open and swung wide, covering them, pressing the tips of their shoes.

"I still would feel safer if she'd let me drip in some Heparin. I don't care what she says, the old guy looked like a clotter to me."

"Give it a rest, Zack, would you? He's fine. They're both fine. You worry too much."

Two figures, a man and a woman, receded down the corridor, their stark white clothing glowing, then fading, then glowing again as they passed from one moonlit window to another like poltergeists.

"Sure, sure. Tell me that when one of them has a stroke. We already had one TIA last month."

Laura grabbed Judy's hand and swung them both around through the open door. With a dull thud that smacked like a flat hand against her eardrum, the oak door closed behind them. They were in the passageway and they had not been seen. Laura realized that she had been holding her breath; she let it out slowly.

Bare, high-voltage bulbs ran the length of the ceiling, glaring on the green tiles which covered the walls, floor, and ceiling alike. It seemed to go on infinitely, like a subway tunnel or a hospital corridor. There were no shadows, no place to hide. Still holding Judy's hand, Laura strode quickly toward the other end: Saxon's Therapy Pavilion.

There was an oak door at this end too. Laura pressed it
open an inch and put her eye to the crack. Three figures, also
in white, were standing in front of an elevator door, their
backs to her. Laura slowly let the door close, her hand still
tightly gripping the knob, her body poised forward on the
balls of her feet. She began counting slowly to ten.

"Look!"

Laura turned. Judy was pointing at the door to Hilltop
House. It was opening. She had no choice now. Laura pushed
open the door in front of her and stepped through, pulling
Judy behind her. Just in front of them the elevator doors were
sliding closed: the three white-clad workers were gone. Laura
closed her eyes, relief surging through her. But only a second
later she heard footsteps clicking in the tunnel behind her. She
looked quickly to her left—an unbroken wall, not a corner,
not a shadow to hide in—then to her right—a short hallway
ending at double doors each with a small glass-and-chicken-
wire window and just beyond the doors, a floor-to-ceiling
rust-red water pipe. The footsteps echoed behind her. Simultaneously, the two women raced to their right, ducking under
the windows and behind the pipe, where they stood side by
side, stiff as matchsticks. The door to the passageway opened.

"She's giving me the first two weeks in August off. I'm flying to Florence the first day."

"Florence? It'll be boiling in August."

"Who cares? After two months here, I need Florence."

It was the same two they had seen before, except this time as
they passed not more than ten feet away, Laura could see them
clearly. Both seemed about thirty; the man wore a neatly
trimmed beard and black-rimmed glasses; the woman's hair
was pulled back in a bun the way Dr. Saxon wore hers, but this
woman's was covered with a net. Their stiff white uniforms
were identical, or almost so. Laura's eyes focused on a batik-
like blotch on the front of the man's coat. It was the color of
blood.

The woman inserted a key in the wall; the elevator doors
parted and the pair disappeared inside. Laura looked at Judy
and nodded. Then the two walked slowly in tandem to the
windowed doors, lifted themselves onto their toes, and looked
in.

Jesus God! The blood drained from Laura's head. It was a

laboratory, a medical laboratory, more sophisticated-looking than any she had ever seen at the museum or anywhere else. From one end to the other were centrifuges, scopes, elaborate consoles with illuminated dials and binocular eyepieces. Laura touched her forehead to the cold glass of the window. What had she expected really—a consultation room with reclining chairs? a hypnotist's light wheel? a padded cell? Laura scanned the far wall. Against it was a rack of beakers and vials, some containing a luminous, yellow-green liquid. Below it, she could see the edge of a laboratory bench strewn with pipettes, a pair of rubber gloves, the still blue flame of a Bunsen burner. And a row of glassine envelopes each containing the barrel of a syringe. Not just one or two, but enough syringes for the entire population of the Institute of Marriage. Laura bit down on her lower lip. This was it, all right. Somewhere in here was the secret of Saxon's Final Session. Somewhere in this sterile laboratory was the doctor's final cure for marital incompatibility. Something brushed against Laura's arm. She turned to see Judy slump against the wall, her face ashen.

"Le-let's—g-g-go," she stammered out loud.

Laura cupped her hand over Judy's mouth. Jesus, she never should have brought her. She had given in too easily, and for an ugly reason: she knew she'd need a collaborator to convince Ted of whatever she saw.

"Please! Get ahold of yourself," Laura whispered. She released her hand from Judy's mouth. "You've got to give me just one more minute."

Judy sucked in her breath and nodded. Laura slowly returned to the door and pressed her head alongside the window. She forced herself to again stare inside. She had to take in everything, record every detail to recite to Ted. Damn him!

From this angle, Laura could see vapor rising from a steam table and, in a stack behind it, several familiar-looking small brown parcels. She strained her eyes to the corners. Good God, there were half a dozen people inside here too, more of the phantom staff in white laboratory jackets, not one she had seen before. This was the real faculty of the Institute of Marriage. They stood in a cluster near the wall. And now they were slowly turning toward the door.

Laura jerked her head away. Immediately she grabbed Judy by the shoulders and half carried her to the tunnel door, then pushed her through ahead of her. Hand in hand, they started down the tunnel toward Hilltop House. They had not taken more than ten steps when they both froze.

The whine pierced the air like a siren. It was the most terrifying sound Laura had ever heard, shrill, fast, like a tape at high speed. It was at once human and mechanical. A cry for help. A machine out of control. Laura's head spun. For several seconds, she could not move. Then, pulling Judy behind her, she raced the length of the tunnel, their footsteps echoing on the tile walls, blurring the whine.

There was no one at the other end, not a soul in the foyer or back corridor of Hilltop House. Out in the garden, they could hear the band playing, the voices and laughter on the terrace. It was only then that the tears burst from Judy's eyes.

"Oh God!" she wailed. "I'd hoped . . . I'd only hoped . . ."

"Have you ever been in love, Dr. Hobson?" Mrs. Goodwin opened her sad brown eyes wide as she looked up at Wade from the examination table.

Wade smiled nervously and looked away. Here he was, four hundred miles from Washington, interviewing the one person who might make sense of the peculiar web surrounding the Saxon experiment, and his overriding emotion was shyness. He had felt it the moment Dr. Berman had ushered him in to the patient's room, and the reason was not merely her unsettling, dolorous eyes. No, the reason was that the widow Goodwin bore a remarkable and disturbing resemblance to Rachel: the color and cant of the eyes, the narrow nose, the jut and flesh of the lower lip. Even the question was characteristic of her, although surely Rachel would have invested it with a touch of winking irony. Florence Goodwin had asked it with perfect ingenuity.

"That's not an easy one to answer, do you think, Mrs. Goodwin?"

Berman stood with the technician just inside the door, listening quietly. Ever since Mrs. Goodwin had been given permission to transfer to the private clinic in Maine, she had stopped talking with the entire Memorial staff, Berman included. Yet for almost a half hour now she had been conversing attentively with this Hobson fellow from NIMH.

"Oh, yes, it's a very easy question to answer," Mrs. Goodwin said, her eyes brightening. "That is, if you *have* been in love. Then you simply answer, 'Yes.' It's as clear and easy as saying, 'Yes, I've been in London.' "

Wade laughed.

"Well, I have been in London," he said, "and I must sadly admit that I've never felt so definitively in love as I felt I was definitively in London."

"How sad, indeed. Being in love is far more interesting. And certainly more pleasant." The widow smiled. "Especially in winter."

Wade laughed again. This was the second woman who had completely charmed him in a single day and both were former patients of Elizabeth Saxon, hardly a bad recommendation. Certainly he would have preferred having dinner somewhere with Mrs. Goodwin to this. But everything Dr. Berman had told him about her history—the delayed hysteria, the hunger for phenylethylamine, even that bizarre business about her late husband's decapitation—somehow fit into the pattern which Wade had tried to piece together on a cocktail napkin during the evening flight up here. He had drawn a triangle and in one corner put the name "Adonski," and under it "violence control"; at the second angle, he had put down "Saxon," and under her name, "Tyrazepam—memory loss"; at the last he had written down "Tillie Josephson—epilepsy?"

Wade looked up. Dr. Berman was gesturing with his hand to his watch. They only had forty-five minutes left to do a neurological work-up. Berman had concocted an emergency to get them in at this hour and had called the technician away from her favorite sitcom to assist them. Wade nodded, then looked back at Mrs. Goodwin.

"We're going to be doing a couple of tests now," Wade said. "Nothing serious and it doesn't hurt. The technician will have to shave a couple of small patches on your head, but they certainly won't show when you comb out your hair." Wade looked at Mrs. Goodwin's hair; it was darker, richer-looking than Rachel's. "There was one more thing I wanted to ask you, Mrs. Goodwin. What does this love sensation feel like? I mean, do you feel it in any particular part of your body?"

"I don't know. I feel it in my heart, I suppose, and in my head. And other places." The widow looked directly back into his eyes, ignoring the technician, who had begun snipping her hair. "You make it all sound terribly clinical, Doctor."

Wade stepped back as the technician taped the first electrode to her scalp.

"Yes, I suppose I do," he said.

10:20 P.M.

"Hey, is anybody listening to me?" Ted held both hands open in front of him as he paced back and forth across the sitting room of their cabin. "I agree with you. All of you. There's obviously something going on here that we haven't been advised about. And that's wrong." He stopped in front of John, who was sitting in the wicker settee next to Judy. "All I'm saying is that before I sneak out of here in the middle of the night after having contributed almost four thousand dollars to the place, I'd sure as hell like to know what they are doing here and why we haven't been told about it. I'd like some honest answers, face to face with Saxon, tomorrow morning at a reasonable hour. Now is that so irrational?"

Laura clenched her hand.

"Not irrational, Ted," she said. "Idiotic. You don't seem to get it, do you? There isn't just something wrong with this place. It's dangerous. We're in danger here, Ted, and I think we ought to get out of here right now. If we can."

Ted sighed loudly, pursing his lips as he exhaled.

"Look, folks, I hope I'm not disappointing anybody if I tell you that I don't think this place is any more dangerous than Club Med." Ted looked pleadingly at Laura. "Honey, you've had some pretty exaggerated ideas about this place since we got here. But then I'd thought you realized that yesterday at dinner."

Laura stared back at her husband. At this moment, it was not a question of whether or not she could ever love him again. The only question was how she had ever loved him. The man understood absolutely nothing about her and, worse, he did not trust her.

"Damn it, Ted, do you believe that Judy and I saw what we said we did or don't you?" Laura's voice was ice-cold.

"Of course I do," Ted said. "I believe you saw some sort of chemical laboratory or other. Or maybe it was an infirmary. And I'm sure you heard somebody scream bloody murder. Although I, for one, certainly would expect to hear somebody

173

really let it out at a no-holds-barred marriage-therapy session. I mean, I believe everything both of you said. But I'm just not sure I can come to any precise conclusions from it, at least until I get some answers from Saxon. Is that really so idiotic? You tell me, John."

John tilted his head from side to side, as if weighing Ted's argument, but then he blurted out, "Hey, all I know is that I've never seen Judy this frightened in fifteen years. That's why we've got to go. And as far as the money is concerned, I'll have my lawyer contact hers and see if we can work something out."

John began easing Judy to her feet. Somehow they both looked so old just now, slack, listless. There seemed to be more defeat than fear in Judy's eyes.

"If we're going to leave, we might as well get started right now," John said. He shook his head. "It's a damned shame. Everything else about this place is, you know, terrific."

Laura and Judy embraced, rocking back and forth.

"Call me as soon as you get home tomorrow," Judy said.

"Of course."

Judy abruptly hugged Laura closer, putting her mouth to Laura's ear. "You can come with us now, you know," she whispered.

Laura pulled back reflexively. She actually caught herself resenting Judy for even suggesting that she leave without Ted. But why the hell not? Ted's stubbornness was his own idiocy; she wasn't obligated to stay in danger for even one more hour because of it. Let him meet her at home tomorrow with a full report on his face-to-face confrontation with Saxon. Laura bit down on her lower lip. No! With the fears she had about this place, she couldn't leave Ted alone here for even a night. Damn it, she *was* still married to him.

"Thanks." Laura hugged Judy again. "We'll leave first thing in the morning."

John and Judy walked slowly out of the cabin, hands at their sides, not touching. Ted turned and started for the bathroom.

"There's just one goddamned thing," Laura said to his back. "You're staying up with me, Ted. We aren't closing our eyes tonight."

Friday

2:15 A.M.

"Greg, I'm not going through this again. Now either you call Jeckman or I will. Is that clear?"

Wade could hear Greg Horowitz clicking his teeth together in his bedroom four hundred miles away.

"Listen, I'm definitely going to call him," Horowitz said. "I'm just sitting here trying to figure out what the optimum way to proceed is. Now don't misunderstand me, Hoby, but on your word alone—I mean, without any material in hand—I can't even wake The Wizard up, let alone get an investigation going. How quickly can you fly down here with everything?"

Wade tapped his finger on the manila envelope on Berman's desk. Inside were Mrs. Goodwin's electroencephalogram, her X rays and CAT scan reel; the data of a neurological examination, now evidence of the most bizarre and horrifying medical crime he had heard of since the war.

"I could be there in four hours, five at the most," Wade said. He looked across the office to Dr. Berman and nodded. "But I'm not leaving this hospital without custody of the patient. I think she's in danger as long as Saxon knows where she is."

"Hoby, get on the first plane you can. We can take care of everything from this end, including the safety of the patient. But I need that material, those X rays, to get things going here."

Again Wade raised his eyes. Berman had opened the office door and was looking out into the hallway, where Mrs. Goodwin lay sleeping on a rolling stretcher. Horowitz was probably right, they'd need some kind of tangible proof in Washington before they could take any action. But he did not dare leave Mrs. Goodwin in this hospital while he took his case to Jeckman, no matter what guarantees Horowitz gave. Even Berman was sure of that. Horowitz had to be pushed.

"Greg, there's one aspect of this business that I didn't go into before." Wade paused a second; he wanted to be sure Horowitz was listening to every word. "We've got a P.I. in animal behavior, a man named Adonski at the Harvard-MIT Primate Center who we've been funding a couple of years for violence-control studies. Now it looks very much to me like he and Saxon are in this together. They applied to us for separate grants, but this Adonski's been funneling all his equipment up to her for use on human subjects. Greg, I don't think we've ever been exploited in such a—a humiliating way before. It just makes all of us, right up to the top, look like we're running things with our eyes closed. If the critics of NIMH were to get ahold of this . . ."

Wade let the sentence dangle. He wished he could enjoy manipulating Horowitz more.

"Hobson, let me put you on hold for a moment. I'll see if I can find Jeckman."

Wade cradled the phone against his shoulder as the line clicked. Berman still stood by the open door, his eyes dazed. The young resident probably could not believe that any of this was happening; he probably could not believe that any of this *could* happen. Wade could. They had finally taken modern psychology to its logical extreme: the dehumanization of our fondest sensibilities.

Out in the hallway, the widow Goodwin stirred in her sleep, turning her face toward Wade. A beautiful woman. He had to help her.

"You still there, Hoby?"

"I'm here, Greg."

"Look, The Wizard agrees with you one hundred percent. He's going to arrange to have the patient released to you and he's going to bring both of you directly down here. You'll be picked up within the hour."

"Good." Wade felt his heart accelerating. He had done it. He had been playing this mad hunch all week and now he was being vindicated.

"Oh, one thing, Wade. What was the name of that doctor at Memorial who's helped you there? We may need an affidavit from him."

"Berman," Wade said. "Fred Berman. He deserves a great deal of credit for this."

"Sure," Greg Horowitz said. "But you're the hero, Hobson."

2:50 A.M.

Laura turned the wooden skirt hanger back and forth in her hand, considering whether or not to steal it, then scowled and tossed it into her open suitcase. It was not the time to be weighing the ethical niceties of petty theft. Let Saxon take it out of their four-thousand-dollar tuition. Laura looked slowly around the bedroom, checking to see if there were anything left to pack.

Ted lay flat on the bed in his tennis shoes and shorts, taking the nap she had finally permitted him. Wearing the tennis shoes had been one of her conditions—she wanted them both to be ready to run, if necessary—and Ted had made a joke about it, a silly joke from the good old days before they were married when they had sometimes been in such a hurry to make love that they did not get all their clothes off. Laura could barely remember what that kind of passionate urgency felt like. She sighed. Oh, yes she could; this very afternoon while spying on Affy and Guy she had remembered it quite well. Kneeling there in her bathing suit, she had felt the memory like a warm drug spreading through her body. Laura turned away from Ted. That damned oak bed. It sat there like a judge's bench.

She looked at her watch. Seven hours at the most and they'd be gone from here. She would call Judy right away. They would have to figure out what authorities should be told about Dr. Saxon and her institute. Perhaps Jerzy could give them some advice. But after that, how long would it be before she would be making jokes about I.M.? A month? Two? Laura smiled to herself. Funny, in her fantasy she was joking about I.M. around the kitchen table with Ted. It was a family joke.

3:10 A.M.

Berman picked up the phone on the first ring.

"Dr. Berman? This is Nellie downstairs. I have a message for you from Dr. Russell. He would like to see you immediately in front of the Neurological Work-up Room."

"Thank you. I'll be right down." Berman replaced the receiver and looked up at Hobson. "It's Russell, my chief. Word travels fast around here. I guess I'm in for a dressing down for an unauthorized use of expensive equipment."

"I'll talk to him, if you like." Hobson smiled ironically. "I think I can convince him there were extenuating circumstances."

"Let me try first," Berman replied. "In some sadistic way I might actually enjoy seeing Russell's face when he hears what's happened."

The older man nodded. "I'll be here," he said.

Berman paused a second in the hallway to look down at Mrs. Goodwin, still asleep on the stretcher. Dr. Hobson had revealed nothing to her after he had made his discovery. He had just continued with that strangely intimate patter that the two of them had commenced the moment they had met, talk of love and loneliness at a level that would only confuse the teaching psychiatrists in this hospital. He wondered how Hobson would finally get himself to tell her what he had found.

Berman took the elevator to the third floor, then walked to the end of the hallway and turned to his left. The door to the Work-up Room was open, the fluorescent lights on. Russell was probably really looking forward to this. No doubt he'd come in for his shift an hour early just to talk with him. He was probably in there gathering evidence now. It wouldn't be hard; Berman had signed all the logs himself. Russell was probably thinking he could knock him off the rotation for this, screw him good. Berman stepped into the room.

"Dr. Russell?"

When Berman first felt the prick of pain at the base of his spine, he reached back his hand as if to swat at a horsefly. But then his knees popped under him and he spun to the ground. And lying there, fully conscious, he saw his attacker above him: a pleasant-looking young man with a smile on his face and a syringe in his hand. Berman tried to get up. He could not. He could not move at all. The man had injected a muscle relaxant directly into his spinal cord.

The young man gathered up Berman like a rag doll and carried him back into the corridor, then through one open door and past another. He was hefted onto a table and strapped to it. Berman strained against the drug to keep his eyelids up. On the wall just in front of him, he could make out the palm trees, the surf, the setting sun—the pretty pastel mural which was meant to calm patients about to undergo radiological therapy. Berman's heart raced. He could hear the soft whirr of the motor as the young man lowered the betatron columnator directly over his forehead.

Berman willed his head to move, begged it to roll away. Not an inch. Not a millimeter. He heard the young man close the door behind him in the leaded control room.

The six thousand rads the betatron beamed into Berman's skull instantly reduced his brains to the consistency of scrambled eggs. He was dead within seconds.

3:35 A.M.

"My car is next to the kitchen loading platform. The east service elevator should be our best route, don't you think, Doctor?"

Wade nodded. He was relieved that Jeckman's young emissary had everything under control. He was exhausted and would need some rest before presenting his findings to Jeckman and Horowitz and whoever else would be waiting for him in Washington. And sometime before that—on the plane, perhaps—he would have to tell Florence Goodwin where he was taking her and why. He was not looking forward to that at all. He hoped there was a bottle of vodka to be found somewhere between here and the District of Columbia.

The young man grasped the handles of the rolling stretcher by Mrs. Goodwin's head.

"Do you think you can manage the other end, Dr. Hobson?"

Again, Wade nodded. He placed the envelope containing the test results on the stretcher between Mrs. Goodwin's feet and took hold of the handles.

"I'd like to give Dr. Berman just one more minute," he said.

"I wish we could," the young man said. "But we're running a bit late as it is. I'm sure he'll understand."

Wade hesitated a second, then began pushing the stretcher down the corridor. Maybe they would encounter Berman along the way. After what he and Berman had experienced together, Wade did not like leaving without saying good-bye. At the service elevator, the young man reached into his jacket pocket and withdrew a ring of keys, selected one, inserted it into a slot in the wall, and turned it, opening the elevator doors. The fellow was certainly a master of preparedness, a true Jeckman man. They wheeled Mrs. Goodwin into the elevator and the doors closed behind them.

"Nice-looking woman," the young man said, looking down on the sleeping patient's face.

"Yes." Wade did not much like the casualness with which the young man appraised Mrs. Goodwin. A typical NIMH condescension about it. But that was not all that bothered him; Wade felt a certain possessiveness toward the woman. He looked at the young man, wondering how much the people in Washington had told him about Mrs. Goodwin's condition.

At the first basement, the elevator doors opened and they wheeled the stretcher down the corridor to the food-storage room and then through it to a rear door. The young man had arrived complete with a bona fide transfer and custody clearance for the patient, but he said everyone concerned thought they should make their exit as inconspicuous as possible. Wade could believe that. The Wizard was about to have the biggest public-relations problem of his career and needed all the time he could buy.

The young man vaulted off the edge of the loading platform and pulled open the rear door of his vehicle, a small van. Wade was surprised when he first saw it, although he did not really know what he had expected. They eased the stretcher onto a platform in the back of the van and strapped her to it.

In the cab, the young man sighed.

"It's going to be a long night," he said.

"It is already," Wade replied.

"You wouldn't want a drink, would you?" The young man smiled.

Wade hesitated, wondering if this fellow would report a drink to Jeckman, but then he saw him pulling an unopened bottle of Polish vodka from the glove compartment and the hesitation passed. The young man twisted off the cap and handed it to Wade. Wade raised the bottle between them.

"To a safe journey," he said, and he took a long swallow of the odd-tasting liquid.

"To love eternal," the young man replied, smiling.

Wade attempted to smile back, but he was already passing into a leaden unconsciousness.

7:45 A.M.

"Good morning and welcome to your fifth full day at I.M. This will be a special day for you, Ted and Laura Esposito. Today you will experience a rebirth of your relationship. Today is your Final Session."

Laura tore the print-out sheet straight down the middle, placed the pieces on top of one another, and tore again and again until the pieces were no bigger than petals of a daisy.

"No," she said to herself as she dropped the pieces back into the breakfast basket. "Thank you very much, but no."

Behind her, Ted had just turned off the shower and now stepped through the bathroom door rubbing himself vigorously with a towel. In spite of the fact that Laura had sat quietly on the packed suitcases for six hours before awakening him, Ted had insisted on a shower before they left.

"Hey, it'll be my last decent shower in who knows how long," Ted had argued. "I've told you about that dribble that passes for a shower at my apartment, haven't I?"

Laura had flinched when he said it. So Ted did not intend to come back to Charlestown and live again as a family. But why should that surprise her? Whatever in the world should have made her think he would do otherwise?

Ted threw the towel onto the window seat and stretched athletically before pulling on his shorts. For effect, Laura thought. He was purposefully showing her what a fine specimen of a man she was losing. An adolescent ploy, really. He was actually trying to make her feel guilty for dragging them away from here.

"Shall we take the bags with us or pick them up later with the car?"

"I'd rather take them now, Ted," Laura said. "We can each take one." She handed him the lighter one.

Ted took a long gaze around the cottage, sighed, and pushed open the screen door to the deck.

"I don't suppose you'd like to have a last continental

184

breakfast on the porch, would you?''

"No," Laura said. ''We'll get something on the road.''

Ted shrugged and started down the steps.

"That could be hours," he grumbled.

"Not if we get out of here fast," Laura said. She still had hopes of getting him to postpone their confrontation with Dr. Saxon until they were all back in Boston. Maybe his hungry stomach would do it. She followed behind him on the footpath, not saying a word. At the driveway, Ted swung left toward Hilltop House. So, it was going to be Saxon before breakfast. Laura suddenly felt very tired; she set down her suitcase and took a deep breath before picking it up with her other hand. She stopped. From the corner of her eye, she had seen the benches in the pocket rose garden below them and this morning a second couple sat next to the vinyl "lovers." She turned, shading her eyes. She took one step toward the garden, then another. No! God, no!

"Ted," Laura called softly. He was already yards away from her up the drive, but she did not dare to raise her voice. "Ted."

"What?" Ted looked down at her, the beginnings of exasperation on his face. Laura beckoned to him frantically with her hand, her eyes returning to the couple on the second bench.

"What is it now, Laura?"

Laura pointed. She watched his eyes go first to the vinyl statue and then to the pair on the adjacent bench, a man and woman locked in a passionate kiss, the man's fingers running through her hair.

"Jesus Christ!" Ted's mouth dropped.

The couple finally ended their kiss, then turned their heads slowly, and smiled warmly at Ted and Laura.

John and Judy had never looked happier.

"Hi! We were hoping we'd run into you two this morning," John said, waving them toward him.

Laura could not move. She felt Ted's hand on her back, propelling her forward. Judy was rising from the bench, her pretty round face flushed, her eyes somehow different, younger, deeper, more liquid. Laura clenched her jaw. Judy's eyes were the eyes of a woman who had made love all night. Judy looked at Laura and then at the suitcase in her hand.

"Hey, you aren't going, are you?" She looked concerned. "I mean, the doctor isn't making you leave, is she?"

Laura ran toward Judy, screaming. "My God, what's happened to you?"

She grabbed her by the shoulders, shaking her, staring desperately into her eyes.

"Judy! What happened? What did she do to you?"

Judy locked her arms around Laura's waist and pulled her to her. She kissed Laura on the cheek.

"I'm just so goddamned happy, I don't know where to begin," Judy said, tears of excitement in her eyes. "All I can say is don't let anyone ever tell you that sex is an overrated part of marriage."

Laura pushed her away to arm's length, still holding her shoulders and shaking her. "Judy! For chrissake, listen to me, will you? Try to concentrate. Maybe it's not too late. Maybe we can still get you some help. But I have to know what happened to you. Everything. Start from when you left our cabin last night."

John suddenly rose and clasped Judy around the waist, gently tugging her away from Laura.

"God, that really seems like a million years ago, Laura." Judy shrugged coquettishly. "It's been a very long night, as they say."

"I'll bet it has," Laura said sharply. "Now I want to know what happened during every minute of it."

"Hey, lighten up," Judy said, smiling warmly. "What difference does it make? Last night . . . last year. . . . What's happening right now is the only thing that counts. What you're feeling right now. That's the only reality there is. Think about it, Laura."

Laura felt her hands trembling against Judy's shoulders. Oh God, she could not lose control now.

"Now listen to me, Judy," she said evenly. "You and I snuck into the Therapy Pavilion last night. Just nod if you can remember that."

Judy smiled.

"Of course I remember that," she said. "All that sneaking around. It was fun in a way, wasn't it, Laura?"

"It was also frightening," Laura said, not taking her eyes from Judy's. "Do you remember what we saw, Judy?"

Again, Judy smiled. "Of course. How could I forget an adventure like that?"

"My God, Judy, aren't you worried about what they've done to you? To you and John?"

"Worried?" Judy laughed, a high-pitched, girlish laugh. "On the contrary, I've never been less worried in my life. I feel so . . . so comfortable, Laura. I feel so pleasantly comfortable with this man of mine." She leaned her head against John's.

Laura dropped her hands from Judy's shoulders and stepped back beside Ted. She looked up at him. He was looking from John to Judy and back again, his own face blank.

"Laura, there's something I've wanted to tell you since we met. But until today I've never really felt close enough to you to be able to say it." Judy smiled beautifully. "Laur, you kind of trap yourself by always wanting to know what's going to happen long before it happens. That's how you cheat yourself out of ever feeling anything new. Some of the best feelings take you by surprise, you know."

Laura stood numbly. There was nothing more she could say. For almost a full minute, all of them were silent.

"There's just one thing I'm wondering about." Laura held her breath. It was Ted, his voice low, neutral. "Last night you were in a hurry to get out of here. Now who decided that you'd stay—was that you or Dr. Saxon?"

For an instant, Judy's brow furrowed, a slight tremor pulsing along her jaw. John grabbed her by the shoulders and shook her. He stared at Ted.

"Look, Ted, we know you and Laura aren't really getting along very well and, believe me, that concerns us." John's voice was soft, sincere. "But instead of taking it out on us, friend, why don't you get some help? That'd be a more constructive approach to your problems, don't you think?"

Ted looked calmly back into John's eyes.

"You're crazy." Ted said the words in a matter-of-fact tone, as if he had just solved a simple equation. "You are both absolutely crazy." He lifted both suitcases in one of his arms and grasped Laura's hand with the other.

"Let's get the hell out of here," he said.

"Yes, let's." Laura said the words as unexcitedly as she was able—she did not dare jinx the moment—but she was feeling such an immense relief that she could barely contain it. Thank

God, Ted finally understood that this place was completely mad; Ted and she *were* on the same wavelength after all. For the moment, that knowledge eclipsed her fear and her sadness for Judy and John. She ran down the driveway toward the parking lot, holding her husband's hand tightly.

At their car, Ted pulled out his wallet and untaped his spare key from inside the bill compartment. He shoved the suitcases into the trunk and unlocked the doors. The engine caught on the first try. Seconds later they were speeding down the final quarter mile of the magnificent spruce-lined drive that led out of the Institute of Marriage. Laura stared out her window, barely breathing, her eyes flicking from tree to passing tree. Five minutes and they would be out of here.

Ted slowed to a halt as they approached the iron gate. The same collegiate-looking boy who had greeted them Sunday now stepped out of the gatehouse, holding his clipboard with one hand, scratching his head with the other. He ambled in front of the car to Ted's window. Absently, Laura observed that he was still carrying the same dog-eared copy of *Walden Two*.

"Hi. Beautiful Maine morning, isn't it?" The young man ducked his cheery face level to Ted's half-open window. "Living right here is the next best thing to camping out, don't you think?"

Ted said nothing. Outside the window, the young man was flipping through the papers on his clipboard, the spike-topped gate looming behind him like a row of spears.

"Either I slept through yesterday or you're leaving a day early," the young man said, again smiling broadly.

"We're leaving early," Ted said evenly, not looking at him.

"Really? Why's that?" the young man asked.

Laura saw Ted's fingers tighten around the steering wheel. She leaned down, pressing her cheek against Ted's hand and looked up at the young man.

"There just didn't seem any reason left for staying an extra day." Laura smiled as warmly as she could muster.

The young man leaned forward so that his eyes peered over the lip of the glass. He seemed to be studying Laura.

"It *is* beautiful here," she murmured. "But sometimes it's lovely just to go off somewhere alone. Just the two of us."

She raised her head, looking into Ted's eyes and then,

abruptly, she grasped his head and pressed her lips to his in a passionate kiss. Immediately Ted responded, his arms locking around her neck, his lips parting. It was the most marvelous kiss Laura could remember and for a moment she almost forgot about the impression it was supposed to make on the young man just outside their window. When they finished, Laura nestled her head against Ted's shoulder and smiled contentedly. The young man smiled back.

"I'll get the gate," he said and sauntered back toward the gatehouse.

Laura put her mouth to Ted's ear.

"By God, we fooled him," she whispered.

She felt Ted smile.

"Hell, we almost fooled me," he whispered back. He touched her cheek with his hand and again turned his lips to hers when he suddenly jerked back his head.

"He's picking up the phone," he said in a low monotone. "I think I'd better find that gate switch myself."

With a small movement of his left hand, Ted unlatched his door.

"Slide into the driver's seat as soon as I'm out and nose the car through the minute the gate starts to open. I'll jump in once we're outside."

He was out the door, sprinting toward the gatehouse before she could think. She slid behind the wheel, her heart beating rapidly, her eyes fixed on the gate.

"Please, God," she whispered. "Just get us out of here. That's all I want. Please."

From the corner of her eye, she saw Ted enter the gatehouse door.

"Ted!"

Laura screamed a second too late. The two men in white coats had already grabbed Ted from behind and were twisting him to the grass. Laura stared, paralyzed with shock, as one of the men planted a foot on Ted's shoulder and yanked up his arm while the other pierced the crook of his elbow with a syringe.

Laura pushed open her door, but it was all over in a second. They grabbed her by both arms, their fingers digging into her flesh. Laura did not resist. It was Wendy and Arnold.

"They should have never admitted you to I.M. in the first

place," Arnold said. He pressed one of her arms back in a half
nelson while Wendy opened the car's back door. He shoved
Laura in. On the other side, a white-coated man was pulling in
Ted. Ted's eyes were open wide, his pupils dilated in a frozen
stare of helplessness. Laura's heart ached for him. Tears
slipped from her eyes.

Wendy slammed the door shut. She bent down and looked
coldly through the window at Laura.

"You simply don't deserve it!" she snapped.

The white-coated man behind the wheel pulled it hard to the
left, turning the car completely around, then paused as Wendy
and Arnold pulled ahead of them on the white motorcycle like
marshals leading a parade. Ted swayed clumsily against Laura,
but the man sitting on his other side yanked him straight up by
his shoulders. Laura reached down and took Ted's hand in
both of hers. It was cold, lifeless. She squeezed it tightly.
Forgive me, she wanted to say. We never should have come
here.

She looked out her window. They were passing the cupid
fountain and, glistening in the morning light, the golden
cherub suddenly looked grotesque to Laura. Obscene. She was
about to turn her eyes away when she saw the rose garden appearing between the trees ahead of her. She pressed her face
against the window. Yes, there were Judy and John still embracing on the bench. Suddenly they looked up and for an instant Laura's and Judy's eyes met. Judy smiled magnificently
and then put her hand to her lips. She was throwing Laura a
kiss.

Laura pulled herself back against the seat. She did not look
at anything but Ted's hand in hers until she heard the slam of
a gate behind her. She was inside the walled courtyard of the
Therapy Pavilion. This time she was going in through the
front entrance.

Immediately, Laura's door pulled open and two pair of
hands reached into the car for her. Outside, two other staff
people were bracing Ted between them as if he were a
wounded football player. She was escorted behind him to the
bow-shaped foyer—once, no doubt, the lobby to the
chapel—then up a flight of stairs to a wood-paneled corridor.

"She wants them in conference room two," the man
holding Ted's right arm said, pivoting left. He pulled a key

ring from his belt and unlocked an oak door, then pushed it open.

"As is?" another said, "or do you think the bride needs a relaxant?"

"As is," the first man said. Laura and Ted were seated next to each other on a leather library couch. "The doctor wants to talk with her."

The four white-coated men filed out the door, the last closing and locking it behind him. Laura turned and looked at Ted. His eyes were still glazed over, the muscles in his face flaccid, rubbery-looking. She eased herself slowly to her feet and stood in front of him.

"Ted, sweetheart. Please look at me." She squatted level with him, reaching out her hands to his face. Ted's eyes swiveled in his head. For a second he seemed to stiffen, but then he fell back limp against the couch. Tears filled Laura's eyes.

"Oh my God, I'm sorry about this. I'm sorry for both of us. I never should have let go of our marriage in the first place." She buried her head in his lap. "That was the biggest mistake I ever made."

Laura was quiet for a moment, then slowly pulled herself to her feet, and paced toward the window. She looked at Ted's still face.

"I do care for you, Ted," she whispered, "very much."

A flash of color caught her eye and she looked out the window. The courtyard was just below her, its gates open, the familiar, brightly painted van circling to the main entrance of the pavilion, now backing up to the doors. Laura saw the same handsome young driver jump out of the cab and wave the sentries toward him. She pressed her forehead against a windowpane and looked directly down. Jesus God! Two guards slid a gray-haired, patrician-looking man from the back of the van on a stretcher. He lay faceup, his eyes closed, the top of his collar and knot of his tie peeping over the sheet which covered him. Laura grasped the handles at the bottom of the window and pulled. It opened.

"Ted," Laura said softly. "Whatever happens, I want you to know that I feel very married to you. In the best sense. Just the way we are."

She squinted down into the courtyard. The driver and a

guard were pulling a second body from the van, a middle-aged woman with thick brown hair. They lugged her through the door. The courtyard was empty.

"I wonder if you've understood anything I've said," Laura whispered. She thought she saw Ted's eyelid flutter as she swung her hips over the sill. She hung by her hands for a fraction of a second, then dropped to her feet in the courtyard. In three quick steps she crossed the open space to the van. She jumped in and crouched behind the stretcher rack, pulling a blanket over her. Moments later, she heard the driver return. He slammed the door closed. In a minute, they were moving. Laura did not so much as move a muscle until she heard the second gate clang behind her, then she slumped down onto the cold, rigid floor of the van. She was finally out of the Institute of Marriage.

Now she had to get her husband out.

12:25 P.M.

Wade felt his consciousness slowly return like an edge of pink light widening over the horizon. His eyelids fluttered, then snapped open. His eyes stared blankly at the darkness around him. He tried moving an arm, then a leg. Neither responded. He was strapped on his back to something, a table or a stretcher. He twisted his neck to his right. He dimly made out a figure lying like a mountainscape beside him. The face was no more than a foot away from his. It was a lovely face, the face of the widow Goodwin.

Now he remembered a dream he had had at some deep point in his drugged sleep. He had been sailing high above his family's estate in a glider and, swooping down, he had seen his father and mother lying in the grass by the lily pond. They were naked and they were caressing one another. Wade had leaned over to take a closer look when he started to fall, but a pair of long white arms snatched him back up onto the glider, which was now a swan. It was the Goodwin woman who had saved him.

Wade smiled to her in the darkness. She smiled back.

In spite of everything, she was still very much human, he thought. Certainly more human than Jeckman or Horowitz or this Saxon or Adonski or anyone else from here to Washington who was tied up in this incredible conspiracy. This conspiracy of involuntary love.

Wade's eyelids grew heavy again and closed as if by the sheer weight of the paradox.

1:15 P.M.

The van halted, its motor still running. Laura heard the cab
door open and close, then a rumble like rolling thunder, then
the cab door opening and closing again. The van jerked forward and then came to a stop. Once more the cab door opened
and closed and this time Laura recognized the rumbling
sound, a heavy garage door. She was in the back of a van in a
closed garage three or four hours away form the Institute of
Marriage.

The blurred echo of footsteps grew dimmer, then ceased
altogether. Laura rocked onto her knees. Gingerly she slid her
index finger out from under her nose; she had pressed it there
holding back a sneeze for so long that her upper lip was numb.
No sneeze now. Maybe her nose had gotten used to the musky,
oddly familiar odor which permeated the van.

She slowly drew down the rear door handle and pushed.
A frame of yellow light burst through, startling Laura.
Somehow she had imagined it was night out there, but that
was sunlight streaming through the garage windows. Laura
stretched one foot to the cement floor, then the other. Her
knees bounced under her. Her whole body felt as if it had been
hanging from chains. She looked around the garage. There
seemed to be two ways out: by rolling up the clamorous garage
door or by going through the small metal door on the opposite
wall, undoubtedly the door through which the driver had
exited. Laura chose the metal door. Opening it, her first sensation was the smell, the same as in the back of the van but with
ten times the intensity. Laura pinched her nostrils. She was
standing at one end of a brown-tiled corridor; at the other was
a second door, opened, fluorescent light shining out. Laura
considered turning back, but the fluorescent light drew her.
She needed to have one look in there before she went on.

The chimpanzees sensed Laura before she saw them and instantly began chattering. Laura shuddered, then forced herself to step inside the room and turn her head. There were

thirty of them, their masklike faces pressed against the bars of
a cage which occupied half the room. For a moment, she
stared dumbly back at them, her eyes flicking from heart-
shaped face to heart-shaped face. Chimpanzees had always
struck Laura as satirists, their facial expressions not sub-
human but an exaggeration of human expressions, like the
takes of a silent-movie comic, and Laura could tell immediately what human response these chimps were parodying. The
animals stood in pairs, their arms intertwined, ecstatic smiles
on their dazed faces, their heads tilted together. They were
caricatures of lovers.

A shiver passed down Laura's spine. She started to turn, but
then her gaze caught on a strip of cardboard taped across the
bars at the top of the cage. The words *Peaceable Kingdom*
were hand-printed in blue crayon on it. The chimpanzees had
begun wandering to the rear of their cage and now, two by
two, leaped onto a scaffold. Again, Laura started to turn and
again she stopped. Sitting on top of a metal file cabinet directly across from the open door was a pile of brown cardboard boxes, the same boxes—Laura was sure—she had seen
the driver deliver to the Therapy Pavilion on Monday and that
she had seen in the laboratory last night. She squinted at the
black-and-white pattern that ran along the side of each box. It
was not a design; it was a string of oriental characters.

Laura stepped cautiously to the file cabinet, reached up,
and removed the topmost box. It did not weigh more than a
pound. She turned it over in her hand, then ran her thumbnail
along the seal, opened it, and pulled out the weightless Styrofoam packing. Sitting in the center were two identical clear-
plastic cases and clipped to the center of each of these was a
tiny metallic cylinder no larger than the tip of a pencil. Laura
had snapped open the first case when, without a second's
warning, she sneezed. It was a great honking blast of a sneeze
that shook the case from her hands and sent the chimps back
to the bars emitting a high-pitched cackle as if they were laughing at her. Their chorus drowned out all sound of the footsteps
behind her. The young driver was coming at her through the
door before she was aware of him.

Laura ran diagonally across the room, not knowing where
she was going, the young man only steps behind her. On the
far side of a cabinet a door appeared. She planted her feet and

yanked it. It opened just as the man's fingers closed on the
back of her T-shirt. She sprang away, feeling the cotton rip in
a straight line up her back. She was in another room now,
much the same size as the first, but there were smaller cages
here, piled like milk boxes on top of benches, each containing
a pair of white rats. Without thinking, she grabbed at one, her
fingers hooking through the mesh, and flung it with all her
force behind her. It hit the young man in both shins. He
sprawled forward on top of the cage, then suddenly yelped like
a wounded animal and rolled off it. Two spots of blood appeared on the palm of his right hand; he had been bitten.

Laura was already pushing through the next door into another cage-filled room. Behind her, she heard the young man
getting to his feet, cursing loudly. Suddenly there was a
whoosh and bang as the beaker he flung at her burst against
the wall. Laura cut to her left and raced through an open
door. She was at the bottom of a stairwell. She sprinted up
two flights, the metal steps clanging and reverberating against
the tile walls as if it were a belfry. There was no way to hear if
the man were still behind her. At the third level, she raced
through the stairwell exit into a hallway.

The sudden sight of college students in their running shoes
and jeans struck Laura as totally surreal. A couple of them
looked up, startled, as she breathlessly burst into the corridor,
but then immediately returned to their intense, peripatetic
conversations. Not daring to look behind her, Laura elbowed
between two students and funneled with them through open
double doors. She was at the top of a canted lecture hall.
Laura followed a step behind a tall, black-haired boy to a seat
in the middle row. She slumped down next to him. The student
looked at her a moment, his dark oriental eyes opaque, then
reached to his belt and pulled a pocket calculator from a
holster. On her left, a heavyset girl sank into her seat.

"Good afternoon." A man with a headful of loose white
curls smiled out from behind the lectern below. "Today I
would like to elaborate on the psychometric model of percep-
tual responses which I began on Wednesday. Now, if we are to
assume that data reception and data recognition are separate
and discrete mental events . . ."

Laura slowly slid down in her seat until she was certain her
head was not visible from behind. The cool chair against her

back made her realize that her T-shirt must have split all the way to the collar. But on either side of Laura the students busily scratched down their notes on the psychometrics of perception, apparently oblivious to the barebacked thirty-year-old woman sprawled almost to her knees between them. Laura sighed. She looked down the curved row of notebooks and pens to a narrow rectangular window. Outside she saw a road busy with cars and bicycles and just beyond it the beginning of a handsome red brick bridge. Laura knew exactly where she was. She was in an MIT classroom, just three minutes across the Charles River from Boston.

3 P.M.

She was, Wade decided the moment she entered the room, the most intelligent-looking woman he had ever seen, Rachel included. He had somehow expected the refinement, but he had not been prepared for that countenance of profound intelligence. He should have been, he reflected. All the women of Elizabeth Saxon's generation who had made their way into medical school were fiercely intelligent.

"How do you do, Dr. Hobson?" she said, extending her hand to him. She spoke as if they were alone in the wood-paneled office, as if the two white-coated men who had brought him in and now flanked him were not there.

Wade did not give her his hand. Dr. Saxon smiled and lightly dropped hers to her side.

"Dr. Jeckman tells me you are interested in my project," she said. "I'd be delighted to show you everything I can."

4:50 P.M.

"Bear with me just a moment longer, all right, Mrs. Esposito?"

Captain Cella smiled at Laura over the top of the six typewritten pages in his hands, a transcript of the statement she had given the desk sergeant an hour ago. It told the whole story, from I.M. to the man who had tried to kill her in the MIT animal laboratories.

"Can I get you anything? Cup of hot tea, maybe? Something to take the chill off your shoulders?" Cella crinkled his eyes. He was looking at Laura's T-shirt, which now hung on her front like a bib.

Laura crossed her arms over her chest.

"I'm perfectly all right, Officer," she said, looking directly into Cella's eyes. "But I think we ought to move as quickly on this as we can, don't you?"

Laura was making every effort she could to control the tone of her voice. After an hour at the District Four office of the Boston Police Department she understood, as certainly no politician could, exactly why crime flourished in the city of Boston: it was because no criminal could possibly move more slowly than Boston police procedure. All that had kept Laura from screaming at any of them was the fear that they might throw her out on the street. If nothing else, she felt safe in here, and after the past twenty-four hours that was a blessed feeling.

"I just want to check over a couple of things here," Cella said, tapping the papers on his desk. "Now you live at Fourteen Monument Square in Charlestown, is that correct?"

"Yes." The word hissed over Laura's teeth.

"With your husband and son, correct?"

"Captain," Laura said. "I read over my statement a half dozen times while I was waiting to see you and I can assure you everything I said in it is correct. Now let's talk about how we are going to get my husband out of there, shall we?"

"I can understand your impatience," Cella said quietly.

"But you have to understand, this is an interstate matter we've allegedly got here. And before I get out-of-state people involved, I think it would be a good idea if we had all our facts in order." The police captain scratched industriously behind his right ear. "For example, there's one little discrepancy that's popped up already. You say Mr. Esposito lives with you on Monument Square and yet we've got him listed as living on Commonwealth Avenue. I don't know quite what to make of that, do you?"

Laura felt the color rise in her cheeks.

"My husband and I were separated," she said evenly. "He moved out for a few months and now he's returning. Does that clear things up?"

"Yes, it does. Very clear. You and your husband have made it up. That's good. Doesn't happen often these days, you know." Cella gave Laura a tight smile. "Now, this, uh, reconciliation must have happened fairly recently, am I correct, Mrs. Esposito?"

Laura bit down on her lower lip; she was sure that if she tried to say anything it would come out in a scream.

"I mean, none of your neighbors seem to be aware of it yet, not even that woman who's taking care of your son." Cella spoke in a casual voice, as if all of this were nothing more than idle gossip. "One of my people just spoke with her and she thinks you two must have worked things out up at that marriage retreat you've been at."

"Jesus Christ!" Laura snapped to her feet and leaned over Cella's desk, her eyes blazing. "I have just escaped with my life from lunatics who still have my husband captured. Now either you're going to help me get him out or you're not."

"Of course I'm going to help you," Cella said softly, wearing a look of genuine surprise. "That's exactly what I'm trying to do now. What I don't think you realize, Mrs. Esposito—I mean, probably just because of everything you've been through—what you don't realize is how difficult it is to understand some of this." He tapped the statement. "Especially for a person like myself. I mean, I, personally, have never been to a marriage retreat. Do you see what I mean?"

Laura stared blankly at the police captain. For the first time in a day and a half without sleep, she felt exhausted. She sat down slowly.

"Now what I would imagine," Cella was saying, "is at one

of these places people get a chance to get things off their chests
that they wouldn't say normally. Blow off a little steam. Get
things out of your system, right?'' Cella thumped his jaw with
his forefinger. "But I suppose that sort of thing could have its
liabilities too. I mean, I don't think I'd ever want to go to a
place like that with my wife. Things could get out of control.
You know, my wife might say something that would really
hurt me. And then we might fight. And maybe, just out of
spite, you see, I would go off with some other unhappily
married woman for a while. I mean, the place has got to be
just full of unhappily married women, am I correct, Mrs.
Esposito?''

Laura pulled herself back onto her feet.

"I don't have to listen to any of this," she said quietly and
walked out of Captain Cella's office.

5 P.M.

"No, no, no, no . . . of course I was the right person to call. I'll pick you up in five minutes."

Laura leaned her forehead against the cool glass of the telephone booth.

"Thank you, Jerzy."

6:15 P.M.

Wade felt the pinch and jab of the needle, then the warm flush of the drug as it entered his vein. He should be feeling anger now, he knew. Fury. Terror. But instead his overwhelming feeling was curiosity.

Was that his feeling or the drug's?

Wade's head spun pleasantly.

Is there a difference?

7:50 P.M.

"Why she had to go, I don't know,
She wouldn't say.
I said something wrong, now I long—"

The song abruptly stopped and Laura's eyes snapped open. For a brief moment of grace while consciousness returned, she could not remember what she was doing with this darkly handsome man who was slowly driving the car along a wooded road. But then memory clanged into place and she sat bolt upright, her heart suddenly accelerating.

"Bad dream?"

"My God, it's worse than a bad dream," Laura said. "How in the name of God could I have ever fallen asleep?"

"You had to. You're human," Jerzy said softly, his bony face dimly reflected in the day's last light.

Laura looked out the window. She saw the pink glow of a laurel bush high on the hill behind the stone wall.

"Was the radio on or did I dream that?"

"I just turned it off. I didn't think we should announce our arrival. We're almost there, Laura."

Laura nodded. She still did not quite believe that they were actually going through with this. But Jerzy had been right: they had no other choice. Even if they could find a policeman who believed her story, it would take a day at the very least to obtain a search warrant from a Maine judge. And Laura could not wait that long. Ted could not.

"American justice is magnificently designed for lawsuits," Jerzy had said. "For an emergency, you do better to handle it yourself."

"Jerzy, she has a whole army up there. Twenty, thirty people. I don't know how many."

"Did you see any of them with guns?"

"No," Laura had said. "But some were carrying hypodermic needles loaded with a tranquilizer or something. Like the kind they got Ted with."

That was when Jerzy had leaned across her and pulled the service revolver from the glove compartment. Reflexively, Laura had drawn away from him.

"This has a little better range than a syringe," Jerzy had said, smiling. "If we're careful, we should be able to get your husband out of there without any interference."

That had been it. Given the alternatives Jerzy was right, of course. And his calm confidence was reassuring. Laura had to have faith in him. Jerzy was the only person she knew who she had been positive would believe her story first time through, no questions asked.

Jerzy cut the engine off and the car coasted to a halt in the pine needle-covered shoulder of the road. Laura shivered. She zipped closed the jacket Jerzy had brought for her.

"How far are we from the gate?" Jerzy whispered.

"It's hard to tell. A good hundred yards, I'm sure."

"Good." Jerzy pulled the pistol from the dashboard and stuffed it into the pocket of his windbreaker. He turned and looked into Laura's eyes. "All you have to do is show me the way. I'll take care of everything else. Are you ready, Laura?"

Laura was silent a moment, her eyes fastened to his.

"No one else in the world would do this for me," she said, quietly.

Jerzy leaned toward her and quickly brushed his lips against hers.

"I want you to be happy," he said. Then he clicked open his door and said, "Let's get this over with."

Laura slid across the seat and came out after him. The only sound she heard was the rasp of tree frogs. Familiar. She had listened to them drone through several sleepless nights. Jerzy was walking stealthily along the wall, looking up from time to time. The light was all but gone now. He stopped, patting the trunk of a thick-barked wild cherry tree.

"We can get across here," he whispered.

He leaped straight up, hooked both hands over a branch, and swung up his legs. For a moment he hung like a monkey, then righted himself, straddling the branch. He reached down his arm.

Laura hesitated a second before grabbing his hand and clambered up the side of the wall like a mountain climber pulling on a rope. At the top, she let go of Jerzy and grasped the branch, then tumbled to the other side. A second later, Jerzy dropped beside her.

"Where do you figure we are on this?" Jerzy pulled out the map Laura had sketched in the car.

Laura held it up to her face.

"Maybe here," she whispered, touching a spot with her finger. She turned her head and pointed. "The driveway is over the hill there. If we walked up that way we should be able to meet it not far from the main house."

"Okay."

Laura saw Jerzy unsnap his jacket pocket and withdraw the gun. He motioned with it for her to go ahead of him and lightly touched her hand as she passed. Laura started slowly up through a grove of dogwood, barely visible in the dark, but then she began taking long, quick strides as she neared the ridge. "Let's get this over with. Let's get this over with." She repeated Jerzy's words to herself like a mantra, trying to numb her fear. She knew these woods. It was the place she had run to after Saxon had humiliated her at dinner; the place where Ted had followed her.

A loud report echoed in the hills on every side of them. Jerzy grabbed Laura from behind and pulled her against a tree. There was another report, then another and another in quick succession, like a firecracker or a repeating gun. Laura's eyes darted. They were only feet away from the driveway. The sound was the backfire of a motorcycle. It appeared on their left immediately, white, luminescent, a man riding on its back, the visor on his helmet down, a long silver column shining in his hand like a lance. The column burst into light. It was a flashlight and it was pointed directly at them.

"Let him come to us," Jerzy whispered, pressing Laura's body against the tree.

The motorcycle halted, its engine still running. Laura saw the rider swing his foot over the back, then pull up his visor. It was the man who had shot Ted with a syringe that morning, the man who had locked them in the room in the pavilion. The beam again shone in her eyes, blinding her. Her heart pounded. They should run. She was sure they should run.

"I knew you wouldn't get far," the man was saying. "I knew we'd find you sooner or later."

Laura felt Jerzy soundlessly spin away from her. The beam of light swung. She blinked her eyes, frantically trying to see.

"Don't move. This is a gun in your back." Jerzy's voice.

Laura leaned against the tree, breathing deeply. She could see Jerzy pull the flashlight from the man's hand.

"Now slowly take off your helmet," Jerzy said.

The man obeyed. His body slumped to the ground the instant the flashlight struck his skull. It was a satisfying sight; Laura could not deny that.

"Let's move fast."

Jerzy stuffed his gun back into his pocket, snatched up the helmet with one hand, grabbed Laura's hand with the other, and led her to the motorcycle. He pulled the helmet over his head, his face suddenly invisible behind the gray visor. He pointed to the motorcycle's sidecar.

"Get in backward," he said. "Good. Now slide your feet back as far as you can and put your head here."

He unfastened the canvas seat cover and pulled it over Laura's head.

"Hold tight," he said.

Laura heard him mount the saddle above her and rush the motor. They lurched forward, Laura's knees bouncing painfully against the cold metal of the sidecar floor, her hips slapping against its side as they took a turn. They must be at the garden already, circling Hilltop House. Everyone would be on the terrace now, drinking, dancing, totally unafraid. Guy and Affy . . . Ginger and Ralph. John and Judy.

Laura heard Jerzy shift down, then pull to a halt. They were at the gate to the Therapy Pavilion.

"That you, Reg?" The guard's voice seemed to come from directly above Laura.

"Yes." Jerzy raced the motor over his voice. It could be any man's.

"Okay. Keep the noise down, though. They're just starting in there."

Laura heard the electronic whine of the gate as it swung open, the jerk and sputter of the cycle as it passed through and again halted. The engine stopped.

"I'm getting off the bike," Jerzy was saying in a low monotone. "Now there's another helmet under your seat. Grab it. And when I tell you it's clear, jump out of there and pull it on. . . . Now!"

The canvas flashed open above her. Laura rolled out of the sidecar in a somersault. Jerzy pulled her up and to the front door of the pavilion. Just inside, he put her helmet over her head.

"Keep your visor down and act like you're in a hurry," he whispered. He touched the pocket that held his gun, then took her hand again. They walked inside.

A red bulb pulsed in the foyer. Beneath it, a woman in what appeared to be a nurse's uniform held a finger to her lips.

"Session's just starting," she whispered.

Laura nodded her helmet, then looked to her right. She pulled Jerzy along the bowed corridor to the stairwell. At the first landing, she looked through the door into the hall: there was no one there. The room Ted and she had been locked in was no more than thirty feet away. She started for it, Jerzy right beside her, but they had only taken two steps when a door flashed open on their right and a man's head jutted out.

"Session's on, damn it," he whispered, indignantly. "Keep this hallway clear."

Laura backed away. Jerzy's hand grabbed her shoulder and swung her around, through an open door into a dimly lit room. He closed the door behind her. Laura leaned against the wall, catching her breath before she raised her eyes. The room slanted up in front of her in four levels of benches, the first three made of chrome and vinyl, the last of oak and leather. The only original, Laura thought; this had obviously once been the chapel's choir loft. She turned around. Where the balcony overlooking the chapel must have been, there were now floor-to-ceiling drapes. Jerzy had taken off his helmet and was walking toward the draped wall. Removing her own, Laura followed behind him. Jerzy reached out and tentatively parted the drapes an inch, then two, three.

At first, the double-glazed glass and the brightly illuminated shapes beyond it looked like a mammoth diorama from the Science Museum, a tableau depicting state-of-the-art medical technology.

Just below Laura on the near wall was a ring-shaped metal apparatus a good fifteen feet in diameter encircling what seemed to be an examination table. On the floor, extending out from under the table, was a pair of trolley tracks which led toward the center of the room, forking along the way and ending at two patient tables side by side, both tilted up and away from Laura. At the near end of each of these tables were identical, squat, stainless steel apparatuses which looked like over-size hair dryers; behind these was a bank of video screens above an elaborate console. And directly across from them was an elevated glass enclosure holding more medical machinery. The plaster cornice and wood paneling on the wall above the enclosure made it clear that it sat where the chapel's altar once had been. This is where Hilltop House's original owner and his wife had offered up their prayers and pledged their sacraments. It was now, Laura knew with complete certainty, the theater of the Final Session.

A door beside the bank of video screens swung open and five figures in hospital green smocks, caps, and slippers marched in. Instinctively Laura ducked her head behind the drapes.

"I'm sure they can't see us," Jerzy whispered. "Not under those lights."

Slowly Laura turned her head back. She needed to watch this, to witness every detail of it, yet she had to force herself to peer down again. Several people in white coats had seated themselves on high stools inside the glass enclosure. All were looking attentively at one of the green-clad people. Laura squinted. The patrician head turned to profile. It was Elizabeth Saxon. The doctor raised her hand. Immediately one of the tilted tables lowered, then spun on its axis like a barber's chair. A man was strapped to it, a gray-haired, pleasant-looking man, his eyes closed. Good God! Laura knew that face. She had seen it that morning when he had been carried in from the van on a stretcher.

One of Saxon's assistants now attached a plug and lead to the wires emanating from the binding sheet at his chest. The heart-monitor screen lit. Another assistant released the man's left arm and wound the sleeve of the sphygmomanometer above his elbow.

The man on the table blinked open his eyes. Dr. Saxon smiled down at him, opening her mouth as if to speak.

The sudden crackle behind Laura made her gasp. She spun around, but all she saw was Jerzy picking up a set of earphones from the front bench of the gallery. He handed her a set, smiling. Laura took them reluctantly and set them on her head before turning back to the glass.

". . . hope you're comfortable. Actually, the whole procedure will be completed in less than twenty minutes, thanks to this elegant machinery. None of this was even conceivable when we were medical students. Remarkable, isn't it, Dr. Hobson?''

It took Laura a moment to realize that Dr. Saxon was addressing the man who was bound to the table.

Wade strained to keep his eyes open. He looked into hers, bright, blue-gray, not a glimmer of insanity evident in them. He ran his tongue around his lips. They were chalk-dry from the Tyrazepam. He was still waiting, like a spectator, for the terror to descend on him. He felt nothing.

"Dr. Jeckman tells me you have two marriages behind you," Saxon was saying. She nodded to one of her assistants and Wade felt himself turn and tilt up again. "That's a good sign, actually. It shows that at least you believe in matrimony, if not the sanctity of it. I'm sure you're a man for whom life is fuller when you are married. Fewer empty spots. Less idle time."

Wade felt hands touch his scalp, then a cold, viscous liquid pouring over it. It gave off a sharp, antiseptic smell.

"Good thick hair," someone behind him said. "I don't see any concealment problems."

He heard a snip, then another. He felt a circle of hair smaller than a dime being cut from the crown of his head.

"It is always the most interesting people who end up alone, isn't it?" Saxon went on in the same intimate tone. "No accident, I suppose. Original minds naturally have a difficult time matching up with others."

He felt his head being lifted, then the snap of the elastic turban as they fitted it over his scalp.

"We're sterile, Doctor," a young woman's voice said.

"Good," Dr. Saxon said. "That's another improvement, isn't it, Dr. Hobson? A few years ago we would have had to shave your head entirely. Not very attractive, really. We'd have people thinking you'd joined some awful religious cult."

Wade opened his jaw. He tried to speak. The words would not come.

The cuff expanded on his arm, pinching his skin, then loosened.

"One twenty-five over eighty."

A dab of cold gel dropped onto his head, now rubbed into the tiny bare patch. The skin immediately went numb. A topical anesthetic. He felt a collar snap into place under his neck, then heard the whirr of the crane as the cold metal bowl settled over his skull.

"There's nothing to worry about, Dr. Hobson. You'll feel nothing. We don't even have to cut a flap anymore. This lovely machine makes its own incision before the drilling begins without spilling a drop of blood. Things are so much neater when you are working in millimeters. Subtler. Computerized microsurgery finds its best expression in this kind of work. There's nothing quite so—you know—accessible as the brain."

Wade forced his tongue, his lips.

"God . . . help . . . me. . . ."

But his words were inaudible under the whistle of the drill as it cut into his skull.

Jerzy caught Laura around the waist just as her knees buckled under her. Her eyes rolled into her head; her consciousness spun to a fine point, then vanished.

Until that sound, everything happening below her had seemed not quite real, as if the glass window framing it had turned it into theater. But the sing of the drill as it touched the bone of the man's skull jolted her consciousness; this was real, this was happening. She had passed out.

"Laura! Breathe deeply now. . . . That's it. . . ."

She had only been out for a few seconds yet she had the sensation of being awakened from a long sleep. Then she remembered.

"Let's go," she said out loud. "Let's find Ted and get out of here."

Jerzy leaned his head down to hers.

"Soon," he said quietly. "You'd better get some strength back first. You look a little pale."

Laura looked into Jerzy's eyes. He was right again; she was too weak to move really fast just now if they had to. It was remarkable how strong he was, how calm he had managed to remain throughout all of this.

"Laura, if it helps any," he whispered, "I can assure you that the patient felt no pain. The brain is insensate, you know.

The numb organ, they call it."

He put his earphones back on and returned to the gallery window. For a moment, Laura stared after him. Then, slowly, she stood and came up beside him. She slipped the headset over her ears and looked down into the operating theater.

Two of the green-gowned staff rolled the table along the tracks, ferrying the man to the large wheel-shaped object just below her. There, they transferred the man to the examination table. Only then did Laura see the black cylinder protruding from his skull like the handle of a knife. Laura's head jerked involuntarily. She sucked in her breath and stared straight down. The man's eyes were open. His expression, if anything, seemed thoughtful.

The doctor's assistants checked the rubber straps which secured the man, then scurried to the glass enclosure on the opposite side of the room joining Saxon and the rest of her staff. Suddenly, the large wheel began to rotate around the man's head.

"Computerized tomography," Jerzy whispered. "CAT scan. They're taking three-dimensional pictures of the inside of his skull. There, you can see it now."

He pointed at a large illuminated screen in the center of the room. It showed a white, mushroomlike object rotating like a globe, a black line emanating from its top. It was the object which they had inserted in the man's skull.

"We're just taking a fixed-point reading to see where we are, Dr. Hobson." Saxon's voice issued softly over the earphones. "Letting the computer take some measurements. We don't want to make any mistakes. We never do. Then all we'll have left is to let one of the computers talk to another for a few seconds and we can finish up."

The man was now being rolled, stretcher top, straps, and all, back to the center of the room. Saxon stepped out of the enclosure, followed by her cadre. She stopped at the head of the table.

"It's a pity we haven't had time to learn more about you, Hobson. I mean other than your medical records. It's not just irregularities like epilepsy we look for, you know. We test potentialities with our games. We derive our greatest satisfaction from the little personal adjustments we can make—a special sensitivity to smell, a hidden phobia, an idiosyncratic erogenous zone. The fine tuning, so to speak. It's remarkable how many of these we're learning to pinpoint in the amygdala and septum. But never mind. Our goal can be reached without such subtleties. I mean, pleasure *is* pleasure, Dr. Hobson. That is the bottom line, isn't it?''

She made a small gesture with her right hand and the table tilted up under the squat, hair-dryerlike apparatus. Two assistants fitted its inverted bowl over his head, then tightened the vises which locked his skull in place. Three screens illuminated above the console: one, a replay of the CAT scan; the second, a live image of the man's skull; the third and largest, a superimposition of the two.

"Stereotactic surgery is too fine a craft to be left to the shaky hand of man. It's still done that way in the rest of this country, but I would never allow it. Not when the difference between heaven and hell in the temporal lobes can be a matter of millimeters. You are in better hands than mine, Dr. Hobson.''

Laura saw a flurry of activity inside the enclosure. Now, two more screens lit and, line by line, computer read-outs appeared. Dr. Saxon studied them. The others watched her expectantly.

"Thirty-six insertions, Dr. Hobson," she said. "The minimum, actually. The universal loci of love, one of my people calls them. Most are in the pleasure centers of the superior temporal lobe, but we've found other very effective loci in the hypothalamus. A good basic mix, really. In combination, they get quite a production of phenylethylamine going in the system.'' Saxon paced back to the operating table. "Amazing how the brain can intoxicate itself, isn't it, Doctor? Produce its own nectar. Its own aphrodisiac. Its own love potion. Now there's where we should be doing our research, shouldn't we? Discovering their own needs and desires. Helping them to become self-reliant. That's what mental health is all about in the end, wouldn't you say?''

Dr. Saxon looked over at the glass enclosure.

"All right," she said, nodding.

Laura stared at the large screen. White lines were descending from a single point at the top of the skull. She looked at the patient's face. He was blinking his eyes. Laura felt herself go completely numb. She was sure she was watching a man die. Murdered.

"We use only platinum electrodes," Saxon continued, her

tone almost cheery. "Fine as angel's hair, but expensive nonetheless. Worth it, of course. They're indestructible, like eternal love."

On the screen, Laura saw the thirty-six electrodes reach their destined loci. They looked like an inverted fan inside his brain. Saxon was inspecting the print-out on one of the monitors.

"Good," she said, half aloud.

Two of her assistants were releasing the vises from the man's skull. The bowl lifted off, revealing the black cylinder still protruding from the top of his head. Now a third assistant attached an alligator clamp to the cylinder. It was connected by a long wire to the console, like a jumper cable to a car.

"We're just going to find a level now, Dr. Hobson," Saxon said. "It can be a little unnerving until we locate that happy medium between your upper and lower stimulation thresholds. Do be patient with us."

Everyone stood quite still. Saxon paced slowly to the console, quickly snapped three switches in succession, then grasped a knob between the thumb and forefinger of her right hand. Immediately, all eyes shifted to the patient's face as his wail pierced the air.

It was the same half-human whine Laura had heard last night. Except now she could see the patient's mouth flap open, his face contorting from grimace to wonder to grin and back again so quickly it looked like a fast-motion sequence from an old comedy film. And now, too, Laura realized that the whine was a high-pitched, unbroken string of half sentences, fragments of cries, unfinished laughs—a rush of jangled human thoughts and emotions triggered by the variating charge of an electric current. Laura felt dizzy again. She leaned her head against the cool surface of the window, drawing her breath slowly, not taking her eyes from the man's face. His voice was now sliding octave by octave to normal pitch; the words gradually slowed.

". . . favorite was the columbine . . . Oh, God! Every time! Rachel, do you—? He said, 'Wade, come down from there,' and . . . Yes. Oh, God, yes. This is it. Oh, God . . . yes, don't stop. Yes and yes and yes. . . ."

The words stopped altogether, replaced by a low throaty murmur. His face relaxed, softened, his eyes brightened, now almost glowed. He smiled enchantingly. If Laura had not known that it was all artificially induced, she would have sworn that it was the face of a man who was divinely happy.

"Pleasure, Dr. Hobson," Dr. Saxon said. She had removed her hand from the knob and walked directly in front of him. She smiled. "Pure, undiluted pleasure. No nagging worry can weight it down. No sudden itch on the back can distract you from it. No, this is the pure thing, the uncut stuff. The aim of all the psychotherapies whatever their dogma, when you think of it. Pure pleasure crowds out guilt, numbs anxiety. And, of course, it has an altogether socializing influence. That's the reason so many of our leaders support our work here. Happy people are good, generous, loyal. Undemanding. Yes, the ability to experience pure joy is the very essence of mental health." She suddenly touched her hand to the man's brow, then turned back toward the console. "It's what makes us human," she said, quickly snapping down the three switches.

Laura stared at the man's face. For a full minute he continued to smile, to exude total bliss, but then, in slow, ticlike quivers, his face hardened, his smile contorted into a grimace.

"My God! What are you doing now?" The man spoke sharply. It was the first complaint Laura had heard him utter.

"Please bear with us, Dr. Hobson. You'll be feeling so much better in just a moment." Saxon held her arms in front of her as two aides slipped sterile elastic gloves over her hands. "It is not pain you are feeling, but the absence of pleasure. The removal of its source." She walked behind the patient. "Not that I underestimate the power of that deprivation. It is the origin of our cruelest emotions—jealousy, despair. We can endure pain for years without losing our will to live, but suddenly subtract pleasure from us and we have nothing left to live for."

Saxon was silent a moment, seemingly isolated in thought, but now aides began pulling a surgical mask across her face and her eyes focused on the skull top in front of her. Saxon unscrewed the cylinder from the man's head.

"The final steps are done by hand," she said. "They needn't be, but there's no chance for error now and this gives us all a greater sense of participation."

"Please!" The man's voice again. Pleading.

An aide held something out to Saxon. Laura squinted. It

was a clear-plastic case, the same as she had found in the brown parcel. Saxon removed something from it with small tongs and now inserted it in the cylinder.

"The electrode leads are anchored in your skull bone, all attached to a disk no bigger than a Sen-Sen." Saxon fitted a chrome plunger in the cylinder and slowly pressed down. "And now we've fastened the transceiver and battery, both marvels of Japanese microminiaturization. The battery is charged by the fluctuations in body heat. It works amazingly well—too well, in fact. No one suspected that the charge would hold for weeks after a body went cold. The late Mr. Goodwin certainly proved otherwise."

Saxon grasped the entire cylinder in one hand and turned. "The incision is no bigger than a match head, so not a stitch is necessary." She lifted the cylinder from his head. "And the tissue covering our skulls is so thin that with a drop of cortisone and a dab of vitamin E gel you'll be mending by morning."

Two aides pulled the elastic turban from the man's head. Dr. Saxon touched his hair, rearranging it with an almost affectionate gesture. Even from directly above, it was impossible for Laura to see any indication that the man had just undergone extensive psychosurgery. Saxon pulled off her surgical gloves as aides released the man's collar and began unfastening his restraint straps. Under the sheet, the man was wearing slacks, an open shirt. Someone untaped the heart-monitor leads from his chest and buttoned his shirt.

"There. We want you looking presentable," Saxon said, smiling. "First impressions do abide."

Aides stood on either side of the patient as the table slowly tilted down.

"Easy now," one said. "It takes a minute to find your balance."

The man was eased to his feet. He stood unsteadily in front of Dr. Saxon, a look of utter desolation on his fine face.

"Done and done," Saxon said. "The simplest solutions to our problems are usually the best; it's the theorists who like to make the human psyche more complicated than it really is."

Saxon raised her hand, signaling two assistants who stood behind the patient.

"In the end, Dr. Hobson, it seems that Oscar Wilde's

definition of love fits the best. Love, he said, is simply grati-
tude for pleasure.''

The aides had now paced soundlessly to a door thick as a
bank vault's directly behind the patient. Laura stood on her
toes, her forehead still pressed against the glass, following them with her eyes. She watched, dumbfounded, as the
woman stepped into the operating room.

Wade could sense her presence before he saw her, before he
heard her voice. And in that same instant he felt an overwhelming thrill of excitement, a warmth spreading across his
chest and in his groin, an aliveness, an eagerness bursting inside of him. It was like that thrill of pleasure which he had felt
a few moments ago, yet now there was a new dimension to it.
As he reflexively turned and faced Florence Goodwin, he immediately understood what that dimension was: he not only
felt supremely happy, he felt fulfilled. Gazing into Florence's
eyes, he knew, as he had never really known before, what it
was to be in love.

"A very simple model, actually," Dr. Saxon was saying in
back of him. "Your transceivers match. Mrs. Goodwin can
only receive your signal and you can only receive hers. You
stimulate each other's electrodes whenever you are in range—
up to ten miles in good conditions, although, of course, it's
strongest when you are very close. You alone can thrill each
other. You alone can make the earth move with pleasure. You
will fall in love with one another every day of the year. You
are connected eternally on the same wavelength.''

Wade's hands touched Mrs. Goodwin's. He drew her to
him.

"How very nice to see you again," he said, barely conscious
of the people around them.

"Yes. Very nice indeed."

Mrs. Goodwin's smile was truly the most beautiful Wade
had ever seen.

"A perfect model of love," Dr. Saxon was droning in the
background. "A perfect model of harmony, responsiveness,
connectedness. Of joyful interdependence."

Florence pressed Wade's hand to her lips.

"It's so wonderful to be in love again," she murmured.
"How very lucky I am. After . . . after—" She suddenly
looked confused, a tiny tremor disturbing her lips, but an

instant later she was again smiling beautifully at Wade. "After I lost Harold, I never thought I would be blessed again. Oh, God, how very lucky we both are."

Wade took her into his arms, touching his cheek to hers, sighing with pleasure. This was it, all right. This was the very feeling he had spent his life searching for, whether he had known it before or not. It was what he had hoped to find in Rachel's arms. What he had half expected to find at the bottom of the next drink. He had yearned for it. He had tried to force it. He had given up on it. He had denied that it was possible, that it even existed. And now here it was, as undeniable as the beautiful face touching his. Florence pulled her head back and gazed up at him, her eyes twinkling.

"So, what do you say? Is it better than London?"

Wade smiled.

"Why, it's almost as good as Paris," he said, winking, and they both laughed. By God, she even had the same sense of humor he did. They were absolutely the perfect match. He looped his arm through hers and started for the open door.

"We'll have to keep you in the pavilion for the night," Saxon was saying. "But you'll have your privacy, except for a couple of quick interruptions to take urine specimens to see how your phenylethylamine count is doing, not that I have any doubts. And do be gentle with him tonight, Florence. This all comes as a bit of a shock to his system, you know. . . ."

Wade heard Dr. Saxon scurry behind them. It was as though she dreaded their leaving her, excluding her completely. Wade turned and looked warmly into her eyes.

"Yes?"

"You've both had enough Tyrazepam to make you forget everything that's happened," Saxon said. "But you've known about our techniques for longer than just this evening, haven't you, Dr. Hobson? You *will* remember every once in a while."

Wade tried to focus on what Saxon was saying, but at the moment it was difficult to think about anything but how sweet it was going to be to make love to Florence Goodwin.

"Somehow I don't think that will make a difference, do you?" Saxon said.

Wade was through the door before he comprehended what Dr. Saxon had been saying and then he felt a wave of anxiety sweep through him, pulling him down. His face quivered with it. He grasped Florence around the waist and looked deeply into her eyes.

"I swear to God . . . I—I was falling in love with you before . . . before they did anything to me," he said, his voice trembling.

"Of course," Florence replied. She touched his cheek with her hand. "I know that."

"It's so important that you do," Wade went on. "Otherwise . . . otherwise . . ."

Wade's anxiety was all but gone, eclipsed by a rush of love for this dear woman. And vanished with it was the rest of his thought.

Laura stared blankly at the door as it closed behind the couple. From the moment they had brought the woman into the operating room and she and the man had touched hands, Laura had been transfixed by the two of them. They seemed so genuinely happy, so deeply in love, yet, incredibly, none of it was real. None of it! Now, below her, Saxon took a seat inside the glass enclosure while several assistants began cleaning the surgical equipment. Laura blinked her eyes. For most of the past half hour she had almost managed to forget about herself, but now she felt her heart accelerating. There was no longer any reason to wait. It was time. They had to find Ted and get out of here now. She pulled her face back from the observation window and removed her earphones.

"Jerzy?"

She turned.

"Jerzy?"

Louder.

"Jerzy?"

A feeling of terror descended on her. Laura ran between the benches, swinging her head from one side to the other. Nowhere. He was nowhere in the room. She dashed up the aisle to the door, her heart thudding inside her chest. She put her hand on the knob and turned. She pulled.

"Jesus God!"

It was locked. She was locked inside here. Laura sank to the floor. Her head was spinning. She leaned back against the wall.

"No," she whispered to herself. "No . . . No . . . No . . . No . . ."

Then she abruptly stopped and held perfectly still. Of course! Jerzy was out there getting Ted on his own. Less risk that way, especially considering Laura's faint. He had somehow locked her in for safekeeping until he came back. And he had slipped out without a word because he did not want an argument from her. It was the way he did things. Laura took a deep breath and let it out slowly.

"You always make things harder for yourself, don't you?"

Laura froze. For a split second, she thought she was hearing Saxon's voice over the earphones.

"You want to know everything before it happens, yet you are disappointed that there is no spontaneity in your life. No wonderful surprises."

Laura stared at the far wall. Saxon's voice was coming over a speaker box suspended from the ceiling.

"I have such wonderful plans for you and Ted."

Oh, God! No!

"There is so much potential in both of you. You could be the perfect couple."

Laura's whole body was shaking. She bit against her lip.

"I'm very sorry I frightened you, Laura." Saxon's voice was low, intimate. "I've known you've been up there for some time, actually. I could see you on my monitor down here. I can see you now. Why don't you come back to the window so we can look at one another face to face?"

For a long moment, Laura did not move. Then she suddenly stood, grabbed the door handle, and yanked at it again and again, tears streaming down her face.

"Come now, Laura," Saxon said, sternly. "You're not going anywhere. But no one is coming in to get you either. Come to the window and let me try to explain all of this to you in a way that you can understand."

Laura turned slowly and walked down the aisle. She pressed her palms against the glass and looked down. Saxon was alone in the operating room, seated on a stool at its center. Laura stared through her tears at Saxon's clear, aristocratic eyes.

"You have nothing to explain," Laura said evenly. Her voice sounded stronger than she had expected it to. "I saw everything. All your precision machinery, your electronic wonders. I saw what you did to that poor man. I understand very well: you're more dangerous than I could have ever imagined.''

Saxon was shaking her head slowly, like a disappointed parent.

"Really, such righteous indignation from you, of all people." Dr. Saxon got off of her stool and took a step toward Laura. "Why, I've never come across anyone who demanded so much from a relationship as you, Laura. You were willing to let your husband and son wait indefinitely while you held out for your miracle . . . your magic, your enchantment. You wanted passion and romance all wrapped nicely in the security and warmth of your family. You wanted to be dazzled by the same man every day for the rest of your life. And when I promised you that it was possible, you were the first in line to sign up.''

Laura watched Saxon pace below. She hoped to God that Jerzy had not been spotted on her monitor, that Saxon had no idea that at this very moment he was prowling through the pavilion with a gun in his hand. Laura clenched her fists against her thighs. She knew that nothing must happen until Jerzy came back for her. She had to keep Saxon talking.

"You know damn well I would never have signed up if I had known it was this," Laura said loudly.

"Please!" Saxon raised a finger up at Laura. "You know as well as I that you don't save marriages with cold negotiations or confessional encounters. It always comes down to just one thing: you either love one another or you don't. As simple as that. And you also know that as surely as we grow older, love burns out. Even in the best of families." Saxon smiled. "So we really only have one choice: let a marriage die its natural death or reactivate that feeling of love in it." Saxon paused. "You do understand that love is simply a feeling, don't you, Laura?''

"It may be a feeling," Laura said. "But it's not just something you can make happen with a piece of wire and a radio.''

"No?" Saxon laughed softly. "I've often wondered why it is that romantics like you always believe they understand science better than scientists." She returned to her stool. "Do you have any real idea why you ever feel what you feel? Why you ever fell in love with Ted in the first place? You always thought it was something chemical, didn't you, Laura? Something physical? A feeling over which you had no control? Now what can you possibly think is the difference between that feeling and the one I can give you and Ted?''

"You just can't do that!" Laura shouted back. She was trembling. What in the name of God was taking Jerzy so long? "You just can't tamper with people's brains!"

"Tamper? My Lord, Laura, you would have cried out in rage at Dr. Barnard's first heart transplant. You would have screamed murder at the insertion of the first pacemaker. If it were up to people like you with your misguided sense of natural purity, there'd be millions dead whom we could have helped."

Laura suddenly lifted her eyes. The door behind Saxon was opening and two figures in white were guiding a patient on a rolling stretcher into the operating room.

"We don't tamper, Laura," Saxon went on, not turning her head. "Like all necessary surgery, ours corrects a flaw in nature. We cure the disease of loneliness and alienation. We stem the epidemic of broken families."

The aides lifted the patient onto the operating table nearest Saxon. Laura stared. Jesus Christ, it was Ginger! One of the aides was already dousing her long red hair with the oily antiseptic. The other was removing a pair of scissors from the steam table.

"But for some unfathomable reason, it is the brain that you purists find sacrosanct. We can operate on stomachs and substitute kidneys, but if we so much as touch the brain, we are suddenly tampering with nature."

Laura watched as the aides pulled the sterile turban over Ginger's head and now rotated the table.

"You've seen my work, our Soul Mates," Saxon raised her voice. "They all still answer to the same names they did before they came here. They still have the same sense of being themselves. The only difference between them and you is that they are happy, Laura. Truly happy, loving people."

Laura slammed her open hand against the window.

"If there is no difference, Doctor . . . if you are doing nothing wrong, why in the name of God don't you tell what you are doing before you bring us here? Why must it be such a secret that you even erase our memories of the surgery after it is done?"

"Because of alarmists like you!" Saxon said impatiently.

"You purists with your obsession for freedom . . . or rather the illusion of it. You people who insist on believing that something inside you—something other than your brain—chooses what you feel . . . what you do . . . whom you love!"

Laura turned her head. A second stretcher was rolling through the door. A man lay on it.

"You want a choice, Laura?" Saxon said. "I'll give you the very choice you've been avoiding for much too long. Are you committing yourself to Ted or aren't you? Do you want to love and be loved by him? Or are you willing to let him go?"

The man was lifted onto the operating table.

Ted!

Laura slumped to her knees. Her body trembled uncontrollably. They had doused Ted's hair, clipped the circle of his crown, pulled on the elastic turban. And now his table tilted back, side by side with Ginger's. The aides began to fit each of their skulls into the inverted bowls which housed the drills.

"Shall we let them share this joy?" Saxon said. "Shall we put them on the same wavelength?"

The scream burst from Laura's mouth:

"Jerzy! Now!"

Immediately the far door to the operating room swung open and Jerzy bounded through. Everyone stared at him. No one moved.

Laura's heart thumped in her chest. Thank God! Thank God! She pressed her face against the glass.

"Dr. Adonski," Saxon said warmly. "We've been waiting for you. We're just beginning a session."

Laura stared. A spasm racked her body, knocking her head against the glass. Jerzy was shaking Dr. Saxon's hand.

"I think you know everyone," Saxon was saying. "Even Ginger, if I'm not mistaken."

"Yes," Jerzy said. "Ginger is also one of my finds."

The blood had drained from Laura's head. She fought desperately to remain conscious.

"Jerzy. My God, why? WHY?" Laura's cry echoed in the operating room.

Jerzy smiled up at Laura, his dark eyes shining.

"But you know I've always wanted you to be happy," he said, as aides pulled the green operating gown over his outstretched arms. "I thought if you could see with your own eyes how simple and painless it was, you could accept my gift.''

Dr. Saxon raised her hand and everyone was still. She paced beside Ted and touched the side of his face with her hand. Laura saw his eyes blink open in a daze.

''It's your choice, Laura,'' Saxon said. ''Will you take this man to be your own?''

Epilogue

"But with a great deal of hard work and perhaps a little bit of luck, you *can* have it both ways. You *can* create a marriage that combines the comforts of home with the excitement of an illicit affair, the warmth of family life with the cool romance of solo adventure. Yes, you have a very good chance of having it all!"

Several people rose to their feet in the hotel ballroom, applauding enthusiastically. Laura turned in her chair, looking from one eager face to another, and again an unidentifiable sense of foreboding sent a shiver up her spine.

"Before we go on," Dr. Saxon was saying, "I see we have a few old friends with us tonight." Saxon looked down, smiling shyly. "Well, it's not actually pure accident. I asked some of my favorite couples to drop by and say a few words to you." She looked directly into Laura's eyes. "Why don't you and Ted get us started, Laura?"

Ted was up immediately. He leaned down and swept Jonah —giggling all the way—onto his shoulders, before reaching for Laura's hand. For a moment, Laura did not move. She shook her head. For some reason, she had been having trouble focusing her thoughts all day. Finally she stood and marched behind her husband and son to the front of the hall. She turned and looked out at the audience.

"On our way down from Beverly tonight," Laura began, her voice trembling, "I told my husband that I was nervous because I hadn't prepared anything to say. And he told me, 'Well, you don't have to prepare, Laur. Just tell them what's in your heart.' "

Laura closed her eyes and breathed deeply.

"And in my heart," she said, "I know that I must be the happiest woman alive."

Author's Postscript

Wavelengths is a fiction from start to finish, yet consider my inspirations:

> Perhaps it wasn't what [Muktananda] said that struck me, but how he said it . . . I felt as if a huge pool had opened in my heart . . . and the pool was full of soft air, and I was floating on it. It was the most intensely sensual feeling I ever had. It felt so good that my first reaction was a sharp pang of guilt, a feeling that I had stumbled into some forbidden region, perhaps tapped a pleasure center in my brain, which would keep me hooked on bodyless sensuality, string me out on bliss until I turned into a vegetable . . . then I forgot about thinking, and just let myself drift on.

> —SALLY KEMPTON
> "Hanging Out with the Guru"
> *New York* magazine

> [At California's proposed Center for the Prevention of Violence] it would be possible to try out the so-called Schwitzgebel Machine, a means of "implanting tiny electrodes deep within the brain," connecting them to small radio transmitters, and monitoring—perhaps even controlling—the behavior of violence-prone individuals or probationers—or indeed anyone else—by remote control.

> —PETER SCHRAG
> *Mind Control*

The main characteristic of love and friendship is precisely that stimuli coming from a favored person are interpreted as more agreeable than similar stimuli originating from other sources, and this evaluation is necessarily related to neuronal activity.

—JOSÉ M. R. DELGADO, M.D.
Physical Control of the Mind: Toward a Psychocivilized Society

Love is all there is, it makes the world go 'round . . .

—BOB DYLAN
"I Threw It All Away"

Bestselling Books for Today's Reader